# "You Sound Like a Real Hollywood Wheeler-Dealer!"

Cassie said, laughing.

"I'm not sure I really want to be a Hollywood wheeler-dealer."

"Oh? What do you want to—"

Her words were cut off by the pressure of James's mouth. She melted against him, revelling in the embrace she had been anticipating all evening.

"You know what I want," he murmured, winding his fingers through the inky cascade of her hair. "I want to do this." He nibbled the sensitive spot below her ear. "And this." His lips slid to her shoulder as Cassie turned her head to allow him easy access. "What *I* want to know, though," he breathed against her skin, "is just what *you* want."

---

## LUCY HAMILTON

is happily married and is the mother of a young daughter. She writes in her spare time and, she says, she looks forward to "translating a lifelong affection for books into a new career."

Dear Reader,

Thank you so much for the many letters I have received from you praising our Silhouette Special Edition series. Your comments and views have proved to be very informative and have been a great help to us in establishing Special Edition as a firm favourite amongst romance readers.

Special Editions have all the elements you enjoy in Silhouette Romances and more. These stories concentrate on romance in a longer, more realistic and sophisticated way, and they feature greater sensual detail.

I hope you enjoy this book and all the wonderful romances from Silhouette.

Please continue sending your suggestions and comments by writing to me at this address:

Jane Nicholls
Silhouette Books
PO Box 177
Dunton Green
Sevenoaks
Kent
TN13 2YE

# LUCY HAMILTON
# Shooting Star

Silhouette

Special Edition

Published by Silhouette Books

Copyright © 1984 by Lucy Hamilton

Map by Ray Lundgren

*First printing 1984*

**British Library C.I.P.**

Hamilton, Lucy
    Shooting star.—(Silhouette special edition)
    I. Title
    813'.54[F]          PS3558.A4431/

ISBN 0 340 36566 8

---



Printed and bound in Great Britain for
Hodder and Stoughton Paperbacks, a
division of Hodder and Stoughton Ltd.,
Mill Road, Dunton Green, Sevenoaks,
Kent (Editorial Office: 47 Bedford
Square, London, WC1 3DP) by
Richard Clay (The Chaucer Press) Ltd.,
Bungay, Suffolk

# Shooting Star

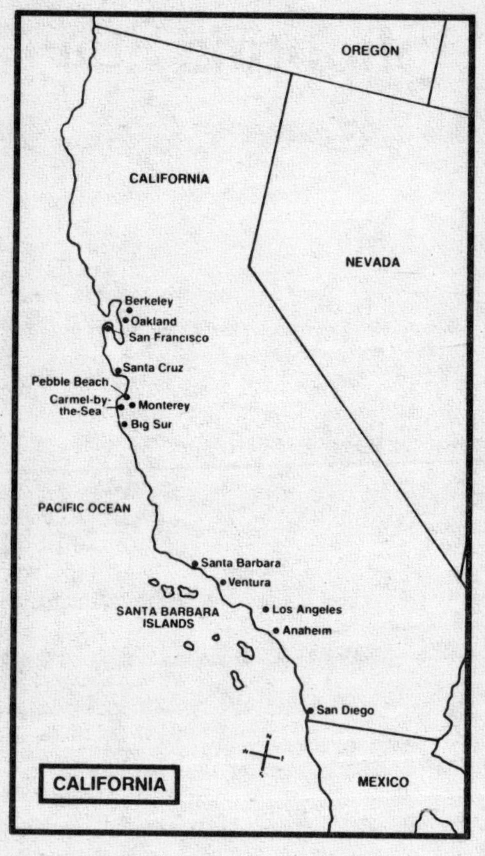

OREGON
CALIFORNIA
NEVADA
Berkeley
Oakland
San Francisco
Santa Cruz
Pebble Beach
Carmel-by-the-Sea
Monterey
Big Sur
PACIFIC OCEAN
Santa Barbara
Ventura
Los Angeles
SANTA BARBARA ISLANDS
Anaheim
San Diego
MEXICO
CALIFORNIA

# Chapter One

"What a day!"

By the time Cassie slid her tray onto a table in one corner of the large cafeteria, the dinner-hour crowd at Los Angeles General Hospital was already thinning out. She was joining a group of other residents, doctors doing post-medical school training in their respective specialties, and she knew they would understand her lament when she dropped into a chair, groaning.

"I have never, repeat never, seen so many pregnant women in my life!" She shook her head wearily, gazing out the window at the panorama of Los Angeles spread out below them, beautifully smog-free after a heavy rainstorm that morning. "I think every woman in LA is planning on having her baby today!"

"Is our Chief Obstetrics Resident feeling just a bit busy tonight?" Mike Benton, a third-year resident in Internal Medicine, grinned across the table at her, and Cassie nodded, her mouth full of ham sandwich. "Well, don't let it get you down, kid, because you're not alone. I think I've had more admissions on Medicine in the last twelve hours than in the last two weeks, and they just keep coming!"

"So do our deliveries." Cassie returned his grin as she answered. "I'm not even sure how many women have had babies already today, and there are still several upstairs in labor. And, by the way, why aren't you up on seven practicing medicine, if you're as busy as that?"

"Because I left a medical student up there practicing medicine, so I could come down here and eat!"

"Smart boy!" Cassie joined in the laughter around the table. "I left an intern up in Labor and Delivery, but he's had exactly two days of obstetrics since his third year of medical school. I think he's more nervous than the patients!"

"Don't worry, Cassie," chimed in a Pediatrics resident named Jeanne from the far end of the table. "You'll have him whipped into shape in no time!"

"Cassandra the Terrible strikes again!" Cassie grimaced comically at her cohorts. She was as amused as they by the nickname the interns and medical students working under her direction had bestowed on her. Those who considered her "terrible" were those who had mistakenly assumed that their small, cameo-lovely Chief Resident could be pushed around. As they learned, to their cost, looks could be deceiving.

Cassie was barely five feet, three inches tall and slender, with a perfect oval face and below-shoulder-length silky black hair which she coiled into a shining knot at her nape for work. Her eyes were large and smoky gray, framed by absurdly long lashes, and her voice was low and sweet and slightly husky. Until they witnessed it for themselves, her subordinates found it difficult to believe that those soft eyes could be ice-cold and piercing as daggers, or that her husky voice could clip out a lacerating assessment of a less-than-adequate performance. They made that mistake only once.

Now Cassie let the dinner-table conversation swirl around her as she ate her sandwich, a salad that was only slightly tired-looking and a piece of surprisingly good cherry pie. She ate quickly, less concerned with the taste of the food than with the necessity of fortifying herself for the long and busy night ahead. There had been four laboring women upstairs when she left for dinner, all of whom would deliver some time before morning, and she had already spent a long, tiring day helping babies into the world. As she swallowed the last of her pie, washing it down with cold milk, the beeper in the pocket of her green scrub dress sounded, summoning her back to work.

"What timing!" Mike laughed, and Cassie grinned, shaking her head.

"It's not so bad, really. After all, I did get to finish eating this time, didn't I?" Still smiling, she walked to the house phone a few feet away and dialed the switchboard operator. "This is Dr. Mills. What's the message?" A pause. "Okay, I'll call her." She punched out another number and waited while the call went through. "This is Cassie," she said when the evening charge nurse on the Labor and Delivery unit answered. "What's up, Grace?" She frowned at what she heard. "You *are* joking, aren't you? You can't be serious!" The residents at the table looked up curiously as her voice rose. "Well, who authorized . . . Oh. Of all the ridiculous things to have to do! . . . Yes, I know it's not your fault, Grace; I'm sorry. I'll call Dr. Hammett."

She leaned one shoulder against the wall as Dr. Hammett's telephone rang, turning toward the table to meet several pairs of interested eyes. Cassie didn't ruffle easily, and they all wanted to know what had provoked this uncharacteristic outburst. She shrugged at them and turned back to the phone.

"George, this is Cassie Mills, I just got the message about . . . Of course, I understand, but this couldn't have come up at a worse time. . . . Yes. . . . Yes, I appreciate that. Accuracy *is* important, of course, but—" She paused, listening to Dr. Hammett, head of the Obstetrical Department, and scowling at the dull gray linoleum beneath her feet. "George, we've got pregnant women coming up through the cracks in the floor tonight! Can't this wait until—" She closed her eyes with a sigh of defeat and listened for several moments. "All right, I'll do it. But I'm warning you, George, if he gets in the way tonight, he goes!" With a muttered imprecation she banged the receiver back onto its cradle.

She stalked back to the table to collect her tray, but Mike

reached out to hold it down. "Not so fast," he told her. "What's going on that has you so steamed?"

"You wouldn't believe it!" She exhaled loudly in exasperation. "Tonight, of all nights, Dr. Hammett wants me to show James Reid around Labor and Delivery because he's going to be doing a movie adaptation of that book *New Life. Tonight!* As if I didn't have better things to do with my time than baby-sit an actor!"

"That's the price you pay for working in LA, kiddo," Mike said unsympathetically. "It'll be interesting, though, James Reid being *here.*"

"Interesting?" breathed tall, blonde Jeanne, rolling her eyes to heaven. "Interesting is something new in a medical journal. James Reid is *fascinating!*"

"Oh, come on, Jeanne," Cassie scoffed. "You wouldn't want an actor tagging along after you!"

"Honey, James Reid can tag along after me any time he wants to!" Jeanne asserted. "If he's interested in Peds, you just send him along to me!"

"Believe me, I would if I could! You may want him tagging along with you, but for myself, I don't know what I'm going to do with him!" With laughter, and more than a few ribald comments drifting after her, she grabbed her tray and marched away.

She was still simmering when she stepped out of the elevator onto the fifth floor, which housed the Obstetrical Unit, and walked through the doors of the Labor and Delivery suite. It was obvious that the news of the movie star's imminent arrival had preceded her, for a knot of people had gathered at the nurses' station, bubbling and chattering with excitement.

"Have all our patients had their babies and gone home already?" Cassie asked gently, her smile taking the sting from the words, while her meaning remained clear. There was a great deal of shuffling and stammering as they drifted away to return to their duties, leaving Cassie with Grace Walsh, the evening charge nurse, and Dee Woods, one of the unit's registered nurses, who would brief her on any changes in their patients' conditions since she left for dinner.

"Well, Grace," Cassie grinned as the last of the crowd disappeared, "what's the status report?"

"Apart from the news flash about James Reid, you mean?" Grace, fifty, silver-haired and efficient, with a dry sense of humor, grinned back at Cassie, her blue eyes sparkling with amusement. "I didn't mean for that to be broadcast, by the way, but one of the student nurses took the phone message and shrieked 'James Reid' at the top of her lungs. Every non-laboring female on this floor was out here looking for him inside of ten seconds."

"Well, I hope they can refrain from fainting dead away when he gets here," Cassie said dryly. "We're going to be busy enough tonight without worrying about the James Reid Fan Club. Did George tell you when he's due to arrive?"

"In about an hour. George said seven or so."

"Let's get some work done while we can, then. Have there been any more admissions since I left?"

"One, but her labor is still in the early stages, and we got a call from one of the Clinic patients, who will probably arrive in a couple of hours. She's in labor, but it's slow yet, and she lives fairly close. I told her to stay home where she's comfortable until the contractions get down to five minutes."

"I'm glad you did. It could get crowded around here before long. How about the others?" The three of them bent over the charts, reviewing the status of each of the patients currently in labor. Most of them were doing well, both physically and emotionally, but Dee Woods frowned as she opened the last chart.

"I wanted to speak to you about Mary Jo Sutton, Cassie." The tall, striking black woman was frowning in concern as she tapped Mary Jo's chart with her forefinger. "She's only seventeen, and her husband's eighteen, and they're both scared to death, even though her labor has been perfectly normal so far. The trouble is, she's so scared and tense that she's making it harder on herself than it has to be."

"Has she had any childbirth classes?" Cassie asked, knowing already what the answer would be.

"Not a one." Dee shook her close-cropped black curls. "No childbirth preparation at all, barely any doctor's care during pregnancy, and her mother-in-law, who lives with them, has been telling her horror stories for weeks."

"Oh, great," Cassie groaned. "Why do women who have already had children feel they have to scare the next generation to death? That little girl needs all the encouragement she can get, not old wives' tales. Does she trust doctors and nurses?"

"She seems to, and I've assigned the most sympathetic nurse we've got to stay with her until she delivers."

"Good idea." Cassie closed the chart and handed it to Grace. "I'll go see our new admission, and then talk to Mary Jo for a while." Dee nodded agreement, and together they went to see their patients.

Small and thin, with lank blonde hair and enormous, frightened blue eyes, Mary Jo looked even younger than her seventeen years. Her husband, standing at her bedside gripping her hand, was as thin and as frightened as she was. He looked up sharply as Cassie pushed open the door, and his face, boasting the merest beginnings of a beard, was stiff with the strain of concealing his fear.

"Good evening." Cassie smiled. "I'm Dr. Mills, Mr. Sutton, I'm going to take care of your wife this evening."

"Evenin' ma'am." He ducked his head in shy greeting, but kept a grip of his wife's hand.

"How do you feel, Mary Jo?" Cassie stepped to the bedside and took the thin wrist in her fingers, finding the reassuringly strong pulse. "Are your pains getting any stronger, or changing in any way?" She hated to use the term "pains," but Mary Jo wasn't ready to learn any new terminology now, so Cassie used words she would understand.

"They're getting harder, ma'am, a little at a time," the girl replied, then gasped and stiffened as another contraction began.

Cassie rested one hand on Mary Jo's swollen belly, judging the strength of the contraction as the girl's nurse calmly coached her in the ritual of slow breathing and relaxation. As the contraction ended and the girl sagged against the pillows, Cassie smiled encouragement at her. "That was a good, strong contraction, Mary Jo; everything seems to be going fine. I'm going to examine you now, to see how far along you are."

A short time later she had reassured the young couple that the labor was progressing perfectly normally, had allowed them to listen to the fluttering beat of their baby's heart, and had answered their questions, calming them both as best she could. Between her reassurances and the presence of the nurse, things were under control, and Cassie left the labor room feeling good about the night ahead.

Feeling good, that was, until she glanced toward the nurses' station, her eye caught by the crowd which had reassembled there. It appeared that half the Labor and Delivery staff was there, clustered in an adoring crush around the tall figure of James Reid, who was easily recognizable from his photographs. The hero of the hour was smiling lazily down at the circle of upturned faces around him, and Cassie's lips tightened in irritation at the sight. That man had no business being there in the first place, and she was not going to allow him to disrupt the smooth running of the unit.

Since Grace didn't appear to be around to disperse the mob, Cassie exchanged a knowing glance with Dee and quickened her step, intending to break this up once and for all. She had taken only a few steps, though, when a delivery nurse peered out into the hall.

"Dr. Mills?" she called urgently. "We're having a baby in here!"

"Be right there!" Cassie called in reply, doing an abrupt about-face. "Break that up for me, will you Dee?"

"Consider it broken." Cassie nodded to Dee and raced away to the delivery suite, sparing no more than a glance for the movie star. She spared no thought for him, either; her concentration was all on Mrs. Miller and her new son as she directed Craig Marshall, the intern, in the delivery.

An hour later she stripped off her soiled gown and gloves, discarded her disposable cap, shoe covers and mask in a trash hamper, and splashed her face with cold water before leaving the scrub room for the nurses' station.

"Karen said it went well, Cassie," Grace greeted her. "That's one down."

"Mm-hm, and who knows how many to go," was Cassie's unoptimistic reply.

"Cheer up; it can only go on all night!"

"Don't remind me!" Cassie lifted Mrs. Miller's chart from the rack and took it to a small desk in the corner, where she slumped into the hard chair and pulled a pen from the pocket of her lab coat.

"Coffee or soda?" Grace asked from behind her, and Cassie replied without looking up.

"Thanks a million, Grace. Coffee, please."

"I can afford to be generous." Grace placed a steaming mug at her elbow. "I get to go home at eleven thirty."

"That's right, rub it in!" Cassie took a cautious sip of the scalding coffee and resumed writing. "By the way, what happened to the fan club meeting down here?"

"Oh, Dee and I sent them back to work. Mr. Reid showed up while I was with a patient, and by the time I got back here, the grapevine had done its job. We shut Mr. Reid in the on-call room and threatened everyone else with the wrath of Cassandra, and they went back to work. Now they just keep peeking out the doors and around the corners, looking for him."

"As long as they're working," Cassie said absently, and turned her full attention to the chart as Grace walked away, chuckling softly.

"Uh . . . Dr. Mills?" The hesitant murmur which interrupted her a few minutes later belonged to a nursing student who stood timidly behind her.

"Mm-hm?"

"Uh . . . Mr. Reid is . . . uh . . . waiting for you."

"Let him wait. I'm busy."

"Uh . . . Dr. Mills, he's—"

"Look," Cassie scowled in irritation at the page before her, "I know he undoubtedly thinks he's the greatest thing since pockets, but he's going to have to wait until I have some free time. *If* I even have any tonight."

"But, Dr. Mills—"

"He can *wait!*" Cassie bit out, her exasperation breaking through. "It's our patients who are important around here, not someone who's just here to sight-see. And you can tell him that for me!"

"That won't be necessary." The deep male voice came from directly behind Cassie and brought her around sharply in her chair. "You just made your feelings very clear." James Reid, star of stage and screen, smiled lazily down at Cassie from his considerable height, a glint of amusement and male interest lighting his eyes.

If it were possible, James Reid in the flesh was even more impressive than his screen image. His thick, wavy dark hair glinted with reddish highlights beneath the harsh fluorescent light, and the hard planes of his face were thrown into sharp relief. His face wasn't pretty like many actors', but strong and cleanly carved and intensely male, with high cheekbones, a square jaw and a firm, well-shaped mouth. His eyes were deep-set beneath straight dark brows, their clear green color even more striking in person, and he was bigger than Cassie had expected, well over six feet with broad shoulders and strongly muscled limbs. All in all, he was devastating.

Never would Cassie let him see just how devastating. That glint of patronizing male amusement in his eyes had caught her in the raw, and she would be damned if any man, movie star or not, would patronize her. She might have apologized for her rudeness in other circumstances, but not now.

As far as Cassie was concerned, she had nothing to apologize for. She had been stating a simple fact, albeit rather tactlessly. He was the interloper here, and he could, and would, await her convenience. It might be a salutary lesson, she thought, for him to discover that he wasn't always first in the line of importance. She smiled sweetly up at him.

"I'm glad you understand my position, Mr. Reid, because you'll also understand me when I say that I don't have time right now to chat." She turned back to the chart, ignoring the student nurse's shocked gasp.

"That's all right." He dragged another chair up beside the desk. "I'm here to observe, so I'll observe." Cassie shrugged her indifference, but as she finished writing her notes on Mrs. Miller's chart, she was acutely aware of him at the edge of her peripheral vision, positioned just where he could watch her face as she worked.

He was so close that she could feel the warmth of his body and breathe a subtly spicy hint of aftershave, and Cassie found herself writing more rapidly, eager to end this stiflingly close proximity. It was a very effective tactic, she admitted to herself, for few things could be more unnerving than being closely scrutinized while reading or writing. His little ploy was working beautifully, but not for anything in the world would Cassie have let him see that.

When she flipped the chart closed at last, suppressing a sigh of relief, she turned to Grace with only a passing glance for the actor waiting beside her.

"Grace, I'm going to check on Mary Jo Sutton. If anything's happening with the others, let me know, please."

"Sure thing, Cassie."

"All right, Mr. Reid." She pivoted to find him close behind her, and had to tip her head back to look all the way up to his face. "I have to check on a patient, and then I'll meet you in the on-call room. I believe you already know where that is?" She answered his murmured reply with a curt nod, spun on her heel and walked quickly away.

Mary Jo was doing fine, as were the other patients. There had been no new admissions, and Cassie quickly ran out of reasons to put off facing James Reid. She had begun to feel a bit embarrassed about facing him again, knowing she owed him an apology. The trouble was that he probably expected her to be feeling guilty, and she resented that.

She wasn't usually so prickly; in fact, she thought resentfully, she was ordinarily a very courteous, pleasant person, but somehow James Reid rubbed her the wrong way. He probably expected women to fawn over him the way most of the staff had been doing, but he'd soon discover that Cassie Mills didn't fawn over anyone, even if she did apologize. She left Mary Jo in the care of her husband and nurse, with strict instructions to call her if *anything* happened, and went to find James Reid.

He was waiting for her in the on-call room, a combination lounge and bedroom for residents and staff physicians who were waiting for patients to deliver. The bedroom end of the L-shaped room held two narrow beds separated by a night-stand with telephone, while the lounge area boasted a battered sofa and armchair, a coffee urn and another tele-phone. The overall tiredness of the plastic and chrome decor left a lot to be desired, but Cassie was usually too tired herself to pay much attention to the aesthetics.

As she pushed the door open James Reid rose from the armchair and lifted the coffee mug he held. "Like some?"

"Please," Cassie replied, even as she noted the courteous gesture with faint surprise. Somehow she hadn't thought of the famous James Reid as the type of man who would rise when a woman entered the room, and this inconsistency with her expectations was vaguely disturbing. "Black, no sugar," she replied to an inquiring glance from the object of her thoughts, and kicked off her shoes before she dropped onto the sofa, lifting her legs to stretch them out on the lumpy cushions as she leaned back against the armrest. "Thanks." She accepted the steaming mug he handed her and sipped gratefully, relaxing into the corner of the sofa and letting her eyes fall closed.

She took another sip, and then a long swallow of her

coffee, and after a moment summoned the energy to glance at her watch. She saw that it was nearly 11:30. "It's going to be a long night," she sighed, thinking of Mary Jo.

"So it seems." Cassie blinked in surprise. Her statement had been rhetorical, she hadn't expected a response, but now she pushed herself slightly higher against the cracked vinyl and regarded James levelly.

"Well, Mr. Reid, they told me you were coming, but not what, exactly, you intend to do here."

"Observe," he replied succinctly, meeting her gaze with that infuriating hint of amusement in his brilliant green eyes and raising Cassie's hackles again.

"Very droll, Mr. Reid, but I don't really have the time for word games. You have no doubt gathered that I don't want to play tour guide, so why don't you just tell me how I can show you what you want to see and get you out of my hair?"

His facial muscles didn't move, but Cassie saw something flicker deep in his eyes before he spoke again. "You're very blunt, aren't you?"

"I suppose so. I'm not usually rude, though, and for that I do apologize. I've had a long and busy day, and I have a long and busy night ahead of me, and on the scale of importance around here, you don't rank very high right now."

"I see." He was silent for another long moment, sipping his coffee and gazing at the far end of the room. "Dr. Mills, I'm not here to be shown around on some kind of ten-cent tour and then sent on my way. I'm going to be playing the lead in the film version of Mercer's new book, *New Life,* but in addition to that I'm writing the screenplay. Have you read the book?"

"Hm-mm." Cassie shook her head in a quick negative. "I seldom read so-called 'medical' fiction, Mr. Reid." She grinned wryly. "It so rarely lives up to reality."

"So I understand." He grinned back. "And that's why I need the sort of assistance you can give me. I don't want to fall into any of the clichéd traps that have become so common."

"Do you mean that your movie won't have any handsome young interns carrying on with student nurses in the linen closets?" Cassie drawled. "I'm crushed!"

"No interns in the linen closets, no over-sexed nurses and no omnipotent doctors who effortlessly solve all the problems of the world." He grinned. "I'm anxious to make this as realistic as possible, because I feel the story is dramatic enough without that kind of sensational embellishment. It's a novel about an obstetrician practicing in a large city hospital like this one, and about his personal struggle with right and wrong and the choices he's confronted with. The author of the book is an M.D. himself, so I believe the plot is authentic enough, but I want to get a feeling for the setting before I begin adapting it for the screen. I've known George Hammett for years, and when I asked him to suggest a doctor I could observe and talk with, he said you would be his first choice."

"Thanks a million, George," Cassie murmured. James ignored the interruption.

"What I want to do is spend the next six weeks with you, see what you do, talk to you about your work and your life."

"Six *weeks?*" Cassie had stopped listening when she heard that and simply gaped at him in astonishment. "You *are* kidding, aren't you?" He shook his head. "Well, how much time do you intend to spend here? A day or two . . . a week?"

"I'll be here whenever you are."

"*All* the time I'm here?" He nodded. "But *I'm* here over one hundred hours a week!"

"To the extent that I have no other committments which cannot be rescheduled, I'll be here when you are."

"You really should see a psychiatrist, you know. You're obviously either a fanatic or a masochist. Anyway, I can show you what you need to see in—"

"It's not just that," he interrupted. "I want to feel what you feel, the exhaustion, the ups and downs, the long hours and days. I want to get into your skin, to really understand."

Cassie studied him over the rim of her mug, then laid it

aside and dropped her head back against the arm of the sofa again. "And George okayed this, and I don't have any choice, do I?" He shook his head again, and she closed her eyes wearily. "Great. Just exactly what I need."

"People aren't usually so distressed at the thought of my company," he said dryly, and Cassie frowned.

"I'm sorry if I've pricked your delicate ego," she retorted sarcastically, "but in case you missed it, I have a job to do here. Your presence isn't exactly going to make that easier."

"I won't get in your way."

"You can bet on that," she said flatly. "I already told George that I wouldn't tolerate your presence if you did, but you're going to disrupt this unit all the same." He raised his eyebrows in inquiry, and she scowled again. "Did you or did you not notice the small riot you caused just by walking off the elevator tonight? I think we can safely anticipate that happening with monotonous regularity when you appear, and who do you suppose is going to take care of the patients if the staff are all following you around in panting admiration?"

"The novelty of my presence wears off after a short time," he said.

Cassie shook her head. "There are far more people passing through this unit than the few you saw this evening, the other two shifts, for instance, not to mention the unauthorized personnel who will be finding reasons to come up here once your presence becomes common knowledge. Hospitals are the worst gossip mills in the world, in case you didn't know, and having you around is an open invitation to every female in the place. No, Mr. Reid," she said, sighing softly with fatigue, "however long you stay here, or around me, whether it's six weeks or six minutes, you are going to be a colossal nuisance." Her eyes were closed, and she slid lower to rest her head more comfortably on the cushions. "And there's not one thing I can do about it, however much I'd like to throw you out." Her eyes remained closed as she drained her coffee and set the empty mug on the floor. "And make no mistake,

Mr. Reid," she added after a moment, "I would dearly love to throw you out. Bodily, if need be."

James declined to respond to the jibe, and only smiled into his cup as quiet seeped into the room. For some minutes neither of them spoke, so he glanced over at her, mildly startled, when Cassie muttered something unintelligible. Her small, round breasts lifted beneath the soft cotton of her scrub dress as she sighed, moving, with a little nestling squirm, to settle herself more cozily, and James realized in surprise that she had fallen asleep.

As he watched she turned her face away from the light of the ugly floor lamp, cradling her cheek in the palm of her hand. Now that he could look at her without the distraction of her sharp tongue he realized, with some surprise, that she was actually a beautiful woman. His first impression of her, swathed in a surgical gown which camouflaged her body and made her look, if anything, even smaller than she actually was, had been that she was a child dressing up in adult's clothing. His reaction as she told him so plainly that she did not want him there had been that of an adult confronting a fractious child—amused and patronizing.

He had done her a disservice, and she had realized he wasn't taking her seriously, so it was hardly surprising that she was antagonistic. Even so, James wasn't accustomed to being told that he wasn't wanted. When the person telling him his presence was a nuisance rather than a pleasure was a young, lovely, presumably unattached woman, his interest was inevitably piqued. In this case, though, his interest wasn't just piqued, it was entirely captured, and that irritated him in some subtle way.

When George Hammett, a long-time family friend, had suggested that James use Cassie Mills to gain the background and insight he needed to write this screenplay, the older man hadn't mentioned anything personal about her at all. In fact, George had avoided the issue. When James had expressed surprise that his friend's choice of mentor was a woman, and asked what she was like, George had talked on and on about her professional abilities and never even mentioned something so trivial as her age. Could he be match-making, the old devil?

James grinned at the thought, for if the tabloid press was to be believed, there was no man in America less in need of a matchmaker than James Reid. Especially not since he was frequently seen with Marise Marshall. Marise was good for his image, as well as being a reasonably witty dinner partner and a complaisant "friend." Perhaps a bit too complaisant; she had lately been seen about town with a producer currently engaged in planning a new horror epic. James didn't begrudge Marise her ambitions, though.

Neither of them had any illusions about their relationship. For James, Marise was the sort of woman he was expected to escort: stunningly beautiful, a starlet unlikely ever to be a star. And for Marise, James was her ticket to the "right" parties and restaurants, and to the powerful people. No doubt she was seeking a part in that horror movie, and James wished her luck. It was just the type of part she was perfect for, with a minimal wardrobe and a great deal of terrified screaming to make up for the lack of acting talent.

Cassie moved in her sleep, and James blinked, his attention drawn back to the present. He studied the sleeping woman for a moment, wondering at the contrast between her and Marise Marshall; two more different women would be difficult to find. Where Marise was tall, with artificially brilliant red hair and a figure that could only be described as startling, Dr. Mills was petite, almost doll-like, slender and delicately boned with a figure no less female for its slightness, and hair which owed none of its raven sheen to the hairdresser's art.

It was hard to think of her as a hard-working physician when he saw her like this. Her face was perfect, and serene in sleep, a delicate oval with clear, almost transparent ivory skin. Her features made up an elegant whole, large gray eyes thickly fringed with jet-black lashes, small straight nose and sweetly curved mouth. Her hair gleamed like polished jet in the harsh light, beautiful even when scraped back into that knot at the nape of her neck.

She moved again, turning onto her side as she sought a comfortable position, and her green scrub dress twisted beneath her, riding up to bare one slender thigh almost to the hip. James glimpsed a froth of ecru lace at the top of her leg, obviously decorating some feminine undergarment, perhaps a wispy teddy, a tantalizingly sexy contrast to her severe demeanor. No woman who wore lacy things like that could be as cold as Cassie Mills seemed to be.

His eyes flicked to her face, innocent and almost childlike in repose, then back to her legs, satiny smooth with an even, golden tan and that tempting wisp of lace. With abrupt, jerky movements, he shoved himself out of the armchair and strode across the room to snatch up a light cotton blanket folded at the foot of one of the beds. He shook it out and gently covered the sleeping Cassie, then dropped into his seat again, deliberately distancing himself from her.

How long had it been since she'd slept, James wondered, resisting the urge, which washed through him with startling force, to go to her, to loosen her hair from that knot and let it run through his fingers like black silk, to take her small, tired body in his arms and hold her while she slept. He took a deep swallow of his coffee, welcoming the burning heat in his mouth, the slight discomfort bringing him back to reality, for of course he was going to do none of those things.

As he sat watching Cassie sleep the life of the huge hospital went on outside the door which closed them in together, making this small, rather ugly room a temporary haven of privacy. James' eyes never left her, and he moved only to lift his mug to his lips now and again. As he sat watching her he came to a decision. He could have gone to George Hammett and told him he would find another doctor to observe, but he would not.

When he realized just how busy Cassie Mills actually was, he had half-decided to seek out someone else, but now he knew that he would force her to spend the next weeks with him, whether she liked it or not. She had become more than a means to an end, and though he admitted to himself the unfairness of his methods, he would nevertheless employ any means at his disposal to study this small dynamo, to know her.

She slept for nearly an hour before the telephone shrilled rudely by her head, startling James, but merely bringing her awake enough to reach for the instrument on the lamp table.

"This is Cassie," she said huskily into the receiver. "Gotcha . . . Mrs. Resznycki? . . . What's her dilation? . . . Good. . . . Okay, I'll meet you in room two."

By the time she replaced the receiver on its rest she was alert, swinging her feet to the floor to slip them into her shoes, glancing at James as she rose, her voice and demeanor brisk and businesslike once again.

"Are you squeamish?" she asked abruptly, and he shook his head. "Does the sight of blood bother you?"

"Not that I know of."

"Okay. Have Grace get you some greens and get changed, put on a mask and a cap, and I'll meet you in delivery room two. All you have to remember is to keep out of the way and keep quiet."

"Just a minute," he said. Cassie paused with a hand on the door and turned back toward him, clearly eager to be on her way. "Won't she . . . Mrs. Res . . . Resznycki . . . object to having a stranger in there?"

"This is a teaching hospital," she explained, none too patiently. "Our patients understand that medical and nursing students, residents and others will be involved in their care. Allowing observers in the room is up to our discretion. As long as you stay where we tell you to and do as you're told, it's my guess that for once nobody will even notice you. Now, come on. They're waiting!" She vanished out the door, and after an instant's pause James followed her.

*        *        *

Hours later, the glow on the eastern horizon brightening rapidly toward morning, Cassie paused outside the on-call room, breathing hard, striving to control her simmering anger, preparing for the confrontation to come. She was about to give James Reid a piece of her mind, and she didn't want to forget any of the scathing words she had mentally prepared.

It wasn't only that he had been attached to her like a millstone around her neck, and not just for a day or two, but for six weeks, or that everywhere he went he started a small riot, but to top it off, despite the fact that he had been very clearly instructed to observe as unobtrusively as possible, he had committed the unpardonable sin of voicing an interruption in delivery. After witnessing two deliveries, both of which were uneventful and during both of which he had kept himself silent and well in the background, he had accompanied the rest of the team into the delivery room for the birth of Mary Jo Sutton's baby.

That delivery had been somewhat different from the others, not because something had gone wrong, but because Mary Jo, young and unprepared and frightened, had begun to cry out with each contraction as her labor neared its climax. Many women did this, some screamed, some swore, some cried or laughed uncontrollably, and the delivery team knew and accepted this as part of the range of normal responses to the stress of childbirth. James Reid, however, had apparently been disturbed by the girl's cries, and by what he judged to be the callousness or indifference of the physicians and nurses.

Mary Jo was about to give birth, encouraged by the team to work with her contractions, and crying out with each one, when James could stand it no longer. As Cassie concentrated on her first glimpse of the baby's hair, James stepped from the corner he had occupied, demanding anxiously, almost angrily, "Can't you *do* something for her?"

Cassie couldn't leave Mary Jo, couldn't even look up, but she murmured "Cathy," to the circulating nurse, who muttered a quiet response and firmly ushered James from the room. In a few short minutes Mary Jo had been delivered of a healthy, seven-pound son, and had relaxed into the post-birth euphoria, her previous distress forgotten in the magic of meeting her baby. Her husband was reassured when things ended well, but Cassie had seen the fear in his face when James spoke out, and she resolved to talk to Billy Sutton later, to explain James' non-professional status and his outburst.

She was just glad that the outburst had prompted nothing worse, for husbands, distressed by their wives' or the staff's behavior, had been known to become abusive, and even violent. A remark like James' could act as a spark to the tinder of a husband's worry.

James had spoken out of turn, but he would be in no doubt about his place in the scheme of things when Cassie finished with him, nor in any doubt as to the constraints on his behavior in the future. She took a final deep breath and swung open the on-call room door.

# Chapter Two

James had been seated in the worn armchair, but when Cassie entered the room he rose and moved behind it, facing her as the door swung slowly closed behind her. Dressed in a wrinkled, sweat-dampened scrub dress, her hair rumpled from the cap she had worn, and shadows of fatigue showing in her eyes, she shouldn't have looked at all formidable, but in some undefinable way she did, and James held himself erect, braced for the onslaught to come.

"How dare you?" she breathed. "How *dare* you interfere in the practice of medicine? Who the *hell* do you think you are? Do you have any idea of the possible consequences of an outburst like yours?" She took a quick step away from him, too agitated to stand still, then spun to face him again, fixing him with a frigid glare. "One of the most important aspects of the physician-patient relationship is trust, but it's a fragile thing at best, and in a moment of stress like delivery it's even more delicate and more vital. Laboring women have been known to endanger their lives and the lives of their babies by trying to climb down from the delivery table, and husbands have been known to become violent with less provocation than you so generously provided." Her words were heavily sarcastic, and a dull red flush began to creep up James' neck.

"Wait a minute!" he broke in. "I didn't know that—"

"My point exactly!" Cassie snapped. "*You* didn't know, but *I* did!" He stood still beneath the lash of her tongue, seeing, like many before him, not the quietly lovely, mellow-voiced Cassie, but Cassandra the Terrible, impressive in her authority and intimidating in her ire. "You will do me the courtesy of remembering, Mr. Reid, that you *don't* know what is going on around here, but that I do. That is, as I understand it, the reason you are here. You are here to observe and *nothing* more! Either keep that well in mind or leave now!" She regarded him with distaste for a moment, much as she might have looked at a particularly unpleasant insect, then turned toward the door. "I'm going to have a shower and then go to breakfast. The men's shower is just past the nurses' station, if you want to stay." She stalked out of the room, leaving the tall man staring after her, a curious expression lighting his brilliant green eyes.

In the end, he stayed, though Cassie hadn't been at all sure that he would, and had been wondering how she would explain to George Hammett that she had driven Mr. Reid from the hospital after only one night. He was waiting for her in the on-call room, though, when she returned from showering and changing into a fresh scrub dress, and walked beside her in silence through the halls and down the stairs to the cafeteria. Neither of them spoke until they were seated in the most unobtrusive corner of the large room.

"I didn't expect you to stay." Cassie could feel his gaze on her, but kept her own fixed on the piece of toast she was buttering.

"Are you glad I did?"

She laid her knife carefully on the side of her plate before looking up. "Do you want me to be honest," she asked with an artless smile, "or polite?"

He gave a shout of laughter which drew eyes from all around the room, but Cassie relaxed fractionally. He might not really be able to jeopardize her position if he tried to, but he could certainly make her relationship with George difficult, and the laughter could be a sign that he would perhaps not carry a grudge. "Be honest, by all means!" he laughed. "I wouldn't know how to deal with polite dissembling from you."

Cassie grinned. "I am capable of tact," she told him. "In

the right circumstances. However, I have an unfortunate tendency to be somewhat . . . direct, at times. To answer your question, I'm glad that my chewing you out didn't drive you away, but I still think you're going to complicate my life by being around all the time, and I don't relish the idea of complications."

"I can understand that." James chewed a forkful of ham and eggs thoughtfully. "I'm sorry to be an inconvenience to you, but not sorry enough to leave. I've been chewed out before, and no doubt I will be again, but I do have to admit that you're one of the best chewer-outters I've ever been dressed-down by."

"Somehow," Cassie tipped her head to the side and studied him for a moment, "I find it hard to picture you being chewed out by anyone, least of all me." It was true; as she sat across the small, plastic-topped table from him, she found it difficult to believe that she had actually read the riot act to James Reid. With his striking looks and his aura of power, he appeared to be the kind of man who was never crossed in anything, and yet she had dressed him down with no more consideration than she would have shown a careless medical student. He had allowed her to get away with it, this time, because she had been in the right and they both knew it, but she didn't think for a moment that he would allow it again.

He was smiling as she studied him, though, and commenting that some directors would chew out the Devil himself if they thought he was capable of improving his performance. "I appreciate your being honest with me, and being angry with me if I deserve it," he went on, "because I'm here to learn."

"Well, you've already had a few lessons. What did you think of it?"

"The first time, or the second . . . or the third, when you threw me out?"

"Don't make it sound like that! You've already agreed that you deserved to be thrown out." She grinned again. "The first time, just to do this in the logical way. Had you ever seen a baby born before?"

"Never." He shook his head for emphasis.

"You did pretty well, then. Medical students have been known to pass out or throw up on occasion, and lay people are notorious for it!"

"I don't deserve any credit for that; I've never been squeamish, but I was surprised by a lot of things." Cassie raised one eyebrow in inquiry. "Most of all, I was astonished by how hard the mother was working. I know it's called 'labor,' but I never before thought about why that term is used. I found myself wondering how she could keep up such an effort for so long, how she could bear the pain. I wondered how her husband felt, too, watching her go through it, but helpless to do anything for her."

"I think many people feel that way at first. And the second time, were your reactions any different?"

"They were." He nodded thoughtfully. "The first time I didn't really see, didn't notice, anyone but the mother, but the second time I saw the father, his concern for his wife . . . and I saw the baby." He looked down at his plate for a moment, his expression almost sheepish. "She was so tiny, and so beautiful. I wanted to hold her myself."

Cassie nodded, smiling her understanding. "You feel that way when you look into those eyes as they see their world for the first time, so young and yet so wise. I think the instinct to reproduce is probably the most basic human instinct of all, and the sight of a child, especially a newborn baby, arouses feelings in us that we can't explain any other way."

"Do you ever become accustomed to it?" he asked. "Do you ever get bored or jaded?"

"Not really," Cassie said slowly. "That's why I love it, despite the terrible hours and the unpredictability. Some nights when I'm on call we don't have anything to do here but sit around and play pinochle; on other nights we never stop running. I get tired, physically tired, from nights of no sleep, and I get tired of being called away from dinner parties and movies, but I never tire of seeing a baby born."

James met her eyes for a long moment, his expression serious, almost somber, then he nodded. "Thank you."

"For what?"

"For giving me a serious, thoughtful answer. I think George was right when he said you'd be the best person for me to learn from."

"That's very flattering, but I'm not—"

"It's really you!" gasped an excited female voice from behind Cassie. "You're *James Reid!*" The voice rose to a squeal, and Cassie turned to see a teenager in a candystriper's pink-and-white pinafore hurrying toward their table, pen and paper in hand. She sighed in exasperation and turned back to James, a commiserating remark on her lips. It died unuttered, for in place of the man who had discussed the night's experiences so thoughtfully with her was James Reid the movie star. Smiling, charming, he rose as the teenager neared, agreed happily to sign an autograph for her and one for her best friend, and thanked her for a gushy compliment on his last movie.

As if the ice had been broken by that first fan, people all over the cafeteria, mainly women and girls, were suddenly rising and surging toward their table.

And James stood waiting for them, an expectant smile on his lips, apparently prepared for a lengthy session of signing autographs. Cassie watched in something approaching disbelief, which became cynical comprehension laced with self-reproach. Now she was seeing the real James Reid, world-famous star of stage and screen, the consummate actor who had just given a masterful performance for Cassie herself, neatly convincing her of his sincerity and his interest in her and her world.

Her face set, her eyes cold, she rose so abruptly that her chair slid across the linoleum with a screech of protest. "I have to do rounds," she snapped to James, who looked across at her in surprise. "Then I'll be in the Clinic, if you're interested." Without waiting for a reply she spun on her heel and stalked away, hearing behind her a chorus of female voices singing the praises of James Reid.

It was her own fault, of course, but she felt like an absolute fool for having believed for a moment that someone as accustomed to the wealth and glamour of Hollywood as James Reid would seriously be interested in her feelings about her work. It had been a terrific piece of acting, she had to admit that, and it had been her own flattered ego which had led her to believe everything he said without question, but it wouldn't happen again, she'd make sure of that.

Her resolve was still firm as she sat in the small Clinic office, waiting for her first patient to arrive at 8:15, and rereading the note, left for her by a secretary, which said that James had gone home to change and would join her at the Clinic later in the morning. So much for his much-vaunted intention to stay with her every minute of the day, she thought in disgust, unfairly ignoring the fact that he had probably come to the hospital the night before unprepared for an extended stay. Well, she didn't give a hoot if he didn't show up at all; she'd do better without someone tagging along all the time, anyway.

Perhaps fortunately, the buzzer on the desk intercom interrupted the increasingly peevish train of her thoughts. She reached out to push the button.

"Yes?"

"Mrs. Allen is here, Dr. Mills. She's waiting for you in room one."

"I'll be right there. Thank you." Cassie clicked off the intercom and gathered up her stethoscope and Mrs. Allen's chart, glad to have something to take her mind off James.

Her schedule was full that morning, with no breaks between appointments, but a cancellation at ten o'clock left her a few minutes free. She was at her desk reading a page of patient notes when a cup of coffee magically appeared in the center of the page. She looked up from the desktop with a grin lighting her face even before she saw who had brought the coffee. She didn't need to see, for only Gail Anderson would do this.

Slowly Cassie leaned back in her chair, narrowing her eyes and drawling, à la Humphrey Bogart, "What do I owe ya' for the java, honey?" Gail stood with one hip jutting out, ostentatiously chewing imaginary gum, the archetypal diner waitress.

"It'll be two bits, toots. The sugar's free." The two of them held their "characters" for another moment, then simultaneously broke up, laughing uproariously.

"You're wasted here," Cassie gasped. "You should be in movies or something!"

"Which reminds me . . ." Gail dropped into a chair opposite Cassie, her brown eyes alight with interest.

"Oh, no, not you, too!" Cassie groaned and studied her friend with amused resignation. Tall and slender, with dark auburn hair and a generous sprinkling of freckles, she didn't quite fit the image of a Head Nurse, but despite that she was Head Nurse of Labor and Delivery. At thirty she was a year older than Cassie, but she looked younger than she was, and was also pretty and cheerful, with a sometimes wacky sense of humor and a gentle yet effective authority which kept her unit running smoothly even in times of crisis. Now she grinned back at Cassie and nodded.

"Of course, me too! Are you kidding? You can't have America's heartthrob following you around the hospital and refuse to tell me every little detail! You know better than that. Now, tell me!"

Cassie threw up her hands in surrender. "I don't know how you can do this to me when you're supposed to be my friend, you know. That man is the *last* thing I want to waste time talking about."

"Oh, come on, now. How bad can it be to spend all your time with the sexiest man in America?"

"You forget that you also have to deal with the fans and the autograph hunters and half the hospital staff following you around and getting in the way. Didn't they tell you we could hardly get anything done last night because practically the entire L and D staff was hanging around in the hall just to get a look at him?"

"But he's *worth* getting a look at!" Gail breathed, and Cassie laughed again.

"With a husband as handsome as yours, you can't be that interested in worshipping a movie star from afar! After all, you have Steve right there at home, and he's gorgeous!"

"If you say so," Gail laughed, but her grin faltered and her laugh sounded forced. She shrugged. "They say familiarity breeds contempt, don't they?"

"Gail, is—"

Cassie never got to ask if anything was wrong, because Gail went on speaking as if she hadn't heard her. "Now, tell me what James Reid could have done in one night to get you so mad?"

Under cover of drinking her coffee, Cassie studied her friend for a moment, seeing lines of strain around her mouth and eyes that she hadn't noticed before. She would have pressed, but Gail's face, her manner, made it clear that a door had just been firmly closed on the issue. With a soundless sigh Cassie relented. If Gail wanted to talk about it she would, in her own time.

She told Gail the whole story of James' unexpected presence, beginning with the telephone call at dinner the night before and ending with the cafeteria autograph session that morning, sparing no detail of his interruption of Mary Jo's delivery. Gail made suitably sympathetic noises, but it was apparent to Cassie that she still felt that the benefits of spending one's days with James Reid far outweighed the drawbacks.

"You know, he still doesn't sound all that bad," she said when Cassie had concluded her list of grievances. "He's inexperienced, after all, and anyone could misinterpret what happens in the delivery room."

"That's easy for you to say," Cassie replied sullenly.

"You're not the one who's stuck with him for weeks to come."

"No, but I'd like to be!" Gail rolled her eyes heavenward as she stood, picking up their empty cups to return them to the cafeteria.

"You can have him!" Cassie snapped. "Personally, I'd just as soon spend my time with a good book as with all that Hollywood phoniness!"

Gail paused in the doorway to favor Cassie with an openly skeptical glance. "Methinks the lady doctor doth protest too much!" she fired back, and disappeared down the hall, cackling with laughter.

Not five minutes after Gail's departure the object of their discussion tapped lightly on the office door and then slipped inside. Cassie had looked up idly at the noise, but she stared in disbelief at the apparition which entered. James was plainly dressed in gray flannel slacks and an open-necked shirt, but wore, apparently as an attempt at disguise, a battered tan fedora and dark sunglasses. Considering the fact that she had never seen anyone off the screen wear a hat like that, and the additional fact that the morning haze had not yet burned off, so it was still gray and dreary outside, Cassie thought she had never seen a less effective disguise in her life.

"What on earth," she asked as he dropped into the chair Gail had recently vacated, "is all this?"

"I was trying to be inconspicuous." He shrugged, dropping the hat onto a lamp table and tucking the sunglasses in his pocket.

"You're about as inconspicuous as a brass band! I thought actors were supposed to be good at assuming different identities, but you might as well have your name on the back of your shirt."

"It's not that bad, surely. After all, I don't see anyone asking for an autograph." There was a bite to his words, in response to Cassie's own sarcasm, but she was vindicated by the knock on the door which prevented him from saying more.

"Dr. Mills?" whispered a soft-voiced and obviously nervous student nurse. "I'm sorry to interrupt, but I wondered if I could have Mr. Reid's autograph? I'm a real big fan of yours, Mr. Reid."

Cassie smiled thinly at James and rose. "I rest my case. Of course you may have Mr. Reid's autograph; he has plenty of time for that kind of thing, but I have patients to see." She picked up her clipboard and pen and swept out of the room before either of the others could do more than stare in surprise at her fast-disappearing back.

By the time she was ready to see her next patient, a lab coat had been found for James, and, without asking permission, he fell in step beside her as she walked to the examining room. That omission, she knew, was deliberate; he knew the answer she wanted to give, and he had denied her the opportunity of giving it.

It rankled that she should be so easy for him to read, and though he followed her instructions to the letter for the rest of the day, doing his best to blend into the woodwork, his presence rankled, too. In spite of his cooperation, her resentment smoldered, nourished by the persistence of the fans, hospital staff, patients and visitors alike, who interrupted them to gush compliments at James and beg for autographs, handshakes and even kisses.

Gail was no better than the rest of them, in Cassie's jaundiced estimation, lying in wait at the nurses' station, where she could see everyone leaving the elevator, and planting herself in the corridor so Cassie had no choice but to make introductions. Gail even said all the banal things Cassie had already listened to at least a thousand times as she suffered through a lunch with James that amounted to a cafeteria press conference, and Cassie's insistence that she and James had to get to work was barely civil, cutting Gail off in mid-sentence.

She took no offense, though. "That's right," she grinned knowingly at Cassie, "I'm sure you two have a lot of things to do." Her voice was heavy with innuendo, and Cassie's scowl deepened. "I'd love to talk to you some time when you're not so busy, though, Mr. Reid. The movie business is just fascinating to me."

"Since when?" Cassie muttered under her breath as James made a charming reply, not meaning him to hear, but made aware that he had by the glint of amusement in his eyes as he turned to accompany her down the hall.

Though it wasn't particularly busy, the afternoon seemed endless to Cassie, and she found it increasingly difficult to hold her tongue and her temper as yet another person stopped them to say, "Oh, Mr. Reid, I just *love* your movies. . . ."

It was after seven when she checked out; she had a throbbing headache, and she was nursing a profound sense of personal grievance against the man she considered responsible for it all. He waited while she changed and collected her purse and black bag, then walked beside her as she marched briskly through the corridors, eager to leave the hospital—and James Reid—behind.

"I'm off duty now," she reminded him as they entered the elevator which would take them to the ground floor and the parking garage. "I'll see you here at six-thirty tomorrow morning."

"And not a moment sooner?" he supplied with a humorless smile. "I'll walk you to your car." He moved beside her as the elevator doors slid open and she walked out.

"That isn't necessary," she snapped. "I think I'm capable of finding my own car."

"I'm walking you to your car." His voice was calm, ignoring her sarcasm as he had ignored it all day, but his lips tightened, and Cassie knew her ungracious refusal had angered him. She was a bit ashamed of herself, too; she knew perfectly well that he hadn't deserved that, but she wasn't about to back down and apologize, not after the day she'd had. He escorted her through the echoing vastness of the parking garage, dim and chilly in the January evening, after the day's earlier warmth. If she were perfectly honest with herself, Cassie knew, she didn't really mind an escort; darkness came early in mid-winter, and by the time Cassie left the hospital in the evenings the parking garage was nearly deserted and potentially dangerous, despite the security patrols.

Her car was one of several remaining in the area reserved for doctors, and she faced James with her keys in her hand, anxious to dismiss him and be on her way. "Thank you for the escort. I'll see you tomorrow." She reached to slip her key in the door of her small Japanese sedan, but his words stopped her.

"I know you're tired," he said, "and you won't feel much like cooking, so I'll take you to dinner." Not, will you have dinner with me, Cassie noted, her temper rising again, just a calm assumption that she would passively comply with his wishes.

"No. Thank you."

She didn't even pretend to be polite, and perhaps that was what finally ignited James' own temper. She reached for the lock again, but a large hand closed on her upper arm and he hauled her roughly around to face him. His face was dark with anger, and Cassie felt a pang of apprehension; he was far stronger than she was, and just about angry enough to take advantage of that.

"Look, lady," he growled, pushing her back against one of the huge concrete pillars which supported the structure, "you don't have to like me, that's okay with me. In fact, after the way you've acted today, I quite frankly don't care if you like me or not. If you're mad at me for some reason, then tell me why. If I did something wrong, let me know what I did and I won't do it again, but stop sulking like a little kid who didn't get her way!"

"I am *not* sulking!" Cassie snapped, stung to fury by his attack, and only when the words had been uttered did she realize what she sounded like—a small child who hasn't gotten her way. Even as the realization dawned and she felt an embarrassed flush warming her cheeks, James burst into derisive laughter.

"If you're not sulking, then what would you call it?" Cassie could only glare at him in frustrated rage, knowing she had no defense, and he pressed the point. "Look, if there's a problem, then it needs to be worked out. I'm hungry, and you must be, too, so have dinner with me and we'll get the problem, whatever it is, solved."

Cassie adamantly did not want to have dinner with him, yet she knew that she had no reasonable grounds for refusal, and there was no way she wished to give credence to his accusation of sulking. Unable to meet his eyes and face the knowledge in them, she dropped her gaze to his hands, which were still holding her prisoner against the massive pillar. She hadn't really looked at him that day, but she was struck suddenly by the sheer physical presence of the man. Tall, fully a foot taller than her five feet three, he was lean and hard and tanned. His money and fame didn't seem to have made him prey to soft living and excess, for beneath the perfectly tailored shirt and slacks was no hint of a paunch, and his forearms, bared by the rolled sleeves of his shirt, were corded with powerful muscle.

Her eyes were on a level with his shirtfront and the broad expanse of his chest, close enough that she could see dark hair curling at the base of his throat and feel the heat of his body, so close to hers. As she took a deep breath, which failed miserably to steady her rattled nerves, she caught the faint tang of aftershave, musky and seductive, and was shaken by a frighteningly strong and totally insane desire to be pulled into his arms and held tightly against the hard, strong length of him.

No, she didn't want that. She shook her head, not in answer to his question, but in sharp denial of her own desires, and forced herself to look up into his face. "All right," she said slowly. "I'll have dinner with you."

"Good." He didn't elaborate, didn't comment on her

change of attitude, and with a sigh of relief she stepped away from him as he released her, anxious to put some distance between them. Out of range of the spell of his maleness, she could face him more calmly, and her voice was once again level and cool.

"I'd like to shower and change first, though. Can you give me time for that?"

"Certainly. I have an office in Studio City; I can change there and pick you up in about an hour. If you don't live too far from there, that is?"

"Actually, it should be pretty convenient. I live in Burbank."

"Beautiful downtown Burbank, eh?" He grinned. "An hour is all it will take, then, if that's enough time for you."

"That will be fine." She gave him her address and directions to her house, and allowed him to seat her in her car and watch as she drove away, without the slightest qualm about what she had agreed to. Without a qualm, that is, until he was out of sight and she had time to reflect on what she had done. You'd better hope, Cassandra Lea Mills, she told herself, that you know what you're getting into. You'd just better hope.

Hoping and believing were two very different things, though, and Cassie wasn't nearly as calm as she would have liked to be as she dressed and made up. She had no idea what sort of restaurant James might take her to, so she chose an outfit which would fit in almost anywhere, slim black silk twill trousers and a white silk blouse, cinched at the waist with a wide belt of soft scarlet leather. The blouse, though tailored, was far from severe, relying on the soft fluidity of the fabric and the deep plunge of the neckline to make it an undoubtedly feminine garment. The brilliant red belt emphasized her tiny waist, and when she stepped into black sandals with wickedly high heels and the barest minimum of straps she was satisfied with her efforts.

Her makeup, carefully applied to emphasize her luminous eyes and the curve of her lips, was subjected to an equally close scrutiny, and when the finishing touches of dramatic knots of gold at her ears and her best and most seductive perfume were added, she was satisfied with the effect she had achieved. The woman who looked back at her from the mirror was, despite her size, very much a woman, assured and composed. She wanted James Reid to know that even though she didn't inhabit a world as glamorous and fast-living as his, she was neither childish nor naïve. Her appearance gave her an extra bit of confidence she badly needed after their *contretemps* in the parking garage.

He had been justified in accusing her of childish behavior. Now that her temper had cooled, she had to admit it, and she was ashamed of the way in which she had vented her bad temper on him without even bothering to explain what was wrong. Now that she had proved that she could be childish, spiteful and sulky, she had to prove that she could also be mature, reasonable and intelligent, no small task in light of her earlier *faux pas*.

She caught her hair back from her face on one side, leaving the rest free to swirl around her shoulders, and was just fixing an ebony comb in place when the doorbell pealed. To her disgust she jumped as if she'd been stung and had to take several deep breaths to calm herself before she went to open the door. Her appearance gave an illusion of composure, but her hand shook with a fine tremor as she reached for the knob, and she was suddenly strongly reluctant to face James Reid again.

Taking one more deep breath, she resolutely pulled the door open and smiled serenely up at James. "This is good timing; I just finished changing."

"The result would have been worth waiting for." He smiled lazily back, and a shiver of excitement slid over her skin at the warmth in his eyes. He had only seen her in rumpled, baggy scrub dresses and the rather tired-looking shirtdress she had worn to the hospital over thirty-six hours before, so the transformation came as a surprise to him, as she had intended it should. She was woman enough to enjoy his reaction, that moment when he was off-balance, before the amused, sophisticated mask slipped back into place. There was more than surprise in his eyes, though, there was a sexual appraisal which alarmed her.

He hadn't looked at her that way when she was a hurried, harried resident, and that air of the predator put her on her guard, so that she replied to his compliment with more coolness than she might have.

"Thank you." She gave his flattery the barest acknowledgment and stepped back, inviting him in. "Would you like a drink before we go?" she offered, politely, if unenthusiastically.

"Thank you. Scotch on the rocks, if you have it." James followed her from the tiny, tile-floored entry hall into the living room and looked around appreciatively. Her house was a smallish, two-bedroom stucco bungalow, built in the late forties in the Spanish style, with a red tile roof and stucco pillars and arches framing the front porch. Inside, the walls were painted a creamy white, and the furnishings were traditional, floral prints in shades of blue and rose with a golden oak dining room ensemble and a beautiful golden oak china cabinet that had been Cassie's grandmother's.

The bedrooms were furnished with a mixture of traditionally-styled pieces and family heirlooms, in the predominant blue and rose tones Cassie preferred. Her kitchen wasn't large, but it was cheerful, with counters and a back-splash of bright red tile, and linens and curtains picking up the red, while the bathroom tile was a deep blue which she had accented with many shades from pale delft to indigo. Like many houses built in that postwar period, this one was small but comfortable, with a pleasant back yard and a brick patio outside the kitchen door where Cassie often took her meals on warm days.

Now, as he looked around, she took bottles and glasses from the big oak cabinet, poured Scotch for James and dry sherry for herself, and carried his drink into the kitchen to add ice. To her annoyance he followed her, his bulk making the smallish room seem even smaller.

"Here you are." She pushed his glass into his hand. "Excuse me for a moment; I have to turn the sprinkler off."

"No problem." He stepped back to allow her to pass him, and when she went out the back door and down the two steps to the chevron-patterned brick of the patio, he came along, carrying her sherry. "You have a nice yard."

"What you can see of it in the dark." Cassie found the tap and the "chick-chick-chick-chick-whirr" of the sprinkler out on the grass stopped short. "There is a light, if you'd turn on the switch to the left inside the kitchen door." James reached in to press the switch, and a light mounted beside the door illuminated the patio and a semicircle of the yard.

"Very nice." He looked approvingly at the patio, furnished with a gay red-and-white table and chairs and chaise longue, and edged by lush shrubbery. Two huge hibiscus bushes, one flowering bright pink and the other peachy-orange, flanked the back door, and along the fence separating her yard from the neighbors' were an enormous oleander and several poinsettias, more than ten feet tall and blooming dramatically, at the height of their mid-winter season. "Very nice," James repeated, and Cassie had to smile, because she agreed with him.

"I like it, even though I can't take credit for the bushes. They were here when I bought the house. I planted those," she indicated three terra-cotta tubs along the far side of the patio, "with flowers and herbs and things, but I don't have time to do any real gardening." She turned to go back inside, but James stopped her with a light hand on her arm.

"Could we sit out here? It's not really cold, since it's sheltered from the wind." Cassie looked up at him for a moment and shrugged.

"Certainly. I'll just get a shawl." When she returned she took one of the red-and-white chairs, while James sat sideways on the chaise. "I like it out here. It's my own little piece of nature, even though it's hardly the wide-open spaces." She sipped her sherry reflectively. "There's one thing it needs, though."

"What's that?"

"An orange tree. There was an apricot in the corner of the yard, but it got some awful apricot disease three years ago, and I had to have it taken out, which was like losing a friend. The snails ate most of the apricots anyway, so what I'd really like is an orange tree to replace it. The little ones take forever to bear fruit, though, and I'm not very patient. For now I get oranges from Gail Anderson. You met her; she's Head Nurse of Labor and Delivery."

"I remember. She's tall, with dark-red hair, right?"

"Mm-hm. She and her husband live in what used to be an orange grove, and they have two enormous trees in their yard. She brings me her surplus, but I like the idea of coming out and picking my breakfast."

"Very Californian," James agreed with a smile. "It would give you more shade, too. Have you thought of getting a dwarf-type tree? They bear sooner, and you can get them tubbed."

"Mm-hm, and they're so-o-o expensive."

James laughed with her. "Good point." He glanced at his watch, an impossibly thin wafer of gold, and whistled softly under his breath. "Later than I thought. If you're ready, we should probably be going."

"Yes, of course." Cassie's glass was empty, and she rose to precede him into the house. Her shawl, in sheerly woven cream wool, and a black satin clutch were her only accessories, and when she had collected the clutch she let him escort her to the luxurious, steel gray Mercedes sedan which waited at the curb. It certainly added a touch of class to her faintly dilapidated neighborhood, Cassie thought in amusement, slipping into a sinfully plush leather seat, for nothing more costly than her Japanese subcompact had graced this block in a long time.

"Nice car," she commented, running a fingertip lightly

over the butter-soft burgundy leather after she fastened her seatbelt, and James grinned.

"You don't think I should have brought the Rolls?" Cassie stared blankly at him for a moment, and then burst out laughing.

"Do you have a Rolls?"

"Um-hm." He nodded, and she folded her arms and looked down her small nose at him.

"Well, if you have a Rolls, you certainly should have brought it! After all, why should I settle for second best?"

"My apologies." He gave a half-bow in her direction, his lips twitching with humor, and accelerated away from the curb and toward the freeway. "Nothing but the best for *Madame* from now on."

"Good." Cassie giggled at his expression of dismay, then sat back in the cradling luxury of her seat as he merged with the heavy flow of traffic. She could study him at will while he drove, and now her mind registered what she had been too preoccupied to notice before. He really was stunningly handsome. He had showered and shaved at his office. He looked refreshed, and his hair was still slightly damp, and he had changed into a dove-gray suit that should have looked conservative and dull, and was instead devastating.

It was immaculately tailored, in perfect taste, with no hint of Hollywood flashiness, relying on exquisite cut and perfect fit for its effect. His shirt was a paler shade of gray, and his tie and pocket handkerchief were burgundy with a tiny pattern in silver. He braked to avoid a truck which swung in front of them, and Cassie's gaze was caught by the play of muscle in his thigh as the fabric of his trousers was drawn tight by the movement. The suit was much too well-tailored to be anything so crass as tight, but the lines of his body were discreetly emphasized by the vest which fit close to his lean waist and the jacket which clung to the breadth of his shoulders. The civilized broadcloth veneer seemed only to point up the intense masculinity of the man who wore it. He seemed very big, sitting beside her, and the car somehow smaller, and Cassie was uncomfortably reminded of the predatory light she had seen in his eyes.

He had wanted her then, the way a man wants a woman. The idea frightened her a little. No, she admitted, it frightened her more than a little.

# Chapter Three

Deliberately Cassie pulled her gaze away from the man beside her and stared blankly out the window at the passing city, coughing softly to clear her unaccountably dry throat. Of course he was a handsome, sexy man, the whole world knew that, but that was no excuse for her to get nervous palpitations like a star-struck teenager. She was having dinner with him, not being carried off to his lair, and even the dinner was hardly a social occasion. He'd only asked her out because she was working with him. And because she had acted like an idiot ever since she'd first laid eyes on him, a small voice reminded her.

He had been right in accusing her of sulking, and if he'd chosen to press the point, he could have accused her of a lot more than that. She owed him an apology, as well she knew, though she didn't know if she could bring herself to abandon her pride to that extent. Her father had told her often enough that her pride was both an asset and a liability, for though it prompted her to work very hard to do the best she could at whatever she attempted, it also made apologies very difficult for her. However unpleasant, though, she owed James Reid an apology and an explanation, and she would have to offer them and hope he chose not to gloat.

Thus resolved, she forced herself to relax, and for the remainder of the ride tried to divert herself from self-castigation by guessing which popular night spot he might take her to. To her surprise he bypassed Beverly Hills and the more obvious restaurants, and stopped at last on a quiet street in Westwood, at a restaurant so small and unobtrusive that it was almost invisible. A vast mass of scarlet bougainvillea spilled over the awning in front of an art gallery, and half-hidden beneath it, at one side of the gallery's display window, was a heavy oak door with a small brass plaque which read *Ristorante Fredo*.

The door swung inward on a hallway leading back to the rear of the gallery, and they walked along it to another door. James knocked on this one, and it opened to reveal a small, beautifully decorated and intimately lit cave of a dining room, and a maître d' who bowed deeply to them.

"*Signore* Reid," he nodded, "*Signorina*. If you will follow me." He led them to a table for two in one corner of the room, made private by a screen of palms and other plants, but before James had taken his seat a bellow of "*Jimmee!*" resounded from the kitchen.

Fredo was a very large man, and he erupted from the kitchen, charged across the dining room and clasped James in a bear hug, pounding him happily on the back. Cassie watched in amused amazement as the two men exchanged a laughing, rapid-fire volley of Italian greetings and a few of what Cassie recognized as rather colorful epithets. She sat and enjoyed the show along with the other patrons until the friends paused long enough to notice her, and was amused anew at the crestfallen dismay on Fredo's face.

He smote his forehead with his open palm, then bowed dramatically low, reaching for her hand and pressing a kiss on her fingers. "Why have you allowed me to ignore this lovely lady?" he demanded of James. "I am most ashamed of my rudeness, *Signorina*. If my friend will introduce me to you, I will be eternally grateful."

"Watch out for Fredo when he's grateful." James grinned. "He's dangerous that way. Cassie," he said formally, "this is my friend, and our host this evening, Alfredo Martello, known as Fredo. Fredo, this is Dr. Cassandra Mills."

"*Enchanté*." Fredo bowed again. "I am delighted to make your acquaintance, *Signorina*." With all the solicitous courtesy of an old-world nobleman he inquired after her health, then discussed with them the specialty of the evening and the meal he would prepare for them. It was some minutes before their menu was decided, they were supplied with an aperitif and at last left alone while Fredo departed to oversee the preparation of their food. Only then did Cassie feel her tension returning.

She still had that apology to make, and she still hated the very thought of it. The pride that was so often her nemesis was matched by a bone-deep sense of personal integrity, however, and that integrity would not allow her to evade the issue. She toyed with her glass as silence descended on their table in the wake of Fredo's departure, then took a deep breath and looked up to find James studying her inscrutably. Her color rose, but she faced him without flinching.

"I owe you an apology," she said, and one eyebrow lifted as he watched her, though he said nothing. "You accused me of sulking, and you were absolutely right. I was taking my bad temper out on you, and I'm sorry about that." He nodded. "I'm sorry about that," she went on, "but—"

"There's a 'but' in this, is there?" he asked, a grin lifting his lips, and Cassie nodded firmly, her expression serious.

"Yes, and it's not meant to be a joke."

"Oh, come on, any time you apologize and then put a 'but' on the end of it, it means the entire thing's a joke, doesn't it?"

"No, it doesn't!" Cassie's temper was rising again, and her reply was sharp. "I meant what I said, but there are two sides to this. Your only excuse is that you were unaware of my perspective on things."

"I stand corrected." His grin had faded as she became angry, and now he sat back in his chair, apparently prepared to listen.

"You have to understand how this appears to me," she said. "You were dumped on me, against my will and with no notice, and though you told me it wouldn't be, your presence has been more than a little disruptive. I'm busy eighteen hours a day with just my normal workload, so how on earth can I be expected to function when you, and I, because I happen to be with you, are constantly being interrupted by fans and autograph hunters?"

"That's not my fault," he began to protest, and Cassie pounced.

"Maybe the fact that they ask isn't your fault, but your response to them is. If you act as though you're prepared to give an impromptu press conference any time anyone says hello to you, then it becomes your fault."

"They're my fans, though. I have to be polite to them."

Cassie shook her head. "No, what you have to do is decide which is more important, charming your many fans, or learning about my work. You don't have to be rude to people, but you can't do both at the same time, and if you're not serious about your research, then I see no reason to waste my time and energy on you." She didn't know if she'd just lit the fuse to a keg of dynamite, or simply given him food for thought, but James' face had a certain stillness about it which suggested either anger or thoughtfulness.

Cassie hoped it was the latter; she was a bit leery about arousing his anger again after the scene in the parking garage, but she faced him with outward calm in the tense moment of silence which followed her ultimatum.

At last he nodded slowly. "You're right," he said. "I apologize."

Watching him closely, Cassie felt her lips twitch in an unwilling smile. "You don't do that very often, do you?" she asked, and James frowned, puzzled.

"Do what?"

"Apologize."

"Oh." He grinned. "No, as a matter of fact, I don't. Does it show?"

"Just a little." Cassie grinned back. "Somehow, you just don't seem like the apologizing type." James laughed at that, but Cassie's thoughts were moving in a more serious vein. She had sensed, without being told, that James was a man who made no apologies for his actions, but went through life secure in himself and his judgment. She didn't want to admire James Reid, she was far more comfortable dismissing him as just another narcissistic actor, but she admired anyone with that sort of inner strength, and so, unwillingly, she began to admire him as well.

James swung the Mercedes smoothly in at the curb in front of Cassie's stucco bungalow, put the gearshift in neutral and set the parking brake, but he didn't immediately kill the engine. The cessation of that soft vibration would probably wake her, and just for a moment he would let her sleep. He looked down at the black head nestled against his shoulder, soft hair spilling over his sleeve and gleaming ebony in the light of the streetlamps. She was more than tired, she must be exhausted. He was exhausted himself, and she'd already spent a twelve-hour day in that hospital before he'd joined her yesterday evening.

She had seemed to relax at Fredo's, once she'd gotten her apology over with. He smiled at the memory. It had so obviously been a distasteful task, but one she seemed to feel necessary. They had talked easily as they ate their excellent meal, sharing ever more outrageous stories of their respective careers, and laughing with Fredo, whose uncensored amatory advice had made her blush charmingly. When they finally left, pleading a long day ahead in order to escape the gregarious Fredo, she had chatted happily for a few minutes as they drove away, then fallen silent.

James had glanced over to see if perhaps he had said something to offend her and discovered that she had fallen asleep, literally between one word and the next, succumbing to a mixture of wine and exhaustion. Smiling to himself, he had driven several blocks, only to look down at her again when she slid deeper into her seat and nestled against his shoulder, sighing softly as she became comfortable and relaxing completely when he put his arm around her to cradle her head. Even now she was sleeping so peacefully that he regretted the need to wake her.

He could, he thought, just carry her inside, undress her and put her to bed, but he had an idea that she would resent such familiarity pretty strongly. He wasn't going to risk her wrath again so soon by taking her clothes off as she slept.

Lightly he traced one fingertip down her cheek and across her lips, sucking in a sharp breath as they parted invitingly beneath the caress. It was temptation too great to resist, and he had no intention of trying. Careful not to disturb her, he bent his face to hers and kissed her lips. Just for a moment she responded warmly, instinctively, then she stirred and began to wake.

When she opened her eyes, wide and confused from sleep, struggling to understand where she was and how she had come to be there, the first thing Cassie saw was James, his face bent very near her own, smiling to himself, as though he knew a secret she didn't share.

She blinked at him, focusing slowly as he leaned back in his seat. She remembered the evening now, dinner at Fredo's, her apology, his apology, the ride home. . . . No, she didn't remember the ride home, because she had fallen asleep! And not only had she fallen asleep, she realized, mortified, she had draped herself all over James as she slept. Hastily she disentangled herself, pushing herself away from him to sit stiff and straight in her own seat.

"I . . . I'm sorry," she apologized breathlessly. "I shouldn't have gone to sleep like that—"

"Don't worry about it," James reassured her, easing his length out of the car and bending to grin at her before he closed the driver's door. "After seeing you work, I can understand how it happened." He swung his door shut and strode around to open hers.

Cassie watched him come, her thoughts in turmoil. She was acutely embarrassed at having fallen asleep with James Reid, even more embarrassed by the way she'd been practically lying in his arms, and deeply disturbed by the way she'd felt when she awakened to find herself there. She hadn't been shocked or uncomfortable or any of the things she would have expected; instead she had felt warm and safe.

There had been a rightness about it, as if she belonged in his arms, and Cassie found that incomprehensible. If there was one place on earth where she most definitely did *not* belong, it was in the world-famous arms of James Reid!

Stiff with tension, she let him assist her from the car and managed to walk the short distance to her front door without doing anything stupid, such as tripping and falling on her face. He took the key she extracted from her bag and opened the door, reaching inside to switch on a light for her, though they continued to stand outside.

"I can . . . make coffee?" she offered uncertainly, half hoping and half afraid he would accept, and didn't know whether to be relieved or disappointed when he shook his head.

"Not tonight," he declined with a note of faint regret. "You're exhausted, and I still have a long drive home." He took a step closer to Cassie as he put the keys in her hand, and she tipped her head back to look up at him, knowing with a sudden certainty that he was going to kiss her, and that she wanted his kiss, very much.

He was so near that she could feel the warmth of his body, so near that she had only to sway toward him to be in his arms, her face against his broad chest, her arms wrapped around his waist to hold him close. That desire was so strong that for a moment Cassie thought she could feel his strong, hard body against hers, feel the first gentle touch of his lips, but it was only an illusion. Neither of them moved until James lifted his hand to press his fingertips lightly to Cassie's lips in a caress that was, at the same time, a kiss and not a kiss.

"Goodnight, Cassandra. I'll see you in the morning." His footsteps sounded softly on the pavement, the car door slammed, and as Cassie slipped inside and closed the door, the Mercedes engine snarled into life and he was gone.

She moved automatically about the house, preparing for

bed, but long after he had gone and she lay in her darkened bedroom watching the reflections of street lights swimming on the ceiling, she could feel that brief touch on her lips tingling through every cell in her body. The sensation was not a welcome one. It's going to be awfully unnerving to have him around, she thought gloomily, if I fall to pieces every time he touches me. I wonder if I can stand six weeks of it.

"So do you still want to send him on a long walk off a short pier?"

"I never said I wanted to send him on a long walk off a short pier, Gail Anderson, and you know it!" Cassie tried to frown at her friend, but couldn't keep a grin from breaking through. "I never would have believed it, but he really isn't all that bad to have around!"

Gail stared at her in disbelief for a moment, then she burst out laughing and kept on laughing until tears spilled down her cheeks. "Only you," she gasped at last, "could say, in all seriousness, that it's not 'all that bad' to have James Reid around! You might as well say you wouldn't mind too much if Robert Redford came to dinner!"

"Well," Cassie smiled blandly, "I wouldn't mind *too* much . . . as long as he didn't drop in unannounced." Gail choked on a swallow of iced tea and had to be thumped on the back. They were lunching alone together for the first time in the three weeks since James had been at the hospital, while James met with studio executives, and Cassie was a bit surprised to realize the truth of what she'd told Gail. It really *wasn't* so bad having James around, now that he politely but firmly declined the autograph requests and pointedly avoided interfering or making any comment while she was working.

In fact, they had established a comfortably casual relationship, though it was too soon, she thought, to call it friendship. At first the enforced closeness had been anything but relaxing, as Cassie waited stiffly for a recurrence of the strange electricity she had felt that first evening. It hadn't happened, though, and as the tension and restraint between them eased, the beginnings of friendship developed.

James was no longer a one-dimensional figure to her, and she could manage to forget for long periods that he was famous, a movie "star." To her, he was the silent observer following her through her day, looming behind or beside her in a manner that had given rise to a running Me-and-My-Shadow joke between them.

"Actually," Cassie said thoughtfully as she toyed with the remains of her salad, "it's interesting to me to hear his impressions of things I see and do everyday. He's a good sounding-board when I'm frustrated, he'll celebrate with me when something goes well, and he makes me think, not just about the things I do, but about the things I feel. I think we're actually becoming friends," she concluded, still with that air of disbelief, and Gail smiled.

"Considering your attitude when he arrived, I'd say that borders on miraculous. I wonder, though," she said thoughtfully, "if a *friend* is all he is. Hmmm?" She lifted a knowing eyebrow, and Cassie tried to frown.

"Of course a *friend* is all he is," she said severely. "And it's all he's going to be, too, so don't go trying to make anything more out of it, okay? We're simply professional acquaintances."

"Oh, please!" Gail drawled. "I wish you knew how prissy that sounds!"

"Who? Me? Prissy?" Cassie pursed her lips as prissily as she knew how, and they both dissolved into laughter. Gail laughed a bit harder and a bit longer than her friend, and something in that laughter caught Cassie's ear, a forced note in the giggles which went on a little too long. When the giggles stopped they were followed by a silence which, in its turn, also stretched a few seconds too long. Gail glanced sidelong at Cassie, then quickly down at her empty plate, avoiding her friend's eyes.

"Gail," Cassie said, watching the other woman's fingers toying nervously with her fork, "can't you tell me what's wrong?" Gail's fingers stilled; then, as Cassie watched uncomprehendingly, she shoved her chair away from the table with a screech, jumped up and fled the cafeteria, dodging blindly between the tables. Cassie dumped their dishes on the tray return and hurried after her, finally tracking her down in her tiny office, where she stood at the window, facing out.

Cassie slipped inside and closed the door quietly behind her. "Gail?" Gail turned slowly from the window, and Cassie gasped at the sight of tears streaming down her cheeks. "Gail, can't you tell me?"

"There's nothing to tell!" Gail cried angrily through her tears. "Just leave me alone!"

"No." Cassie's voice was quiet and firm. Gail glared at her, then turned back to the window, arms crossed defensively over her breasts, shoulders hunched. "I'm *not* going to leave you alone. Something's bothering you, a lot, and you need to talk about it. I'm your friend, Gail, and I want to help, only you have to *let* me help."

"Maybe I don't *want* help! Maybe I don't want or need help from anybody, and especially not from you!"

"Gail, don't," Cassie pleaded. "You *know* I'm your friend; don't say things like that." Gail turned slowly from the window, scrubbing tears from her cheeks with the heels of her hands. She sighed, sniffled and sagged into the desk chair.

"I know," she said on a quavery note, "and I'm sorry I said that. This is one time I don't think you can help, though." She dropped her head into her hands, shaking it slowly from side to side. "I don't think anybody can help."

"Try me."

Gail sniffled again, then took the tissue Cassie plucked from a box on her desk. "Thanks," she mumbled, blew her nose noisily and wiped her eyes with angry vigor. "It's up to you. If you want to hear a depressing story . . . ?"

"Tell me," Cassie said quietly, and Gail nodded.

"I think my marriage is breaking up." Cassie sucked her breath in on a shocked hiss, but said nothing, and after a moment Gail continued in a defeated monotone, her eyes fixed on the desk blotter. "I don't see how Steve and I can stay married. I'm sure we're breaking up and it scares me . . . it terrifies me. We want a child. We've been 'trying' —I hate that word—trying to conceive for over two years, but I can't. . . ." Her voice wobbled and she swallowed convulsively. "We want a baby so desperately; we've waited and hoped for so long, and been disappointed so many times. People say you can always adopt, but so many people are waiting for babies, and it takes years and years and years. We've waited and waited already, and I don't think Steve will wait much longer!"

"Have you seen a doctor?" Cassie asked.

"Steve has," Gail's voice shook, "and he's fine!" Her voice rose to a wail, and she burst into tears again.

Cassie passed her several more tissues, and when she was calm, asked, "What about you? Have you been to a specialist, had an infertility workup?" It was a simple request for information, so Cassie was astonished when Gail erupted into furious anger.

"You sound just like Steve!" she shouted, pushing herself to her feet so suddenly that her chair skidded across the floor and crashed into the radiator. "I get enough hassles from him; I don't need *you* hassling me, too!" Snatching a lab coat from the coatrack, she stormed out of the office, slamming the door with a resounding crash. As the noise died away Cassie sat staring at the door in stunned disbelief.

"Something's been bothering you all day," James said. "Can you talk about it?" Cassie sighed and pushed away the tray bearing her uneaten dinner. When she looked up at him he was watching her, concern warming the famous green eyes. Dressed like her, in green scrub clothing emblazoned with "LA General Hospital" and running shoes, he blended well into the hospital crowd, though he wore the greens with more panache than most. The very short sleeves of the scrub shirt bared muscular brown arms lightly dusted with dark hair, while more hair curled in the opening of the V-neck, and the drawstring waist of the cotton pants rode low on his lean hips. He might be dressed like one of the crowd, Cassie thought, but it wasn't at all easy for him to be inconspicuous. "Care to talk about it?" he repeated. "It might help."

"There's nothing to talk about," she said tiredly. "At least, there's nothing I *can* talk about." She was relieved when James accepted her denial without argument and nodded briefly. Gail's problem, and her upsetting reaction to it, had weighed heavily on Cassie's mind all afternoon, and she would have liked to share them with James. It was a measure of her growing respect for him that she felt he might be able to bring a new perspective to the problem, to suggest an answer where Cassie herself could see none, but Gail had confided in her, and she would not break that confidence. She changed the subject instead. "Did you understand why we decided to do a caesarean on Mrs. Rhodes this morning?"

"Because the baby's heartbeat was slow," James replied, leaning back in his chair and looking across the table at her with eyes which saw more than Cassie was saying but respected her privacy. "I'm not sure I understand the reason for the slowing, though."

"It's caused by a combination of factors," Cassie began, but was interrupted by the piercing "beep-beep" of her pager. "Rats!" She pushed herself away from the table. "Let's hope it's something minor." She dialed the operator from the house phone a few feet away.

"LA General switchboard."

"This is Dr. Mills."

"Oh, good, Dr. Mills!" the operator sounded anxious, and Cassie felt herself tensing. "Labor and Delivery needs you, stat. Grace said to go straight to room three as quickly as you can."

"Okay, thanks." Cassie turned to say, "Come on, and fast!" to James, then swung around and left the cafeteria at a trot which became a run as she reached the corridor.

The operator hadn't been exaggerating. Grace was waiting at the door of delivery room three, and her news was grave.

"This is Mrs. Jackson's second pregnancy, the first one went fine, and everything was okay at her last prenatal appointment a week ago, but she hasn't felt the baby move in two days, and we haven't gotten a fetal heartbeat since she came in. She's in active labor, but Cassie, I'm almost certain the baby's dead."

Cassie sighed heavily, hating the tragedy of the situation and her own helplessness to change it. "I'm afraid you're probably right, with that history. How much does she know?"

"No one's told her anything specific, but I think she's guessed that something is wrong."

"Okay, I'll be scrubbed and ready in a minute." Cassie vanished into the scrub room, and after a moment James nodded to Grace and followed, his face as grim as hers.

"Will this be very bad?" he asked, and Cassie's shoulders hunched as she stood over the sink.

"Much worse than 'very bad,'" she muttered, then straightened and turned to him, hands held high to avoid a break in sterile technique. "This is what any obstetrician dreads the most. There's usually a physiological reason for a stillbirth—some undetected birth defect that's too serious for the baby to survive—but it's always a shock, to everyone." She took a sterile towel from the scrub nurse and began drying her hands and arms. "Our job is to help Mrs. Jackson through it now, to make the grieving and shock as bearable as we can." She slid her arms into the sterile gown the scrub nurse held for her, and then into the gloves. She took a deep breath behind her mask and sighed noisily, shaking her arms and loosening her shoulders, deliberately easing her tension before entering the delivery room. "Now let's go do the best job we possibly can." With a new respect in his eyes, James followed her small, erect figure into the delivery room.

"Oh, God," Cassie whispered as she slipped into the on-call room and pushed the door closed behind her. "Oh dear God." She had no idea how long she'd spent with the Jacksons, delivering a perfectly formed, stillborn baby and helping them deal with the blow. Mrs. Jackson had been permitted to see her baby, because it was known that the opportunity to say good-bye would help her deal with her grief, and when her condition was stable she had been taken to a room in the Gynecology wing, away from Obstetrics and the sounds of mothers and babies. Only when she was safely asleep did Cassie leave her, holding herself under rigid control until she reached the safe haven of the on-call room.

Once there, though, the controlled facade crumbled. She walked blindly across the darkened room to collapse on the sofa, bending slowly forward to bury her face in her hands and let the tears come. She was barely aware of the door opening, but when the cushion beside her dipped beneath a heavy weight and arms slid around her, she turned into them instinctively. Aware without opening her eyes that it was James who held her, she was also aware that she needed him, needed his strength and his comfort.

Her tears had slid silently down her cheeks at first, but as she clung to James, her face pressed into his neck, she sobbed out her sorrow and frustration. "It's not *right!*" she cried. "It's such a waste! We're here to save lives, but I feel so helpless, so *useless!*" James gathered her closer, stroking her hair, rocking her very gently and murmuring soothing nonsense until her shoulders stopped shaking beneath his hands and her sobs died away.

He was glad he was able to comfort her; she'd looked so small and forlorn when he opened the door and the light from the corridor had slanted across her huddled form. He smoothed his hand in rhythmic circles over her back as her tears slowed and she breathed in little hiccupping sobs. He was growing aware of the feel of her in his arms, slim and supple and soft, and wearing very little under the shapeless scrub dress. She smelled of antiseptic surgical scrub, and warm, female skin, and a faint trace of perfume she must have put on that morning lingered, and as James lowered his head to rest his face on her hair, he was aware of the first stirrings of his body in response to that oddly erotic mingling of scents.

He could have set her away from him then, because she was no longer crying, but he didn't. Instead he kept her within the curve of his arm as he tipped her face up and gently wiped the tears from her cheeks, then bent his head to kiss her lightly. At least he meant to kiss her lightly, a brief caress of comfort and reassurance, but it became something more. Their lips met, hers softened invitingly, and after an instant's hesitation James' arms tightened, lifting her body against him as he gently parted her lips to seek the sweetness within.

Her response astonished him. It was open and sweet as her lips moved beneath his, answering his kiss, and her hands, which had clutched at his sleeves as she cried, slid up to caress his neck, his shoulders, his hair. The kiss went on and on, and became another and yet another, a hungry, passionate admission of unacknowledged need. She delighted him, the unsuspected strength in her seemingly fragile body, the shape and feel of it, curving and soft, or slender and taut, the way her body molded to his as he pulled her close. His hands moved restlessly over her back, her hair, her shoulders, then down the length of her spine to trace the soft curves there, lightly at first, then more boldly.

God, she was exquisite! Her body in his arms, her hands moving over his shoulders, the taste of her mouth, even the mingled scents of scrub solution and woman set him afire. He wanted her more than he could remember ever wanting a woman; desire pounded through his veins as he touched and kissed her, fanned by her own desire. She might have withdrawn when he traced a line down her throat to the V-neck of her dress, but she didn't, even when his fingers drew the dress aside to caress the upper curve of her breast, then dipped lower to cup its weight, as she gasped softly in response.

She was perfect, tiny and perfect, and he breathed something incoherent against her lips as her fingers followed the example of his, quickly tugging the tail of his shirt free so she could slip her hands inside. She was driving him insane with her touch, and he was driving himself insane touching her, sliding a narrow satin strap off her shoulder, easing the silky fabric of what he guessed was a teddy or camisole away from the warm flesh he sought. Her small round breast swelled into his palm, the nipple tightening into a hard bud at his touch, and he growled deep in his throat as her fingers moved over his torso, delicately enumerating his ribs, tracing the heavy planes of muscle.

Only when he realized what the next step was could James put a brake on his ardor. Yes, he wanted her so badly that it astonished him, but this was neither the time nor the place. When he made love with this woman they would have the privacy and the comfort they needed, not a lumpy couch in a dingy on-call room, with the threat of interruption hanging over them.

With an effort of pure will he forced himself back to sanity, taking his hands from her body to hold her shoulders as he kissed her brow lightly and set her gently away from him. She made an incoherent murmur of protest that was almost his undoing, her fingers clinging as he took her hands from around his waist. Her eyes were soft and blurred with desire, but as he watched they cleared, opening very wide as she realized what they had nearly done, then closing tightly as a hot blush washed up her throat and over her face.

Cassie felt his weight leave the couch as he stood, heard his footsteps cross the room. She risked a glance and was relieved to see that his back was to her, then looked down at herself and closed her eyes tightly again. What on earth got into me, she thought, horrified at her apparent wantoness, embarrassed at the disarray of her clothing, angry at herself and, unreasonably, angry at James as the source of discomfort.

"I didn't intend for—" James began, turning to face her, and Cassie dropped her head, interrupting him.

"It doesn't matter!" she said sharply, then glanced up at him and quickly bowed her head again when she saw that he was tucking in his shirt. This was horrible! She didn't know whether to laugh or cry, for though the situation was rapidly acquiring all the aspects of a bad farce, she was all too painfully aware that only James' control had stopped them from making love right there in the on-call room. She twisted away from his gaze, frantically straightening her own clothes.

"Cassie, I'm sorry about this. I—"

"It doesn't matter!" she repeated, struggling to keep her voice down when she would have liked to scream and swear. The vehemence was there, though, in the barely controlled trembling of her voice, but she didn't dare shout and risk being heard out in the hall. "You don't have anything to be sorry about. I was just as . . . as . . ."

"There's really nothing to be upset about, you know." His placidity infuriated her, though whether she was angry at herself or at him was unclear.

"There's nothing to talk about!" she snapped. "It's *over*, okay? It's over!" She was trembling, and that angered her, too, as she stood waiting for him to leave, wishing desperately for him to leave.

James studied her for a moment, seeing more, she was certain, than she wanted him to. Then, to her profound relief, he nodded. "I'm hungry, and I know you must be. I'll get some sandwiches from the coffee shop and bring them up." It was a statement, not a question, so Cassie said nothing, only watched him leave the room, then collapsed back onto the couch as the door swung closed behind him.

Why had it happened? She slid lower on the cushions, head back, and draped an arm across her eyes. Why had she *let* it happen? She stirred restlessly, seeking a comfortable position, but comfort was elusive in her agitated state. She was mortified by her behavior, utterly baffled by it.

James Reid was indisputably a very sexy man, but she'd known attractive men before and had never behaved this way. She had thought they were building a working relationship, based on mutual respect and on friendship, *platonic* friendship, but that illusion had been shattered quite thoroughly. Cassie wasn't in the habit of self-delusion, and she didn't pretend to herself that what she felt for James was merely platonic friendship. She didn't know when her attraction to him had gone deeper, but it was undeniable. The awful part of the whole situation was that she didn't want to be attracted to him, didn't want that sort of involvement with a man like James, a movie star. His world was so far removed from hers that he might as well have come from outer space; there could be no future in such a relationship.

She shifted restlessly on the couch, then pushed herself to her feet and stalked across the room to flop onto one of the narrow beds. Agonizing over what had happened was getting her nowhere; sleep would at least refresh her for the rest of the night's work. She lay back on the pillow, closed her eyes, and with an ease born of necessity during the long years of medical education, slipped into sleep.

That was how James found her when he returned with ham-and-cheese sandwiches and a cellophane-wrapped packet of chocolate cookies. His foray in search of food had been more a means of distancing himself from Cassie while his ardor cooled than of satisfying a simple hunger for food. Despite that enforced distancing, James knew the sandwich would satisfy only a small fraction of his hunger. He stood by the narrow bed, looking down at her, relaxed in sleep, the light blanket she'd pulled over herself covering, but not concealing, the lines of her body.

With a muttered imprecation he pulled his gaze away and crossed the room to drop onto the sofa. Slumping against the vinyl-covered cushions to eat his sandwich, he reflected gloomily that he wouldn't find sleep as easily as she had. He'd be lucky if he slept at all.

# Chapter Four

Cassie felt more than a little bit foolish as she slipped through the shadows in the parking garage some sixteen hours later, hurrying toward her car. In fact, she felt downright silly, but not quite silly enough to face the postmortem discussion she knew James expected. She had slept undisturbed until 5:45 A.M., an almost unheard-of luxury, and had managed by dint of some rather fancy footwork to avoid being alone with James during the day, and now, in what she freely admitted was an act of craven cowardice, she was sneaking out of the hospital in the winter dusk.

She sighed with relief as she left the parking garage and joined the evening commuters headed for Burbank and home. On this Thursday she felt particularly fortunate to have escaped that heart-to-heart with James, because this was her scheduled weekend to go out with the Traveling Clinic, and she would have four days away from the hospital. She welcomed the respite; the long weekend would be an opportunity for her to sort out her feelings for James, and to stamp down hard on those she considered inappropriate.

She really should have known better. Cassie had to bite her lip to keep from groaning aloud when she climbed aboard the large motor home, outfitted for medical use, the next morning. James was there ahead of her, lounging on one of the benches which could be converted into treatment tables, chatting with two of the other staff members.

He looked up as she climbed the three steps into the van,

and a sardonic smile spread over his face at the expressions which played across hers. Surprise, dismay, a scorching blush which washed up her neck and into her cheeks as she remembered all that had passed between them and waited unresolved, and finally a glower at him for being there. The glower only caused his knowing smile to widen into something that, to Cassie's prejudiced eyes, strongly resembled a leer.

"Good morning, Cassie." His voice was pleasant, but Cassie didn't feel like playing along.

"Hi." Her greeting was little more than a surly grunt, and she pushed past his long legs, ignoring an empty seat beside him in favor of one at the rear of the van. Why, oh why, did he have to be there today?

Of course he's here, she thought, disgusted with her own simplemindedness. Where else would he be? Of course he would know, without my telling him, exactly where I'd be. And of course he's going to fit right into our cozy little group. He was doing that already, she noted sourly; he was the center of an animated conversation with the rest of the staff. As the engine throbbed to life Cassie slumped lower in her seat and composed herself for sleep, trying to ignore the deep, distinctive rumble of James' voice.

The resident staff of LA General rotated staffing of the clinic, which went out every weekend, but the team always consisted of one obstetrics resident, one pediatrician, one family practitioner and one internist, as well as two registered nurses and a driver-paramedic. Their route took them into the remote mountains and desert to visit Indian reservations, migrant camps and tiny towns which would otherwise have no access to medical care.

Ordinarily Cassie enjoyed the challenge of these trips and the camaraderie among the staff, but she had an idea that this was going to be a very long weekend. She knew that James would insist on discussing the situation between them, knew, if she were to be brutally honest with herself, that such a talk was necessary, but she would put it off just as long as he would let her. That was one conversation she wasn't looking forward to at all.

Though she appeared to be asleep as they drove away from the hospital, Cassie wasn't. Instead she was listening, rather unwillingly, to James charming the socks off the rest of the staff. Determinedly she kept up the pretense of sleep rather than join in the conversation, and eventually the pretense became reality.

Three hours later she was awakened by the altered motion of the vehicle as it left the freeway for a narrow gravel road leading into the desert. Others on the staff had dozed as well, but even they were awakened when the narrow gravel road became an even narrower, deeply rutted dirt road before they reached their first stop. A tiny, dusty hamlet of some fifty souls, huddled at the foot of a mountain on the edge of the vast emptiness of the Mojave Desert, it was over one hundred miles from the nearest doctor and welcomed the clinic visits. Their patients were waiting for them, assembled at the town's combination hotel-cafe-tavern-gas station, some of them having traveled from far out in the surrounding area.

"What can I do to help?"

Cassie glanced sharply up at James when he spoke, looking for any hint of mockery. She found none, and nodded, accepting his offer at face value.

"We have to take these," she indicated two large equipment cases she was trying to extract from a storage locker, "into the hotel. They'll have a room we can use for exams."

"Why not use the van?"

"It gets crowded." Cassie left the equipment cases to James and picked up a bundle of disposable examination drapes. "If we use extra rooms as well as the van, we get more done in less time."

"Makes sense." He followed her off the van and into the hotel, where they worked quickly to transform a bare but clean hotel room into an examination room. "What kinds of things do you usually do? Deliver babies?"

"Not if I can help it! We send them to stay in a town with a hospital when they're near term, so they don't risk an emergency birth without care. Mostly I'll do prenatal exams, routine gynecological exams and pregnancy diagnoses. It's pretty routine, though we sometimes discover serious problems in the course of these routine exams."

"What can I do now?" This time Cassie didn't question his motives. If she had a willing pair of hands to help her, she wouldn't quibble.

"Get charts from the van for me, and whatever supplies I run out of. Just run errands, mostly. Dull but necessary."

"No problem. After all, it's not like I'm qualified to do much of anything else, is it?"

"You never know." Cassie grinned. "We may make a paramedic out of you yet!"

He was as good as his word, quietly making himself useful, and they spoke no more than a few impersonal words until the last patient had been seen, the van repacked and they adjourned *en masse* for a late lunch in the cafe. The first faint pricklings of unease stirred when he led her purposefully to the end of the long table where they were to be served, distancing her from the others. Under the cover of the waitress' bustling about as she served the family-style meal, he ducked his head slightly to study Cassie's face.

"What was it?"

"What was what?" she countered blandly, and James shook his head.

"Don't be evasive. What was bugging you yesterday and this morning? And still is, from the look on your face."

"*Nothing's* bugging—"

"I'm not simpleminded, Cassandra! Don't insult my intelligence by treating me that way. Something's been bothering you. You managed to put it out of your mind while you were working, but it's there now. Have some green beans." He ladled a heaping spoonful onto her plate.

"I don't really *want* green beans. And you know perfectly well what's bugging me!"

"Have some chicken; you need to keep your strength up."

He deposited a succulent piece of fried chicken beside the beans. "I know what's bugging—" He thought about it for a moment while he served them both mashed potatoes and gravy. "I can't think what, unless . . . the other night!" he said in triumph. "After the stillbirth. *That's* what it is!" Cassie's angry silence was confirmation, and he frowned at her, puzzled. "It doesn't make sense, though. Why should you be so upset about that?"

"Because it *happened*," she whispered angrily at him, "and it shouldn't have!"

"Why on earth not?"

"Because our relationship is a professional one! At least, it's supposed to be professional. What happened between us was a serious mistake, and one that I regret. A lot."

"You can't be serious," James began, his face a study in amused astonishment, but as he met Cassie's eyes he sobered. "Come on, Cassie, what we did concerns no one but ourselves. Don't make a big deal out of it when it's really not so bad."

"It's bad enough!" Her voice was low to avoid being overheard, but still vehement. "It's the very last thing I wanted to happen, and it was a big, fat, stupid mistake!"

"Okay, if it was a mistake, it was a mistake," James said coldly, pushing his chair away from the table. "But there's no reason to carry on like an outraged virgin. I promise you, your honor is in no danger!"

Cassie kept her eyes on her plate as he left the table, biting her inner lip hard. He hadn't seen her flinch from his words, but they had struck too close to home. Cassie was indeed a virgin. She often felt like an anachronism in a permissive world, yet her inexperience was less the result of any rigidly-held puritan tenets than of a combination of innate distaste for one-night stands and an education which had left her no time to build a serious relationship with a man.

She sometimes felt her lack of experience a handicap, as if it were somehow presumptuous of her to counsel women with partners and pregnancies, yet she knew, or hoped, that she would eventually find a man to love. She'd always believed, naïvely, no doubt, that when she fell in love with a man she would desire him with a full-blooded passion and not the tentative curiosity of her high school days. She'd also believed that when she desired a man, she would love him. James had proven just how fallacious that belief had been.

There was no point in denying that she'd desired him there in the on-call room, and equally little point in denying that she was aware of him in a way she had not been before. He had made her want him once, and he could do it again, of that she was unhappily convinced. But of course she didn't, couldn't, love James Reid.

Love him or not, she was acutely, uncomfortably, aware of him over the next forty-eight hours as they made their way across the desert. He made no further effort to seek her company, acting as a gofer to assist anyone on the team who seemed to need help and socializing with the group at meals and in the evenings. She was fairly certain that no one else was aware that James was avoiding her, but she herself was acutely conscious of it, just as she was acutely conscious of James himself.

She was keenly sensitive to his voice, his presence, aware without looking up when he was near her, as if through a sixth sense. Perversely, though she had essentially told him to leave her alone, she missed the companionship and camaraderie they had shared while discussing her work.

The patients they saw on these trips were some of the poorest in California, people with no other access to medical care, and treating them was both rewarding and heartbreaking. Cassie could see that the work they did moved James and impressed him, but he made no effort to discuss it with her. She didn't love him, of course, and their relationship was a working one, superficial at best, but still she missed talking over the day's events with him, missed it more than she cared to admit.

"Can I join you for a minute? I wanted to ask you about one of the women you saw this afternoon." Cassie looked up, startled to hear James addressing her after the last two days, then nodded.

"Sure. Which woman did you want to ask about?"

James took the seat she indicated on the massive maroon sofa beside her. Their last stop on Sunday had been a tiny hamlet clinging to a range of mountains near the Arizona border, and their accomodation was an elderly Victorian hotel which sat like a slightly seedy dowager in the midst of a cluster of newer and uglier buildings. Cassie had brought a stack of charts to the parlor after dinner, intending to check over and complete her notes while she warmed herself by the fire. It had been chilly since they left Los Angeles, but had turned truly cold that afternoon. Now, at an elevation of nearly five thousand feet, they were on the snow line, with a cold wind whipping occasional flurries of sleet against the windows while the hotel's ancient boiler struggled to send warmth to the radiators.

When James sat beside her, though, Cassie felt a warmth which had nothing to do with the fire chasing the chill from her limbs. James' question, when he asked it, wasn't a difficult one to answer, but then, to Cassie, the question itself was not as important as the fact that James had sought her out to ask it. He didn't leave when she'd answered it, either, but stayed to discuss his impressions of the weekend with her.

"What do you do if a real emergency arises?" James leaned back comfortably into the enormous sofa's maroon velour depths. "I wouldn't imagine it happens often, but you must have to be prepared for anything."

"Well, we are . . . and we aren't," Cassie replied thoughtfully, tucking her feet beneath her and leaning one elbow on the sofa-back. "Serious cases, those which we diagnose but don't have the resources to treat, are usually transported to a hospital, either by ambulance or, if necessary, by helicopter. If something were to happen that couldn't wait that long, we'd just have to do what we could with what we have on hand, I suppose."

"I don't envy you the uncertainty. You could make nine

perfectly peaceful trips and have all hell break loose on the tenth!"

"We try not to think of it." She grinned. "It's just a part of medicine."

"Well, I wouldn't find it very relaxing—"

"Dr. Mills?" The hotel owner's agitated call interrupted James in mid-sentence. "Dr. Mills, could you come in here? It's an emergency!"

Cassie was halfway across the parlor before Mr. Franks finished speaking, with James close behind her. They were led to the hotel office, where the agitated hotelier thrust a telephone into Cassie's hands.

"Uh, hello? This is Dr. Mills." There was a pause, during which James watched her face, trying to read the play of expression there. "Yes, I am . . . *Sí. Obstétrica, sí.* . . . Her *parto* is early . . . is too soon? How many . . . *cuanto semanas?* . . . *Cinco?* . . . *Sí.* Is there a midwife? A *partera?* . . . Good. What does she say?" Cassie listened for several minutes, her face going still and grave, and James wished fervently that he could hear both sides of the conversation. Finally she nodded, though the caller couldn't see her.

"*Sí.* I will come. *Sí.*" She turned to Mr. Franks. "Can you borrow a horse for me?"

"Sure. When do you need it?"

"Now." She turned back to the telephone. "How long is the ride? . . . *Dos horas?* Okay, don't be afraid. She will be all right. *Adiós.*" She cradled the receiver and turned to face the two men, but addressed only the hotelkeeper. "I'll need that horse just as soon as you can get him here, and somebody who can guide me to the village. He says the road's been closed by a mudslide, but they can be reached on horseback."

"That's right, ma'am. My son Cory knows the way; he can guide you."

"Great. I'll be ready by the time the horse is here."

"Two horses," James said, and she looked around at him in surprise. "I'm going with you."

"But what can you do?"

"I speak Spanish."

"It's that obvious that I don't, is it?" Cassie asked with a wry grin. "Well, if you're fluent, you'll be useful. I've examined this girl before, and she speaks a little English, but she won't remember much of it when she's in labor. Two horses," she told Mr. Franks, who nodded and began dialing the telephone as they left his office.

"Do you know what the problem is?" James asked, and Cassie shook her head.

"Not really, only that there *is* one. She's in labor early, and it's not progressing the way the midwife thinks it should. That was the headman on the phone, and the girl is his daughter, so he's worried sick and not very coherent." She swung around the ornate newel post and took the stairs leading up to their rooms two at a time. She paused at her door. "If you don't have cold weather gear, ask one of the guys."

"I'll be okay. Will it really be a two-hour ride?"

"Probably more. It's snowing up there." She vanished into her room and heard James' door close moments after hers.

Quickly she stripped off her jeans and sweater, then donned thermal underwear over her mauve silk teddy. She pulled two pairs of thick socks up over the cuffs of the thermals, and a wool plaid shirt went over the thermal top and was tucked into her jeans. She pulled a heavy sweater over it all, stamped her feet into well-worn cowboy boots and took a heavy fleece-lined suede jacket, an army-surplus waterproof poncho and an ancient, light-gray stetson with her as she left the room.

James, properly attired, caught up with her in the entry hall and followed her out to the van. One of the nurses was already there, packing a bag which could be strapped to a saddle.

"Thanks, Carol. James is going with me, so let's pack another bag."

"Okay. You want forceps?"

"Yeah. Something all-purpose. And a section pack, just in case."

"Right. Cassie do you want me to go, too?"

"I appreciate it, Carol, but do you know how to ride a horse?"

"Well, no."

"Then you'd better not. James and I will be okay. I've been threatening to make a paramedic of him, and there's a midwife in the village."

"If you're sure . . ."

"We'll be fine. Anyway, they'll need you for the clinic tomorrow morning."

Carol subsided with an ill-concealed sigh of relief. Cassie had appreciated her offer, and it would have been better to have a nurse to assist her, but she knew that none of the other staffers were riders, and two hours through snowy mountains was a vastly different proposition from a pony ride at the zoo. She just hoped that James rode fairly well; they couldn't afford to be slowed down.

"Here." She handed him one of the heavy equipment packs and hefted the other herself. "Good thing there are two of us, we can take twice as much."

"What are you taking?" James tested the weight of the bag in his arms.

"Everything I can," was the dry reply, "and even then I can only hope it'll be enough." They left the van for the street outside, where the rest of the clinic staff waited to see them off, huddled in their overcoats against the sleet which was turning to snow, whipped by a rising wind.

"Great night for a horseback ride through the scenic Chemehuevi Mountains," James observed dryly. "Are you sure you're up to it?"

"I'm up to it. I'd better be, since I told them I'm coming. You still have a choice, though, and it's not too late to back out. Are you sure *you're* up to it?"

"I'm up to it." He nodded toward the corner of the hotel, where Cory Franks stood holding three horses and waiting for them. "I think it's now too late to back out, after all."

"This mare's for you, Doctor, ma'am." Cory, a lanky,

sandy-haired eighteen-year-old, held the reins of a compact Appaloosa mare which rolled an interested eye at Cassie as she patted the gray cheek and shoulder before hoisting her equipment pack onto the saddle and tying it in place. "This'n's for you Mr. Reid, sir. Do you really ride in the movies?" The question seemed to pop out involuntarily, and James' teeth flashed white in a grin as he tied his pack on the saddle of a rangy buckskin gelding.

"I ride, yes, although they won't always let me do my own stunts, because of the insurance."

"Yeah?" Cory grinned, intrigued, then remembered the business at hand. "You a rider, Doctor, ma'am?"

"I ride." She hid a grin at the repetition of "Doctor, ma'am."

"That's okay, then. These two," he indicated their horses, "aren't the quietest around, but they're both sure-footed. The last few miles are on a kinda steep trail, since the road washed out, and I wouldn't want you fallin' off."

"We'll be fine," Cassie told him, gathering up her mare's reins and taking a little jump to get her foot into the stirrup. She had already measured the stirrup leathers against her arm and shortened them to the proper length, and she was aware of James' assessing gaze as she swung easily into the saddle and reined the mare in a tight circle to stand beside Cory's pinto. It was obvious that James didn't have much faith in her riding ability, and she returned the favor, watching as he mounted, grinning to herself. She had a little secret that she'd share with him after a while, but first she wanted to see how he handled his horse.

They fell into line behind Cory, Cassie and then James, sent on their way with waves and good wishes from the staff, who watched them ride away with more than a little trepidation.

She had to admit, after a couple of miles, that James handled his horse quite nicely, sitting easily in the saddle, yet controlling the horse when it tossed its head and sidestepped some bit of wind-borne debris. She had been watching him covertly, well aware that he'd been sneaking glances at her in return, and when their eyes finally met they burst out laughing together.

"Okay," Cassie chuckled, "I give up! Where did you learn to ride? I know it wasn't just on a movie set."

"You're right about that. Actually, I learned when I was a kid."

"I thought you grew up in Cincinnati!"

"I did, but I spent my summers on my grandparents' ranch in South Dakota. I learned to ride when I was five or six. How about you?" He grinned. "You didn't learn on Saturday afternoons at riding school, either!"

"Not quite. Actually, I was one of those kids who literally ride before they can walk. My parents ran a small ranch in Wyoming, and there was never a time when I didn't ride."

"Good training for this," James said dryly as the narrow dirt road left the protection of the trees to cross a windswept meadow. "This isn't going to be a relaxing ride through the park."

"No kidding." Cassie tucked her chin lower into the fleece collar of her jacket for protection from the biting wind and urged the mare after Cory's pinto. By the time they saw the lights of the village they had long since abandoned any attempt at conversation. The trail they took past the area where a mudslide had wiped out the road was indeed steep, and treacherous in the snow, which was falling heavily at the higher elevations. Before they reached the village they had been forced to ford swollen streams, scramble up steep slopes and slither down narrow gullies as the wind tore at their clothes and whipped stinging snow into their faces.

Cassie thought the last descent to the village was the worst, made even worse by the fact that the lights of the village beckoned warmly below them as the wind screamed through the treetops above, and the horses practically sat on their haunches to skitter down that final, near-perpendicular quarter-mile. It was a relief to reach level ground unscathed, and a relief as well to see light spill across the single street as a door was flung open.

Their patient awaited them there, in her father's house, one of the few in the village which boasted both electricity and running water. As they reined in their sweating, snorting horses, the short, stocky headman burst out the door.

"*Hola! Señora* Doctor, you have come very fast. I thank you!" He caught the reins to hold the horses for them as they dismounted stiffly, then shouted for someone inside to help with the equipment bags. As Cassie untied hers it was taken from her hands by a shyly smiling young man whom she guessed to be either the expectant father or one of the headman's sons.

"This way, *señora,*" he said softly, and led her inside, while the headman assisted Cory with the horses. He was, as she had guessed, the father-to-be, but according to tradition he sat outside the room where his wife was laboring while the midwife and an assistant were with her. A short, gasping cry as they neared the door caused him to pale slightly, his free hand tightening into a fist. "*Señora?*" She paused outside the closed door. "You will help her, *Señora?*"

"I'll help her," Cassie said as reassuringly as she was able. "Where can I wash my hands?"

"Oh, *sí*. This way." He led her to the bathroom, in an extension built onto the back of the house. With her coat removed and her hands washed, she returned to the bedroom and the waiting husband.

"She will be all right," Cassie told him firmly, and he muttered his thanks before opening the door for her. The girl, Luisa, lay in a big, hand-carved wooden bed, the midwife and assistant on either side. When Cassie entered the room the midwife stepped away from the bed, eyes respectfully downcast.

"Hello, Luisa." Cassie smiled, and the girl managed a wan smile in return.

"Hello, doctor." She stiffened, clutching the assistant's

hand as another contraction began, and babbled something in a mixture of colloquial Spanish and native dialect which was totally incomprehensible to Cassie.

"Can you tell me what she's saying?" Cassie asked the midwife, but the woman only shrugged helplessly.

*"No hablo Ingles."*

Cassie understood that Spanish perfectly, but it failed to cheer her up. When Luisa had relaxed again she touched the girl's hand lightly, murmured *"Momentito,"* and slipped out of the room. James was sitting with Luisa's father in the living room, but he rose quickly when Cassie beckoned.

"What's wrong? Is the girl all right?"

"I don't know; I haven't gotten that far yet. She can't remember any English now, and her Spanish is too fast and colloquial for me, and the *partera* doesn't speak any English at all. I'll have to have you interpret for me."

"But shouldn't her husband . . . or her father?"

"It wouldn't be proper for them to be in there with her, but if you're a 'trained assistant,' as well as an interpreter . . ."

"You're the boss. Do you want me to explain it to them?"

"No, I will. As you say, I'm the boss." The two men agreed readily, their concern for Luisa outweighing the concerns of propriety, and Cassie and James returned to Luisa. "Tell her you're my assistant and that you'll interpret." James did so, and Luisa managed another weak smile. "Now ask the *partera* what's happened so far."

While James spoke to the old woman Cassie quickly unpacked her equipment, laying it out on a sterile towel that she draped over a table, out of Luisa's line of sight.

"I'll have to give this to you verbatim and see what you make of it," James said, and Cassie turned back to him. "She says the girl's water came early this morning and they brought her here and kept everything clean. That her pains started not long after, and they've been hard and fast, but no baby comes."

Cassie thought about that for a moment, then smiled at the *partera*. *"Gracias."*

"*De nada,*" the old woman replied with a shy smile.

"Well, it's time to find out what's going on," Cassie told James, pitching her voice too low for Luisa to hear and understand. "I don't like the fact that her membranes have been ruptured for so long . . . she's been open to infection all this time. Would you get the drape pack out?" James pulled the pack of sterile disposable drapes from the equipment bag, and they quickly draped the bed and Luisa, then Cassie laid her hands on Luisa's swollen belly and began to press and probe.

An arrested look crossed her face, followed by a frown of concentration as she ran her hands over the girl's belly again. "Ask her if the baby has moved very much lately," she ordered James.

"She says at first the baby moved all the time, but lately, not much at all."

"Mm-hm." Cassie extracted a stethoscope from one of the bags and slipped the earpieces into place. "Tell her I'm going to listen to the baby's heart." She saw James nod, though she couldn't hear him with the stethoscope on. She auscultated Luisa's belly very thoroughly, looking for verification of what she'd begun to suspect, and when she had it, straightened slowly, keeping her face impassive but thinking hard.

"What is wrong?" Luisa's eyes were very wide and very frightened, and Cassie quickly smiled reassurance.

"Nothing's wrong, Luisa. I'm sorry I worried you. I just found out why your labor began early, though. You're having twins!"

"*Gemelos?*" the girl breathed, eyes even wider. "*Dos* . . . *two* babies?"

"Two babies." Cassie grinned, but behind the grin she was worried. Twin births were fraught with all sorts of complications and risks, and these were far from ideal conditions for such a delivery.

"Problems?" James asked from just behind her, and she threw him a speaking glance.

"Potentially lots of them. Will you ask the *partera* if she will help?"

James spoke briefly to the old woman, then went on at greater length as she shook her head and backed away. Finally he shrugged in defeat. "She can't possibly interfere with your work," he said.

"What do you mean?"

"As I understand it, she sees you as some kind of super-midwife, and she has turned her patient over to you, lock, stock and barrel." The *partera* spoke again, and her assistant left the room as the *partera* seated herself in a corner. "The other, the assistant, has gone to prepare some sort of post-birth soup for the girl. The *partera* will help with the babies after they're born."

"Looks like it's you and me, then," Cassie murmured. "I hope you've learned something in the last couple of weeks."

"Not half as much as *I* hope so," James muttered fervently, and Cassie had to stifle a slightly hysterical giggle, all too aware that this situation wasn't funny at all.

It became less amusing when she did a careful exam, discovering another problem. "She's fully dilated," she told James quietly, "and the first baby's coming down, but it's a breech."

"How bad will it be?"

"It won't be good. The head is the largest part of the baby's body, and if it comes down first, it helps dilate the cervix. With a breech, the dilation may not be as great, and you may need forceps to deliver the head. Tell Luisa that we'll deliver the first baby very slowly and carefully, and that I may ask her to stop pushing and pant, like this." Cassie demonstrated. "Tell her it's very important that she stop pushing when I tell her to."

James relayed the message and Luisa whispered, "*Sí*," then gasped as another contraction began.

"It's starting to happen," Cassie murmured. "It won't be long now."

And it wasn't. To her relief the first baby was small, and

Cassie slowly, with infinite care, eased her into the world without having to resort to using forceps. Despite her size, she was a healthy, vigorous baby, with a thick thatch of black hair. Once she was breathing normally, Cassie examined her quickly, then handed her to the *partera* and turned back to deliver her twin.

A boy, he was larger than his sister, but positioned properly head-down, and his birth was quick and easy. It was almost three hours before Cassie was satisfied that her presence was no longer required, though, and she could leave the mother and babies sleeping comfortably. Even then, she couldn't immediately go to bed herself, for she was pressed into joining the burstingly proud father and grandfather in toasting the new arrivals. It was hard to say how long the celebration might have gone on had James not stepped in.

"The doctor is tired," he said, then continued in Spanish that Cassie was too exhausted to understand. Whatever he said, it did the trick, for Jorge, Luisa's father, led them to a small house not far from his own, showed them the bathroom and kitchen, pointed out clean blankets in a cupboard, and left them with a last flurry of congratulations and good wishes.

The quiet he left behind when he closed the door, closing them in together, was soothing, comforting, broken only by the crackle of a fire burning brightly in the big stone fireplace. Cassie looked around the clean, welcoming room, which served as both living room and dining room, with a stove and sink in an alcove, then sank onto the sofa with a sigh of relief. James turned from poking the fire to look at her.

"Are you okay?"

"Probably," was the dry reply. He laughed. Cassie dropped her head back against the cushions and closed her eyes. "By the way," she said after a moment, "where's our guide?"

"Cory?"

"Mm-hm."

"I imagine he's sound asleep. They sent him home with one

of the single men shortly after we got here. He's going to guide us down to meet the van tomorrow."

"Oh." They sat in silence for a moment. "How come they put him with a 'single man,' but they put us in here together?"

"They think we're married."

*"What?"* She sat bolt upright, staring at him.

"They think we're married." He shrugged, trying not too successfully to stifle a grin. "Didn't you hear Jorge and his son-in-law calling you *señora?"*

"Maybe. I don't know. I wasn't paying attention. They actually think we're *married?"*

"That they do." The grin broke through that time, and Cassie felt herself blush scarlet.

"It's not funny, James; it's embarrassing! And quit laughing at me!"

"I'm not laughing at you," he said more gently. "I just realized that Jorge is an old romantic, putting us in this little love-nest and all."

*"James!"*

"Okay, okay! I won't say any more about it. Would you like a shower? Jorge fired up the water heater for us."

"Mmm, I'd love a shower. If I can walk that far."

"If you don't, I'll beat you to it," James threatened with a grin, and Cassie shoved herself up off the sofa.

"I'm going, I'm going." She wasted no time peeling off her clothes and stepping under the delightfully hot spray. She emerged refreshed, but confronting a dilemma. When she packed, her mind had been on medical equipment, not a change of clothes; but now, as she stood in the tiny bathroom, wrapped in a big, hand-woven cotton towel, something in her rebelled at the thought of donning those damp, clammy clothes again. She prodded the pile of discarded clothing with a toe and grimaced.

"James?" She opened the door a crack to call to him.

"Yes?" He appeared in the doorway to the living room. "Coming out?" He grinned, making a knowing survey of what little of her he could see.

"Not just yet." Cassie felt herself flushing under his gaze and compressed her lips in irritation. "I . . . ah . . . I didn't pack any extra clothes. I want to rinse some things out, but I don't have anything else to wear. Do you, maybe? . . ."

He took pity on her embarrassment. "As a matter of fact, I did have the presence of mind to pack a shirt. Hang on just a minute." He returned quickly with a tightly-rolled bundle which shook out into a plaid flannel shirt similar to the one he wore.

"Thanks." She smiled, and his face went still for a moment as he watched her expression.

"No problem." He turned on his heel and returned to the living room. Cassie looked after him for a moment, then shrugged and backed into the bathroom again.

The shirt was enormous, of course, but it was wonderfully warm, covering her to mid-thigh. She rolled the sleeves up until her hands were visible, then quickly rinsed out her teddy, thermals and socks, squeezed them as dry as she could in the towel and carried them out to dry in front of the fire.

James was in the little kitchen when she hesitantly approached the living room, but he spared no more than a quick glance at her small, bare-legged figure swathed in his enormous shirt.

"I've made coffee," he told her. "Help yourself." She agreed, then turned away, draping her wet things over a chair by the fire as James left the room. Taking his advice, she poured coffee and curled up on the sofa with the earthenware mug cupped in her hands as if to capture its warmth. Exhaustion was catching up with her, dissolving the euphoria she'd felt, and she sat huddled in the corner of the sofa, staring into the fire.

# Chapter Five

James found her there when he returned, her firelit face bleak, haunted. "I thought you'd be asleep by now."

Cassie jerked around, startled, when he spoke, and her eyes widened at the sight of him. Wearing only his snug-fitting jeans, with his hair still wet and his skin gleaming from the shower, he was magnificent. If anything, Cassie thought irrelevantly, the camera didn't do him justice. On film he was handsome, but in the flesh, with the firelight sliding over his torso in shades of red and gold, highlighting the powerful contours of muscle and bone, catching in the mat of dark hair which spread across his chest and tapered to the waistband of the jeans which rode low on his narrow hips, he was beautiful. His arms and legs were lean and muscular and strong, so different from her own slender limbs, yet complementary, and he moved with an unconscious grace as he crossed the room, relaxed and controlled and utterly male.

Watching him, Cassie was reminded of her own near-nakedness, aware, as James glanced briefly at her clothing drying by the fire, that he knew as well as she that she wore nothing beneath the loose flannel shirt. She stared at the floor as he seated himself beside her, feeling a blush warm her cheeks. She tried, and failed, to make the shirt cover a little more of her, and her blush deepened.

"Aren't you sleepy?" James asked again, leaning into the cushions and resting one arm along the back of the sofa, his hand almost, but not quite, touching her.

"I'm tired, but I can't relax." She looked up from the

carpet to meet his gaze, her eyes troubled. "I keep thinking about everything that could have gone wrong. James, they could all three have died!"

"Could they? It all seemed to go very smoothly."

"I was lucky," she said flatly. "Twins, in a firsttime mother, with the first a breech . . . that would have been a complicated delivery even in a well-equipped hospital. Out here, with the bare minimum of equipment and unsterile conditions . . . I'll have nightmares about it for weeks!" She shuddered, took a swallow of her lukewarm coffee and shuddered again. "Yuck, that's horrible!" She set the mug aside. "Do you realize we might very well have had to do a caesarean right there in that bedroom?"

"Us? Do a caesarean?" James stared at her over the rim of his mug, and Cassie thought he'd gone pale under his tan. "I'm glad you didn't tell me that *before* you asked me to help!"

"It's always a possibility. That's what most doctors have to argue about with the so-called 'home birth' advocates. Nine times out of ten, or even ninety-nine times out of a hundred, babies can be born with essentially no intervention, or interference, if you like, from a doctor, and mother and baby will be just fine. It's the tenth, or the hundredth, case which shows how vital hospital facilities and care can be. In obstetrics, when things go wrong, they can go very wrong, very fast, even in women whose histories indicate that everything is normal, and before you have time to move the patient to a hospital, she or her baby could be dead. Those 'what ifs' are what give obstetricians nightmares."

"Not tonight." James slid close to Cassie and pulled her into the curve of his arm. "No nightmares for you tonight."

"Oh, yeah?" She slanted a glance up at him. "I was okay while I was in there with her, but now—" She lifted a hand and held it out to show him how it trembled. "Look at this. I can't stop shaking!"

"Relax." James took her hand and held it firmly. "Just relax. It's all over now, and everything is fine." He shifted his position, pulling her back against him and bending her head forward so he could gently massage the tense muscles of her neck and shoulders.

Cassie didn't know or care where he'd learned his massage technique, she only knew that it was marvelous, the gentle pressure of his fingers kneading and stroking her skin combining with the soothing rumble of his voice to drain away her tension. At a time when she seemed to have no strength of her own he was powerful, her protector, his strength complementing her weakness, giving her ease, comfort, security.

It seemed so natural to be held in his arms in the cozy warmth of the cabin, while the wind whined and howled through the trees outside, pushing the snow into weird and fantastic shapes. It seemed natural for James to lift her onto his lap as she relaxed, to hold her securely in his arms, cradled against the broad strength of his chest, her cheek resting on his shoulder, rubbing absently to and fro on the smooth, warm skin.

"Thank you," she murmured against his neck, almost purring with contentment, and he cupped a hand around the back of her neck, tipping her face up to his.

"Don't thank me," he whispered. "You did all the work." He cupped her face in his hands, studying each feature, his own face very close. Cassie gazed up into his eyes, drowning in their green depths, drowning in his nearness. She felt him all around her, his thighs beneath hers, hard muscle and rough denim against her naked skin, his arms around her, his skin, warm and smooth beneath her hands, his face, his lips so close to hers.

His lips. She gazed at them, studied them as if she'd never seen lips before, studied the shape of them, the cleanly modeled upper lip, the lower with its slight fullness hinting at sensuality. She'd tasted those lips, and now, Cassie realized, she wanted to taste them again. She reached up to touch them, tracing the ball of her thumb across them. They parted slightly and his teeth gleamed briefly in the fireglow, and then his hand curved around the back of her neck, drawing her up to his kiss.

Infinitely tender, infinitely sweet, their lips met, clung, then parted reluctantly. He gazed down into her eyes, and Cassie watched his pupils widen; then he dropped his gaze to her lips, soft and moist and slightly parted. Beneath her hands, which rested lightly on his chest, she felt the heavy beat of his heart accelerate.

What she was doing was insanity, of course, and somewhere deep inside Cassie knew that, but her judgment was blurred—no, obliterated—by fatigue and the aftermath of tension, by James' intoxicating presence. She didn't care about judgment and consequences at that moment; she only wanted what he could give her. Just why she should want that so badly she didn't know or care; she only knew she needed James.

Made bold by her own ability to move him, she half turned on his lap, sliding her hands up around his neck, her breasts flattening against the hard wall of his chest. She felt his sharply indrawn breath; then he answered her unspoken plea and kissed her again.

This was no kiss of comfort; this kiss was deep and passionate, Cassie's lips parting willingly to his searching exploration, kissing him back with rising delight. For long minutes they clung together; then James drew back fractionally to trace the outline of her lips with his tongue-tip, to lightly kiss her brow, her eyelids, to explore the sensitive spot below her ear in a way that left her trembling as his mouth traveled down the slender line of her throat. When the collar of the loose shirt impeded his progress he muttered something against her skin, freed a couple of buttons and pushed the flannel off her shoulder so that it clung to the swell of her breast as he tasted the creamy skin of her shoulder.

Teasing, he ran his lips along her collarbone, kissed the little hollows beneath it, tormenting her until she breathed, "Please, James. Please," her body arching up into his embrace in instinctive invitation. His hands moved to answer her plea, sliding over the flannel to cup her small, round breasts, teasing the nipples to aching hardness through the soft fabric. James groaned deep in his throat when Cassie squirmed sensuously under his hands, rubbing her body, her breasts, against him, and his hands slid down to her hips and under the shirt.

They lingered there for a moment, as though the soft curves were more than he could resist, then moved very slowly, up over her waist, her ribs, to softly tantalize the undercurves of her breasts. His fingers curved onto her ribs as his thumbs brushed across her breasts, closer and closer until, with a little gasp of need, Cassie melted into him and he found the taut buds again.

Cassie's hands were busy on errands of their own, seeking to give him as much pleasure as he gave her, and James groaned against her mouth as she ran her palms over his back and probed the heavy planes of his chest, then moved lower, exploring his taut belly and tracing a tormenting line along the waistband of his jeans. The muscles there tightened convulsively, and he pulled her around, kneeling on the sofa, to face him fully, between his knees.

He put her arms around his neck, pulling her forward to kiss him as he lightly caressed her back, her flanks, her waist, her hips, lightly at first, then boldly, fanning the flames of her growing desire. Cassie clung to James as if he were her anchor in a roiling sea, aware of nothing but him, the slight roughness of his hands on her skin melting her from within. She knew no shyness when he quickly unbuttoned the shirt and pushed it open to gaze reverently at her body, knew nothing but the desire to please him, to be pleasing to him.

Slowly he pulled her close again, lightly kissing the scented valley between her breasts; then he slowly moved to capture first one pink nipple and then the other until Cassie was shaking. Sensing her need, he moved suddenly, lifting her into his arms to carry her quickly to the tiny bedroom, where another fire burned in a smaller replica of the massive living-room fireplace, and a huge bed covered with a magnificent, hand-woven blanket dominated the room. James let her toes touch the floor briefly, as with one hand he turned back the bedcovers; then his arm slid behind her legs again and he laid her on the crisp sheet.

He moved to join her there, but Cassie propped herself up on one elbow and reached out to stop him. "The jeans," she whispered, and he stood to strip them off. He was more perfect than she had imagined, lean-hipped, muscular, superb.

"You're beautiful." He smiled a little at her words and shook his head as he joined her.

"*You're* beautiful." He slipped the shirt off her arms and tossed it aside, pressing her back into the pillows. "So beautiful . . ."

Her need was as great as his as they kissed and caressed each other with an urgency that could no longer be controlled, until James moved his body above hers. There was no pain for Cassie, only a brief resistance which brought James up short. "What—?" he muttered thickly, but Cassie didn't let him finish the question. She pulled his head down to hers again, moved against him, and with a soft groan of surrender he took her with him to a passion and a fulfillment she had never imagined.

Exhaustion was claiming them even as they returned to earth, and Cassie was only mistily aware of James pulling the blankets over their cooling bodies and tucking her securely against his length, her face in his shoulder and his lips on her hair. She might have imagined the murmur of, "Sweet," as sleep covered her like a warm, dark sea.

Cassie couldn't understand why the wall of the on-call room was white plaster instead of green enamel, or why the window was covered with a black, rust, and white curtain instead of a dusty venetian blind. It didn't make sense, but maybe it would if she slept just a few more minutes. She let her slitted lids fall closed again. It was so warm and comfortable curled up like this, her head pillowed on James' arm—

Her eyes flew open wide. Curled up with James . . . Oh, my God, she thought, it wasn't a dream, it was real! It was real, and I've got to get out of this bed. Right now. But without waking James. She lay rigidly immobile as she listened to James breathing deeply and evenly beside her, apparently still asleep.

Slowly, carefully, she eased away from him, freezing when he moved and muttered something unintelligible. She didn't move until his breathing was even again; then she slid out of the bed, shivering in the chill air as she looked around for the flannel shirt. It lay crumpled on the floor and Cassie felt herself flush hotly as she remembered how it had gotten there. She snatched it up and fled the bedroom.

Everything in the house seemed to silently accuse her: her clothes, dry now, in front of the fire; the sofa where they had kissed and caressed; wherever she looked there were reminders of her wanton behavior. With a low exclamation of distress she gathered her clothes and almost ran into the tiny bathroom.

Her appearance in the mirror was no comfort. Her hair was wildly tousled, her cheeks still flushed from sleep, her lips softened and bruised from James' kisses. Though all she wanted was to turn away, to hide from herself, she stared at her reflected image, studying each distasteful detail, memorizing them to punish herself with. How, *how* could she have done that? And why? She couldn't love James. She barely knew him, yet he could rouse a passion in her that no other man had ever been able to touch.

She didn't know what it meant. She didn't know what *anything* meant anymore; she felt totally out of control of her life, and it was not a sensation she enjoyed. For years, since her high school days in Wyoming, in fact, she had been in complete command of any romantic situation, her emotions untouched, feeling little more than sympathy for the young men who fell in love with her and disdain for those who tried to maneuver her into their beds.

Suddenly her emotions, her desires, were out of control and she had no idea how to deal with that. She did know, however, that she was not ready to face James again, so she splashed her face with cold water, dragged a comb through her tangled hair, jerking at the snarls until tears started to her eyes, and scrambled into her clothes. As quietly as she could, she stole through the house and slipped out the door, leaving James still sleeping.

The snow had ended and the wind had dropped during the night, and the morning air was clear and crisp and very cold. The morning sun, piercingly bright at that altitude, lit the drifted snow and deep-green pines with crystalline clarity, but provided no discernible warmth as Cassie hurried along the street, exchanging smiling greetings with people who were already going about their day's business. They all seemed to know who she was, and she reflected with some amusement that the "jungle telegraph" seemed to work pretty well just about everywhere.

Luisa was waiting for her, smiling and proud, propped up against a pile of pillows with a baby in each arm, surrounded by beaming relatives. After she had examined Luisa and the babies Cassie was introduced to them all, congratulated, thanked, blessed by a priest and offered numerous gifts which she tried to tactfully decline. In the end she accepted a beautifully woven blanket and a pair of intricately worked silver earrings from the families of the two new parents, knowing she would treasure the gifts for both their intrinsic beauty and the sentiments of the givers.

James found her there at the center of the happy crowd, the two equipment bags packed and waiting beside her. Cassie wasn't sure what caused her to look up from the baby in her arms, a prickling between her shoulder blades perhaps, but she turned to glance at the door, and there he was, smiling lazily across the room at her. There was a warm and intimate message in his eyes, intended only for her. Cassie had been laughing, but as she read that message the humor left her eyes and her smile became a stiff facsimile of mirth.

He recognized the change in her. In the instant before she turned her back on him to hand Luisa's daughter to her grandmother, Cassie saw him frown in surprise. She didn't know what he had to be surprised about, though. Surely he hadn't expected her to be pleased about what had happened? Embarrassed, humiliated, ashamed, certainly, but hardly pleased.

She successfully avoided speaking to him as they said their good-byes and prepared to leave, but when they had followed Cory around the first bend of the snowy trail and out of sight of the village he reached over to grab her reins, slowing the mare so they fell farther behind their young guide, out of earshot.

"What are you doing?" Cassie demanded *sotto voce*. "Let go of my reins!" She tried unsuccessfully to urge the mare on with her heels and pull the rein free. "Let *go!*"

"In a minute. I want to know what's eating you."

"You know perfectly well what's 'eating' me!"

"Last night?" His incredulous expression made her even angrier.

"Of course last night! What else? I'd hardly be upset about Luisa's babies, would I?"

"Well, I don't see why you're so upset that we—"

"I *don't* want to talk about it!" Some of the strain she was feeling came through in her voice and her face, and James relented.

"Okay, we won't talk about it . . . for now."

"We won't talk about it. Period," she muttered as he released her reins and she kneed the mare into a canter after Cory's pinto.

James let her get away with that, though it was infuriatingly clear to Cassie that he considered the hypothetical discussion and its staging to be within his control. For the rest of the day, as they traveled back to Los Angeles, he said nothing more personal than "Do you need help with that?" as she unbuckled the equipment bag from her saddle. Her curt, "No, thanks," left him unimpressed; he only smiled knowingly and carried his own bag to the van.

Cassie would have isolated herself from the conversation as she had on the way out, but the others wouldn't allow it, insisting that she recount all the details of their snowy rescue mission and the village birth. Somehow she held her emotions under rigid control, answered everyone's questions and kept up the appearance of someone with nothing more on her mind than home and a hot bath, but the effort was beginning to tell by the time they reached the hospital that night.

James hadn't really participated in the conversation as they traveled, but Cassie had felt his eyes on her every mile of the way, not frowning, not smiling, just enigmatically watching her, as if she were a specimen in a jar. She didn't enjoy the sensation one bit and was vastly relieved to climb out of the van, bid the others good-bye and head for her car.

"Can I drive you home?"

"No," she replied without looking around at James, a step behind her. "I have my car."

"I'll follow you, then. We need to talk."

"No! I don't have anything to say to you!"

"You've had all day to sulk," he reminded her. "You should have gotten it out of your system by now." She opened her mouth to protest, but James spoke across her. "Like it or not, Cassie, something happened between us. There's no point in trying to pretend it didn't, and we need . . . we *both* need . . . to talk about it."

"Look, James, I'm tired and—"

"So am I, so you don't need to worry that I'll stay late. And just to lay your fears to rest: I have no intention of ravishing your tender, young body."

"I never thought that!" she lied, and James raised one skeptical eyebrow at her.

"I'm profoundly relieved to hear it," he drawled with heavy sarcasm, "but I don't plan to discuss this in the middle of the parking garage, so get in." He held the door of her

Toyota while she slid in. "Go home, Cassie; I'll meet you there." He slammed her door and strode away before she could even begin to formulate a retort.

Fuming, Cassie did as she'd been told. She toyed with the idea of ignoring his high-handed command and driving around for hours, or going to a restaurant, but such a childish gesture would accomplish nothing but making her look foolish. She took the quickest route home, and as she turned her headlights off his Mercedes swung into the driveway behind her. Without acknowledging his presence she dragged her overnight bag out of the back seat and lugged it inside, leaving the door open for James to follow her in. By the time he'd closed it behind him and turned the lock, Cassie was halfway down the hall.

"I'm going to shower and change before I talk about *anything,*" she informed him, her voice and manner openly challenging, but he didn't rise to the bait, only nodded agreement. Cassie, a little ashamed now of her surly behavior, turned and went back to the living room door. "You can make some coffee, if you'd like," she said by way of a peace offering. "I'll only be a few minutes."

"Sounds like a good idea," he agreed. "Enjoy your shower." Cassie did, finding it difficult to sustain her anger at James when he was being so agreeable, but aware of the danger of allowing him to lull her into complacency. She rejoined him wearing a pair of jeans and a sweater, with a towel wrapped turban-style around her newly washed hair, ready to listen to what he had to say, but determined to speak her own piece, too.

In addition to the coffee, James had made sandwiches with ham and swiss cheese he had unearthed in her refrigerator, and he offered her a plate as she entered.

"I hope you don't mind, but that hamburger I had for supper just didn't do it."

"I don't mind. It's not often I get waited on." She took a large bite of her sandwich. "I'm hungry, too." They ate in silence for a few minutes, occupied with their own thoughts. Finally James set his empty plate on the coffee table and leaned back in his armchair.

"We have to talk about it, you know."

"I can't see that talking about it is going to make much difference," was the uncooperative reply. James sighed.

"It happened, Cassie. Maybe it didn't happen in the place or in the way we might have wished, but it happened."

"*I* didn't wish it at all!"

"Not much you didn't!" he roared. In the blink of an eye the patient, reasonable James had vanished, leaving in his place an enraged, green-eyed giant. "You can say a lot of things to me, lady, and I may not agree with them, but I won't argue with you, but don't *ever* say *that!*" She stared at him, transfixed by the naked fury which filled his face, carving it into stone. "You wanted me." He was out of his chair, leaning over her as she shrank back into the sofa. "You wanted me just as much as I wanted you. I did *not* take you against your will, and you *will not* lie about it!" He bent over her, hands braced against the sofa on either side of her, trapping her between his arms.

"Say it!" he ordered her.

"S–say what?"

"*Say it!*" He wasn't going to play her game, and Cassie felt a twinge of real fear at the fury in his eyes.

"Okay, I wanted you, too!" she cried. "But that doesn't make any difference in the way I feel about it now!"

James' face relaxed, one corner of his mouth curling in wry amusement as he sank back into the chair again. "What really bothers you about this, Cassie? The fact that our relationship is no longer just professional, or the fact that the relationship is with me?"

Cassie stared at him for a moment, then dropped her head to gaze blindly at the carpet beneath her feet. Finally she shook her head helplessly. "I don't know. I only wish it had never happened."

"But it did happen," James said quietly, unyieldingly. "Why are you so upset about it? You're a woman, not a teenager hiding secrets from her mother."

"Oh, swell. I suppose that also means I'm at liberty to be a tramp. Thanks a lot!"

"I'm well aware that you're not a tramp. It was the first time for you, wasn't it?"

Cassie felt a fiery blush scald her throat and face. "Yes, it was!" she snapped, furious with him for putting her through this embarrassment. "But even if it hadn't been, the problem would be just the same. It shouldn't have happened!"

"I can't understand what's so awful about it. It's not as though anyone's going to sew a scarlet 'A' on your lab coat, Hester Prynne."

"Hester Prynne was married," she pointed out logically, if irrelevantly. "The point is, I didn't *want* this! I didn't want any kind of a relationship with you at all!"

James shook his head, his expression sober, almost grave. "It's too late for that. We *have* a relationship. It's a *fait accompli,* and I have no intention of pretending otherwise."

Cassie had an immediate and horrifying vision of the embarrassment he could cause her at the hospital. There had been considerable gossip about James, and about her, when he first came to the hospital, and she knew that it would take only one soulful gaze, or pat on the fanny, or any public gesture of intimacy, however trivial, to completely destroy her credibility. She had worked hard to establish herself as a thoroughly competent professional, to earn the position of Chief Resident, and her heart sank at the thought that she might lose that hard-earned respect because of her attraction to James.

"What do you mean," she asked him weakly, "when you say you won't pretend?"

"I meant that we'll continue to see each other, of course."

"At the hospital?"

"Well, naturally at the hospital, and outside it, too." He

saw her face change, and frowned. "What's really bothering you? It can't be the idea of a few dinner dates."

"No, it's not dinner dates," she said irritably, and pushed herself up off the sofa to pace agitatedly across the room. She had brought a comb from the bathroom, and now she pulled the towel from her head and draped it around her shoulders as she roughly combed out her hair. "It's the hospital. You don't know . . . ouch!" She winced as the comb caught a snarl, and she jerked at it in frustration.

"Come here." James crossed the room to take her by the shoulders and steer her back to his chair. "Sit on the floor and give me that comb before you end up bald." He reinforced his instruction by pressing her down to sit cross-legged between his knees as he resumed his seat. He took the offending lock of hair and began patiently working the tangle free. "Now, tell me what it is that I don't know."

"It's the gossip." Though she was acutely aware of James behind her, of his long, denim-clad legs stretched out on either side of her, of the faint scent of horses and antiseptic that still clung to him, Cassie found it easier to explain things when she wasn't facing him. His hands moved through her hair, over her scalp, rhythmically combing, smoothing her hair to a swath of black satin, his touch comforting, relaxing, as she tried to make him understand.

"The gossip in a hospital can be just a harmless annoyance, but it can also be destructive. I don't know if you've been aware of the talk about us, but it's only just begun to die down. If there's even the slightest hint that we have any kind of relationship at all, it'll start up again, ten times worse!" She hunched her shoulders, dropping her head forward, and James paused in his combing to briefly massage her tense nape, then straighten her head again. "Fair or not, I, as a doctor, need to have a good personal reputation, and the things that would be said could prejudice that."

"I understand that." A smile entered his voice. "And you don't need to worry that I'll kiss you in the main lobby. I'll be the very soul of discretion when I'm anywhere near that hospital. Away from it, though, I have no intention of acting like a polite stranger."

"But what's the point?" Cassie half turned to look up at him.

"Does there have to be a point?" He smoothed her hair back from her temples, the light touch of his fingers sending a little electrical current down her spine. "Not everything in this life has a point." He had slid his fingers into her hair, and his thumbs were lightly massaging her cheekbones and brow, smoothing away her frown before it could form. "Some things are simply meant to be enjoyed. Like this." He slid his hands down to caress her neck, lifting her face to his gaze.

As James studied her face, Cassie studied him in return, struck anew by his beauty. The strength of the hard-carved face, the warmth which lit his green eyes from within, were so familiar to her now, but had lost none of their potent attraction, and when he smiled . . . When he smiled her eyes dropped to his lips, and her breath caught in her throat at the memory of what those lips had done, what they had made her feel.

Was he right? Were there moments in life which should simply be enjoyed, not analyzed? Was this such a moment? She turned a bit more to kneel on the carpet between his legs and reached up to shyly touch his face, tracing the straight lines of nose and brows, brushing back the thick lock of dark hair which fell onto his forehead, smoothing her fingers over the planes of his cheek and jaw and finally brushing them lightly over his lips. He drew his breath in sharply at that touch, and she felt him stiffen slightly.

"You'll see me . . . away from the hospital?" He held her face between his hands so that she could look nowhere but at him. "You'll see me?"

"Yes."

"Good." He rose, lifting her to her feet with him. She was close enough to be pulled into his embrace, but he kept his hands on her shoulders, holding her so that a slight distance separated their bodies. "Thank you for the coffee and the sandwich, Cassie, and the promise. I'll let myself out." He kissed her lightly, on her brow then on her lips, and was gone while she still stood staring foolishly at the door.

What was the matter with her? She dropped into the chair James had recently vacated. She had fully intended to refuse, to argue that the whole idea was patently insane, that she would not see him. She'd wanted to tell him that her only intention was to wipe the whole episode out of her mind as if it had never been, and instead, he'd had only to look into her eyes and she had agreed to everything he'd asked.

She used to think she was strong-willed, Cassie reflected in disgust. What on earth had gone wrong with her? Her mind supplied the unwelcome answer. James. James had happened to her. She had read somewhere, in a magazine article or something, that James Reid had "hypnotic eyes." Well, he certainly hypnotized me, she thought. She shoved herself out of the chair, quickly stacked their plates and cups, and piled them in the sink. They could wait until morning.

She stepped back into the living room and paused with her hand on the light switch. The cushions of the armchair still bore the imprint of James' weight, and she had a sudden clear vision of him seated at his ease there, big and virile and very much at home. She'd felt at home, too, Cassie admitted reluctantly. She'd felt like purring as James combed her hair, sensuously reveling in his touch, in the suggestion and remembrance of other touches.

She caught herself up before the fantasy could go any farther, slapped a hand across the switch to plunge the room into darkness and marched down the hall to her room. So much for your strong will, Cassandra!

James walked toward her out of the mist, hands outstretched. Cassie ran to meet him, a smile of eager welcome on her lips, her body on fire with anticipation, but the harder she ran, the farther away he was. . . .

Cassie sat bolt upright in bed, staring at the darkness around her, which gradually resolved itself into her familiar bedroom. "Sheesh!" She flopped back onto the pillows, staring up at the ceiling. Not only could the man gaze into her eyes and make her do anything he wanted, he was invading her dreams, as well. She didn't *want* this! She didn't want to dream about him, to want what she'd wanted in her dream. Her mind was filled with vague dream-visions, dim, disturbing images of James and herself, of making love in a firelit bedroom while a storm howled outside.

*Oh, Lord, I want him.* Cassie rolled out of bed and switched on the light, blinking against its glare. With the light on, the dream images were vanquished, but the remnants of the throbbing need they had aroused were still with her.

"Damn!" She stalked into the bathroom to dash cold water on her burning face, then returned to look at her bedside alarm. Four o'clock, and she had to get up at six. She'd never get back to sleep now. In the predawn quiet she heard a "thunk" as the newspaper landed on her front porch, then the rattle of the paperboy's bicycle as he rode on down the street.

She thought about it for a moment, then picked up her robe and went to make coffee and retrieve the paper. Might as well have a good breakfast, for once.

Two hours of leisure spent reading the paper from cover to cover and eating the kind of eggs-bacon-and-toast breakfast the nutrition books all recommended while the sun rose over the Verdugo Mountains east of Burbank were not enough to prepare her to face James. She dressed carefully, as though arming for battle, though she knew that the real battle was not with James, but with herself. Feeling edgy and vulnerable, with the memory of her dreams too fresh for her peace of mind, she wheeled her car into the "Doctors' Parking" area just before seven.

He had to be faced, she told herself firmly; there was no point in delaying the inevitable. Shoulders squared with more bravado than she really felt, she marched through the north entrance of the hospital and almost ran into Gail Anderson, who was rounding a corner in the corridor.

"Oops! Pardon me, I . . . Gail! I didn't realize it was you!

How are you?" Cassie asked the polite question as they each stepped back and steadied themselves after the near collision, but looking at Gail's face, she knew that something was very wrong. Beneath the sprinkling of freckles, her friend's face was pale, and she looked drawn, almost haggard. Even her normally bouncy dark-red hair seemed dull, lifeless. Cassie knew she didn't look that great herself, after the exhausting weekend and too little sleep the night before, but by comparison with Gail she was the picture of robust health.

"I'm fine," Gail said tersely, avoiding Cassie's eyes.

"Are you sure, Gail? You don't look—"

"I said I'm fine!" Gail snapped, her voice strained. "I've gotta go." She brushed past an astounded Cassie and hurried along the corridor as if pursued.

Gail wasn't the least bit fine, but if she didn't want to talk about it, Cassie was very much afraid that there was nothing she could do to help. Gail would be furious if Cassie were to speak to Steve about it, but she was tempted to breach her friend's confidence on the chance that it might help. She continued more slowly on her way, her gray eyes troubled.

Concern for Gail overrode even her own problem with James, though she was uncomfortably aware of his brilliant green gaze on her as she worked. The new awareness in James' eyes was unnerving, and she was ill at ease with him, conversing stiffly, eager for the day to end. Even at six o'clock, though, her day was not over.

"Have dinner with me." She and James were in the on-call room, preparing to change into their street clothes and leave for the day.

"James, I know I said I'd see you, and I will, but I'm really tired, and—"

"And you need a nice, relaxing evening. I'm not putting pressure on you; I just think you need something besides this place to think about."

"I'll go home and read a magazine."

"What a thrill," was James' dry retort.

"I just don't want—"

"Cassie, it's only dinner, for heaven's sake. I can hardly attack you in a public restaurant, so what on earth are you so terrified of? Look," he sighed in irritation, "this isn't some contrived seduction, okay? I'd like a good meal in pleasant surroundings, and I'd rather not be alone. Now, will you come?" Seen in that light, it was a reasonable request, and Cassie felt ashamed and a bit foolish for overreacting.

"Yes," she said quietly. "I'll come."

"Good. I'll pick you up as soon as I've changed at my office." He pushed open the door, then paused. "Cassie?"

"Hmm?"

"Wear something dressy, okay?"

"Oh. Okay." He vanished toward the men's locker room, while Cassie shrugged and continued packing her tote bag.

# Chapter Six

*S*he had surmised the sort of restaurant he had in mind from his instruction to "dress up," so it was no real surprise to Cassie when James pulled up to the entrance of *Ma Ménage*. For one of the best-known and most exclusive restaurants in Los Angeles, it was so unpretentious on the outside as to be utterly anonymous, the only hint of opulence within being a smartly uniformed valet waiting to park the car.

The valet was an extremely handsome young man, no doubt one of the thousands of aspiring actors waiting for a "break," and he took the keys to James' Rolls Corniche with a cocky salute, then pulled away with a roar as they were ushered through the massive oak doors. The maître d', a small, dapper man with thinning hair, smiled unctuously as the doorman admitted them.

"Good evening, *Monsieur* Reid. Will you wish your usual table this evening?"

"Yes, please, Henri. And, Henri?" The maître d' paused.

"*Oui, Monsieur* Reid?"

"I'm not here this evening."

"Of course, *monsieur*." Henri nodded sagely and conducted them to a curved banquette in an alcove, screened from the other diners by a massive potted palm. Cassie had forced herself to calmly follow Henri and refrain from gawking, but she had received an impression of clean, curving, Art Deco elegance. The linens and upholstery were in shades of mauve, rose and ivory, with touches of chrome and pieces of Art Deco sculpture carefully displayed.

It was every bit as stunning as its reputation had led her to expect, and she was positive that she had seen two movie stars and a rock singer as she and James walked to their table. Henri seated her with great care, and Cassie hid a grin, nodding regally at him as he bowed and retreated.

"If you were going to browbeat me into having dinner with you, at least you could have taken me someplace nice," she informed James. He struggled to stifle a laugh.

"You don't like it here?" He looked comically crestfallen. "Aw, shucks, I thought this'd be better than the taco place on Pico Boulevard. Did I goof up?"

"I'll put up with it, just this once." Cassie smiled teasingly. "I don't think I'm dressed for a taco joint." She glanced down at her utterly simple cream silk charmeuse. It had been a fortunate find, a designer dress on the sale rack because it was too small a size to sell easily, and though it had cost more than she could really afford, Cassie had been unable to resist it. Slim-fitting, with a bodice which wrapped closed in a deep V-neckline, short, stand-away sleeves and a straight knee-length skirt cinched by a wide chamois belt, it suited her figure and coloring perfectly, needing only a wide, red bracelet and strappy red sandals as accents.

"You look gorgeous."

"Why, thank you, kind suh." Cassie knew she looked good; she'd spent a lot of time in front of a mirror trying to ensure that she did, but she doubted very much that she looked "gorgeous," and she was most certain that no one living on a resident's salary could aspire to the standard of dress that appeared to be *de rigeur* here. She looked around them, admiring the elegantly stylized decor. "This is quite the little restaurant, isn't it?"

"Have you been here often?"

"Have I? . . . James, you practically need a S.A.G. card and a financial statement to get in the door! The best I can offer is my California medical license and an automated-teller card from the bank."

"It seems to me a medical license is worth more than a Screen Actors' Guild card."

"Sure. That's why I eat at taco stands and you eat here. Don't you read the papers? Actors' salaries are higher than ever, and the supply-demand ratio for doctors is swinging back from a shortage to a glut. You and I occupy different ends of the economic spectrum, Mr. Reid."

The arrival of their waiter prevented James from replying to that, though Cassie could see that he'd wanted to. She was glad they'd been interrupted. Her tone might have been teasing, there might have been a smile on her lips, but she'd meant what she said. The two of them occupied different worlds. This was James' *milieu*, the haunts of the wealthy and famous and powerful. He belonged in this world; he was at his ease among these people with their money and their names, but Cassie wasn't.

She might be dressed in the single most expensive garment she owned, and she didn't think she *looked* particularly out of place, especially since the rock star was wearing a pair of jeans and a sleeveless sweatshirt, but she *felt* out of place. She was comfortable with ordinary people, the doctors and nurses and technicians and patients she worked with every day, but the people here were extraordinary. Being here was just underlining the vast gulf between her and James, and Cassie didn't know whether to be impressed or annoyed.

"What will you have for a first course?"

James' question drew her back from her musings and she shrugged. "Why don't you choose for me, since you're familiar with the menu?"

"Okay. Anything you don't like?"

"I'm not wild about snails, but other than that, I'm not picky." James scanned the menu, then quickly ordered Tournedos Rossini, with a starter of Pacific prawns which he promised would delight her. The waiter departed, and James turned his attention back to Cassie.

"Do you come here a lot?" she asked him.

"Not very often, but it's a good place to come when I don't want to be interrupted, or to find myself on tomorrow's front page. The food's good, too," he added, and Cassie grinned.

"Now I understand what you said to Henri."

"What was that?"

"That you're 'not here' tonight."

"Ah, yes. The soul of discretion, is Henri. He wouldn't have the job if he weren't."

"It must feel awfully confining, having to always be on show for reporters and all."

"It does, but it goes with the territory. Anyone who becomes a performer has to understand that. No one likes to lose all their privacy, but anyone who pursues a career like mine has to know that compromises must be made." He grinned. "Lots of public figures complain about loss of privacy, but how many of them say, 'I've lost my privacy, I don't want to be famous anymore'?"

"Not too many, I must admit. Your career is sounding less appealing all the time, though."

"Yeah, but it's all I got!" Cassie laughed with him as the waiter arrived with their prawns.

"Mmm, you were right. These are wonderful!" Cassie took another bite of succulent shrimp, lightly dressed with a mustard and herb vinaigrette.

"Just stick with me, kid, and you'll—"

"James! James, darling!" The ringing call from across the room mercifully interrupted his Humphrey Bogart impression. Cassie looked around to see a tall redhead hurrying toward them, waving eagerly. Statuesque, voluptuous, dressed in a skimpy, flame-colored dress and a great deal of fur, with diamonds glittering on her wrists and fingers, she looked like exactly the sort of starlet Cassie would have expected James Reid, movie star, to favor.

She behaved in the expected manner, as well, throwing her arms around James, who had risen to greet her, and giving him a long, intense kiss.

"Darling, it's so good to see you! Where *have* you been

hiding yourself all this time? And you *must* introduce me!"
She perched on the end of the banquette beside James,
smiling expectantly at Cassie.

"Actually, I've been at a hospital . . . but not as a patient," he added reassuringly. "Marise, I'd like you to meet
Dr. Cassandra Mills. Cassie, this is Marise Marshall. We
worked together on *Night Thunder,* if you saw that movie."

"I did," Cassie nodded, "and you do look familiar, Miss
Marshall. Weren't you? . . ."

"The villain's dumb girlfriend? That was me." Marise
grinned. "They never did give me enough of a costume in that
one." Cassie remembered the costume, what there had been
of it. "And you're a doctor? A little, tiny thing like you?"
Cassie nodded. "What kind of doctor are you, darling?"

"An obstetrician-gynecologist."

"A baby doctor? I mean, you deliver babies and all? Just
like those doctors who go on TV?"

"Just like them." Cassie grinned.

"My, my. Things are changing all the time, aren't they?"
The question required no answer, and Marise turned to smile
up at James. "Now, what have you been doing at a hospital?"
James briefly explained, and then Marise launched into a
detailed account of everything she had done since she'd last
seen James. Cassie gathered that that had been some time
ago, so there was a lot to recount. Few of the names and
places meant anything to her, so she returned pragmatically
to her prawns, listening with half an ear.

Marise's escort, a plumpish man in his fifties, referred to
only as Harry, joined them after a few minutes, sitting beside
Cassie. He nodded to her when Marise quickly introduced
them.

"Pleased to meetcha. You an actress?"

"No, I'm a doctor."

Harry's grizzled eyebrows climbed up his high forehead at
that. "That so? Thought you were an actress. Interesting."
Harry turned back to Marise and James. Though neither of
them were rude, and they tried without much success to

include Cassie in the conversation, she felt drab beside the glittering Marise and unavoidably shut out of the film-world chat. It was all too clear that she was the outsider.

When the entrée arrived Marise and Harry departed for their own table, but Cassie was too distracted to fully appreciate the fork-tender filet of beef or the crisp endive salad which followed. She was toying with a pear and a small wedge of Brie when James pushed his plate away and leaned back against the mauve upholstery.

"Do you intend to eat that pear, or are you just going to torture it?"

Cassie looked down at the mangled slice of pear and sighed. "I think I've eaten enough. And you were right, James, it was all delicious."

"If you don't want dessert," she shook her head, "then can I offer you a drink at my house?"

He was watching her intently, his eyes hooded by half-closed lids, but she knew that he would miss no nuance of expression that crossed her face. She squelched the impulse to make some not-so-funny crack about coming up to see his etchings and kept her face carefully bland. She wasn't sure that a drink at his house was such a terrific idea, but, on the other hand, this seemed to be her night for getting a look at James' world. She might as well see his home while she was at it.

"Thank you. I'd like that." From the gleam in his eye she knew that he had a pretty accurate idea of what had gone through her mind and was amused by it. His ability to read her mind was getting more annoying all the time, and she resolved to better conceal her feelings. Her ruffled feathers took a few minutes to smooth down, and she walked out of the restaurant at his side, coolly silent.

Curiosity overcame her annoyance when she saw which freeway he took. They had dined in Bel Air, and when he headed west on Sunset Boulevard she assumed he was driving toward Pacific Palisades or Topanga, or even Malibu. But then he completely confused her by taking the San Diego

Freeway south. When he continued past the exit which would have led to Santa Monica, she had to ask.

"Where are we going?"

"To my house."

"Do you live at the airport?" She had just seen the "Century Boulevard/LA International" sign.

"Nope." Cassie lost her patience.

"Don't play games! Where do you live?"

"Sunset Beach, but don't get upset about it, okay?"

"You live clear down in Orange County? I'd have thought—"

"You've always assumed a lot about me, Cassie. I think it's time you learned how much—or how little—of it's true."

Chastened, Cassie subsided into her seat, gazing out at the passing city. Traffic was light, and it didn't take long to travel the thirty-five miles, leaving the San Diego Freeway in Long Beach for the Pacific Coast Highway, which carried them past the marshy emptiness of the Seal Beach Naval Weapons Station and then across the Anaheim Bay Channel to Surfside, Huntington Harbor and Sunset Beach.

The little enclave that was Sunset Beach occupied a narrow strip of real estate between the Coast Highway and the ocean, while Huntington Harbor's marina community lay on the inland side of the highway. A series of short streets, each only a few houses long, led from the highway to the beach, and at the end of one of these, facing the Pacific, was James' home. Beachfront property, as Cassie knew, was always costly, but James' home was modest by the Beverly Hills-Bel Air standards of walled and privately policed movie stars' estates.

Simply styled, with a natural wood exterior, James' house, like its neighbors, was narrow and deep, two stories tall, with a third half-story and a rooftop terrace. Between the garage and the back door was a brick-paved patio, lush with tubbed and potted plants. In front, James told her, was a tiny yard, separated from the beach by a low stone wall. He unlocked a heavy oak door, ushered her under the branches of an enormous schefflera tree and followed her into his home.

The hallway they walked into was floored with terra-cotta Mexican tiles, while the walls were off-white and the woodwork a rich, dark oak. A few steps down the hall was an archway leading to the kitchen, a spacious room with a windowed breakfast area overlooking the patio, and a few steps past that the hallway opened into the living room. This was a large room, the full width and over half the depth of the house, with a wall of windows facing the beach and covered by narrow-slat blinds to dim the force of the afternoon sun. Smaller windows on the sides of the house, in the hall, kitchen and a downstairs powder room, as well as the living room, spoke of the earlier day in which the house had been built, and gave it an open, airy feel.

The white walls and dark woodwork continued throughout, and from one corner of the living room a spiral staircase led to the upper floors. Cassie's preconceived notions about where and how James lived had been shattering one by one ever since he'd taken I–405 south, and a few more exploded as she looked around the room. The decoration was simple, in light neutral and earth tones, with brilliant, crayon-colored accents in the form of throw pillows and pottery and masses of gorgeous plants. Some plants even hung from the wrought-iron bannister, and Cassie looked around her in growing wonder, smiling her approval.

"It's lovely," she told James as he collected his mail from the door slot. "It really is lovely."

"Have a look upstairs while I sort this." He indicated the thick sheaf of mail in his hand. "Then I'll fix you that drink."

"You don't mind? My poking around your house, I mean?"

He shrugged, grinning. "My secrets are yours. What would you like to drink?"

"To be honest, coffee sounds wonderful. I think I've had enough alcohol for one evening."

"Coffee it is." He waved her toward the stairs. "Go look around." She went.

The second floor was as appealing as the first, with two

large bedrooms, each with a bath. The guest room, at the rear, was traditional, with simple pine furnishings and flowered chintz in shades of blue, which carried over into the bath, while James' room was plainer, more masculine. She felt a bit strange standing at the door of his bedroom; it seemed such an intimacy. And that was a pretty silly way to feel, considering the intimacies which had already passed between them, she told herself tartly, and walked into the room.

It was almost as large as the living room below, with the same wall of windows facing the Pacific. Decorated mainly in beige and dark brown, with the same brilliant accents as the living room, and more plants, it was an enormously appealing room. Cassie wanted to curl up in the large recliner by the window and simply sit and watch the surf, as she imagined James must sometimes do. She skirted the wide bed, almost afraid to get too near, which was also silly, of course, and peered into the bath. James used this bath every day.

A sudden, vivid image of him came to her, standing at the sink, shaving, one of the thick, cocoa-colored towels wrapped around his lean hips. . . . Quickly she backed out of the doorway, switched off the lights and left the room.

The spiral staircase led up again to the half-story third floor, which was one large room, with walls of windows east and west and walls of bookshelves north and south. It was furnished with a large desk, armchairs and a sofa, and seemed to serve as a combination library, study and office. Cassie glanced at a few of the titles lining the walls and was reluctantly impressed. There must have been over a thousand volumes, covering a broad range of topics, from the mundane to the esoteric. Here and there on the shelves were mementos of James' career, but there were no self-congratulatory photos of him with other stars, no movie posters, and she didn't see his Oscar anywhere.

Sliding doors led to the roof terrace, which occupied the oceanfront half of the third floor. Cassie glanced around at the comfortable patio furniture, took a deep breath of the crisp, salty breeze, and stepped back inside, her face thoughtful.

She had assumed a great deal about him with very little factual basis, she admitted that, but she wasn't sure she was happier with the truth. She didn't want to like or admire him, yet she loved this house, and she admired what it said about the man who lived there, especially since that man was an extremely successful and famous actor. He could certainly afford to live on a guarded estate in Bel Air, with a pool, tennis courts and a flock of retainers. The fact that he had chosen comfortable simplicity spoke volumes about his priorities and his taste.

The living room was empty when she reached it.

"I'm in the kitchen," James called, then met her in the hallway with a coffee tray. "Go sit down and be comfortable." He shooed her back to the living room and ensconced her on the luxuriously comfortable sectional seating unit which curved around the room, creating a large conversation area. A coffee table made of a huge slab of petrified wood with a massive glass top stood in the center of the curve, with a couple of plants and a stack of magazines making a homey clutter atop it. James poured her a cup of coffee, added the teaspoon of sugar she preferred and passed it to her.

"How do you like the house?"

"It's lovely," she said honestly. "It really is. Not what I'd expected . . ." She realized the trap she'd laid for herself and fell silent. James said nothing for a moment, and she babbled hastily to fill the silence, "I mean, you'd expect a movie star to have a pool and all. Things like that," she finished weakly.

James took pity on her. "I've never thought I needed a pool when I have that," he nodded toward the ocean, "at my door." He grinned, and Cassie relaxed slightly.

"True. A pool would seem a bit . . . superfluous."

They smiled at each other, James with something almost like pity in his eyes, Cassie nervously wondering what was in his mind.

"I like it here," he said after a moment, gazing out into the darkness where the surf boomed hollowly on the beach. "My neighbors are nice people, professionals, businessmen, a writer or two. Actually, the people next door are a doctor and a writer, and we share a cleaning lady, who's twenty-nine and owns her own cleaning business. She does my house in the morning and theirs in the afternoon."

"You don't have any staff? Cooks and maids and people?"

"What for? The cleaning lady and her employees do what I need. I can cook for myself."

"Don't you have to entertain producers and directors and movie studio people?"

"I don't do business here. I *live* here. I pay a small fortune for a very nice suite of offices in Studio City where I can hold meetings and serve catered food. If I have to give a really big party I rent a room in a hotel. The people who come here are my friends, not business acquaintances." James sounded almost angry, and Cassie tried to make a joke.

"I'm flattered, then, since I'm a business acquaintance."

"Don't act stupid, Cassie!" he snapped. "You're a hell of a lot more than that, and you know it." Shoving himself up out of his armchair, he took the empty coffeepot and stalked out of the room.

Cassie watched him go, wide-eyed, wishing she'd kept her big mouth shut. Of course she knew they were more than acquaintances, she could feel herself flush every time she thought about it, and she regretted it bitterly. The problem was that she didn't want to be anything to him *but* a business acquaintance.

She would have preferred that he have a big, ostentatious house with electronic gates and attack dogs and a staff of loyal retainers. As a matter of fact, she wished he had a pool and a tennis court and a hot tub, and a screening room to show his own movies. She wanted him to fit the clichés, because she could dismiss someone like that as just another narcissistic actor, of no importance to her.

James, the private James, was not so easily dismissed, but

she knew that her basic objection still held true. He might live here in relative simplicity, but she knew the going price for this beachfront house had to be in excess of two million dollars. He drove a Rolls; he ate in restaurants Cassie had only read about; he was a major movie star. There simply was no way to reconcile their disparate worlds.

She was gazing thoughtfully out at the darkness when he returned with a fresh pot of coffee.

"We have to talk." Cassie looked sharply around at him. "We didn't get to finish our conversation last night."

"There's hardly any need," Cassie replied sarcastically. "Anyway, this is rapidly turning into a soap opera. 'Tune in tomorrow for the next exciting episode—' "

"Don't worry, this episode is the conclusion."

"I can hardly wait." Cassie sat back, arms folded and eyes wary.

"We have something," James said soberly, "whether you like it or not. We have something together, you and I, and it's too good to throw away."

Cassie shook her head in quick denial. "We're too different. Our worlds are different. You don't fit into my world the way another doctor would, and I don't fit into yours the way someone like Miss Marshall does."

"I'm not saying this to Marise; I'm saying it to you! And I don't recall you mentioning a doctor 'in your life,' either. So, okay, we have different jobs. Since when is that prohibited by law?"

Cassie rose abruptly and walked over to the staircase to stand with her back to him, toying with the leaves of a grape ivy hanging from one of the risers. "It's not just the jobs, and you know it. It's the demands they place on us. I work ridiculous hours, and I'll always have nights when I'm called out to patients. You're finding it interesting right now, but in time it will become an annoyance, a liability. And your job is even worse! You have shooting days which last eighteen hours; you have to spend weeks on location who knows where in the world, and somewhere in there you must have an actor's ego which needs to be stroked." She bent her head, talking to the ivy. "You live and work in another world, James. The people you spend all your time with live in the fast lane. I'm not a fast-lane type. I don't want anything to do with that world."

"Does this look like the fast lane?" James growled from just behind her. "Look at me, Cassie." He took her shoulders and turned her to face him, cupping her chin in his hand and lifting her face to his gaze. "I don't have orgies, Cassie; the very idea is repulsive to me. I don't do drugs; I don't have a 'casting couch;' I have no unusual sexual proclivities, and my money isn't used for shady financial deals. Don't condemn me on the basis of gossip columns and other people's problems. I'm myself, not part of a cliché about the degeneracy of Hollywood."

He was so big and so close that Cassie could feel the warmth of his body, and slowly, carefully, he pulled her closer, sliding his arms around her. She wanted to push him away, to shake her head and say no, but she also wanted to kiss him, to touch him, and that desire was the more powerful. Her hands, which had come up to his chest to push him away, stayed instead to slide over the crisp cotton of his shirt, sensing the warm skin and muscle beneath.

At that small signal of acquiescence James gathered her fully against him, pulling her up onto her toes as he took her mouth. He kissed her gently, delicately, savoring the moment, savoring her as he had been unable to do in their previous feverish embraces. He teased and tasted, nibbling at her lips, tracing their outline with his tongue as they softened and parted in response. He forced her to wait when she was impatient, teasing until she breathed an inarticulate protest and reached up to pull him down to her. Only then would he deepen the kiss, taking what she was so eager to give.

As their kisses grew more urgent he guided her back to the sofa, where he pulled her across his lap. Cradled there, Cassie reveled in being with him. She was lost in the desires he was rousing in her, but when his hand moved to the neckline of her dress she stiffened. Immediately his hand withdrew. He hugged her to him for a moment, pressing her face into his shoulder, then slid her off his lap, arranging her skirt over her knees before reaching for his now-cool coffee. He took a sip and grimaced.

"I need to cool off, but not with cold coffee." He replaced his cup on the coffee table and sat back, slouching comfortably into the cushions and stretching the great length of his legs out in front of him. "I want you to know," he said after a moment, "that I won't rush you, Cassie. You make the rules."

"And if I say we don't? . . ." Cassie was trembling as her overheated body cooled, but her voice was low and level, and she watched James steadily, looking for a reaction.

"Don't make love?" His lips curved in a half-smile. "You make the rules. When we make love, it will be because you ask me to."

"What makes you think," Cassie bristled, "that I would *ever* ask you to make love to me?"

"Because I have confidence in you." James watched her face in enjoyment as surprise replaced anger. "And in myself." Anger returned.

"What you have, *Mister* Reid, is a great big overinflated ego, and one of these days it'll get you in trouble! And, just for your information, I will *not* ask you to make love to me!"

"Come on." James pulled her to her feet, smiling an indulgent, avuncular smile which set Cassie's teeth on edge. "You're getting crabby; it's time to take you home."

"I am not crabby! And don't you take that superior attitude with me, James Reid. I'll . . ." She was still sputtering as he led her out to the car.

"So what are the general criteria you use when deciding whether or not to do a caesarean?" James laid his fork on his empty plate and pushed his lunch tray aside.

"The general criterion is that a section is done in cases in which a normal delivery is not feasible or would pose an undue risk to the mother or baby. In specific cases the decision may be an obvious one, or it may be a matter of experience and judgment."

"What would the obvious ones be?" James doodled on a notepad as Cassie began to list them, ticking them off on her fingers. She paused after a moment.

"You know, if Luisa had had her twins here in the hospital, I might very well have elected to do a section, because it would have been safer for the babies. Actually, this will make more sense to you if I give you a book to read. There are a lot of different indications, and the library has this," she reached over to scribble the title of a book on his notepad, "to explain them all."

"A book might be more practical, but it won't be as good to look at." James grinned wickedly at her.

"Stop flirting! You promised you'd protect my reputation, remember?"

"Mm-hm, and you promised you'd go out with me, so what time will we finish up today?"

"Pretty early, since the Clinic's light today. About five."

"Want to go to a drive-in movie?"

She stared at him for a moment. "Are you serious?" He nodded. "What movie, and what drive-in?" The movie was a recent hit, one Cassie had wanted to see, while the drive-in was in Orange County, not far from James' house. "It sounds fine," Cassie told him. "But why not go to a theater and sit in air-conditioned comfort?"

"Because I can't be anonymous in a theater, silly."

"Ah, I see. . . ." Cassie's voice rose slightly as she abruptly shifted conversational gears. "The most compelling indication for a caesarean is placenta previa, because it's absolutely impossible in that case to deliver the baby normally."

"Because of the bleeding, right?" James didn't need to look around to know that someone was approaching their table, in this case a medical student just beginning his rotation on Cassie's service. Two weeks had passed since James had first taken Cassie to his house, and the two of them had become adept at this sort of conversational camouflage, at living almost a double life. At the hospital they maintained the pretense that they were no more than colleagues, while outside it they spent nearly every evening and free day together.

Cassie had enjoyed those evenings and weekends more than she would ever have thought possible, for time and again James had surprised her. They had done unexpected things: visited the LA Zoo to pet the animals in the Petting Zoo; strolled along Olvera Street, sampling Mexican delicacies and buying a *piñata* in the shape of a big, pink donkey; going to the southern end of Orange County to visit the San Juan Capistrano Mission. James had promised to take her to Disneyland soon, and they had already toured the Queen Mary in Long Beach.

Cassie knew that she wouldn't have done many of these essentially "touristy" things on her own, just as she wouldn't have thought of a drive-in movie, but she knew it would be fun. They shared a confidential glance, and Cassie had to smother a grin as she answered the medical student's many questions.

Cassie thought, or at least she hoped, that she and James were behaving with impeccable discretion, and she also thought, or hoped, that no one suspected the additional dimension their relationship had acquired. She realized that Lincoln had been right, though, when she met with Gail to review some patient records. You couldn't fool all of the people all of the time, and Gail was difficult to fool at any time. She was grinning like the Cheshire Cat when she walked into Cassie's Clinic office with an armload of charts.

"Is he here?" She peered around the door with exaggerated stealth. "Is it safe to come in?"

"Why on earth wouldn't it be safe to come in?" Cassie grinned. It was a relief to see Gail cheerful, because in recent weeks her state of mind had varied from bad to abysmal, with only occasional flashes of cheer. Carefully, Cassie refrained from commenting on the lightened mood, for fear of jeopardizing it yet again.

"Well," Gail sidled around the doorframe and into the office, pulling the door closed behind her, "I don't want to . . . ah . . . interrupt anything, that's all." She dropped into a chair, still grinning.

"Interrupt what?" Cassie looked around and shrugged. "It's just me and the office here."

"Ah, yes, but it could be you and The Great Lover."

"What—? Oh, you mean James." Cassie laughed easily. "You'd hardly have to worry about interrupting, Gail, unless we were deep in a discussion of the indications for a C-section."

"Ah-ah-ah." Gail wagged an admonitory finger. "You might as well stop pretending, Cassie. I've seen the way you two look at each other, the way you smile and talk with your eyes. There's a lot more going on here than this mentor-student business."

"Gail, be realistic, will you? What could be going on between me and James Reid? It's ridiculous!"

"Is it? I'm not dumb, my friend, and I can see the signs." Cassie stared at her in dismay. "You can see? . . ."

"I'm your friend; I know you. Of course I can see."

"This is just what I was afraid of." Cassie dropped her head into her hands. "The whole hospital must know, and that kind of gossip is going to do terrific things for my reputation, not to mention my career."

"This is *not* all that bad!" Gail insisted. "Really, it isn't! *I've* seen it, but I don't think anybody else has."

"Are you sure?" Cassie looked up, afraid to hope.

"Pretty sure. I haven't heard any gossip about the two of you, and you know how it would get around. Anyway, James is only going to be here for another week or so, isn't he?"

"Yes, that's right. I hadn't thought about it, but the six weeks are almost up."

"See? You won't have to keep up the pretense much longer."

"No. I guess I won't," Cassie said, a bit hollowly.

"Okay, then you don't have anything to worry about." Gail grinned again and plopped the stack of folders on the desk. "Now, I want to get out of here by five for a change, so let's get these done."

"A.S.A.P." Cassie took the top folder from the stack and flipped it open before her. "What's the problem with this one?"

"There's a question about the medication she was given. This doesn't agree with the Pharmacy records." Together they bent over the desk. Cassie had to struggle to focus her attention on the charts, and when Gail left her shortly before five she slumped back into the chair, massaging her temples.

James' six weeks were almost over. Funny that she hadn't realized that until Gail had mentioned it. Maybe she hadn't wanted to realize it, she admitted to herself; maybe she'd just wanted to pretend that things would go on as they were indefinitely, refusing to face the possibility of not seeing him anymore just as she'd refused to analyze her feelings for him. James had practically forced her to continue seeing him, though she was reluctantly aware that if she had been one hundred percent opposed to that, he could never have persuaded her, but when his time at the hospital was up, what then?

A short time ago she would have loudly proclaimed her delight at the prospect of James leaving her life, but now she felt empty and alone just thinking about it. Despite all the time they had spent together, he hadn't said anything about what would happen when he was no longer coming to the hospital with her. She hadn't thought to ask before, and now she was afraid to, afraid of what his answer might be.

He laughed aloud when she opened the door to him that evening. Getting into the spirit of a drive-in movie, she had dressed in a pair of tight jeans, ancient sneakers and a shocking pink sweater, and had pulled her hair back into a ponytail, tying it with a pink chiffon scarf. Big pink buttons were clipped on her earlobes and she was energetically chewing gum.

"Hiya," she greeted him, then shouted over her shoulder at an imaginary parent, "Mom! Jimmy's here!" James laughed harder, then looked down at his jeans, open-necked white shirt and tweed jacket.

"I feel like I should have a DA and a black leather jacket."

"Nah." Cassie took his arm and led him out the door. "You're pretty cute, for a nerdy guy."

"I'll have you know I am *not* nerdy! Preppy, maybe, but not nerdy." Cassie collapsed in helpless giggles at his haughty reply, clinging to his arm.

"I couldn't resist," she told him, "but if this won't work for wherever we're going, it won't take me long to change."

"There's no need. What you have on is exactly right for the dinner I have planned for you."

"Oh-oh. I'm not sure I like the sound of this."

"Remember the taco stand on Pico I told you about?"

"We're going there?"

He shook his head. "Not to that one; it's in the wrong direction. But I know an even better one in beautiful, downtown Anaheim."

"Sounds perfect. Can I have a burrito?"

"You can have anything you want."

"Don't make any rash promises, James. I happen to be a confirmed Mexican junk-food junkie!"

"Small potatoes." He seated her in the car and walked around to slide into the driver's seat. "You happen to be looking at the taco-eating champ of the El Toro Marine Air Station."

"You were at El Toro?"

"Mm-hm. I was stationed there for a while, and I set a taco-eating record that, for all I know, still stands!"

"Well, you'll get to prove yourself tonight, buster!"

Cassie laughed and joked as they drove, always aware that her time with James must be savored, for it was passing all too quickly.

# Chapter Seven

$\mathcal{N}$ o, no, the best moment in the movie was when the guerilla army attacked the mountain fortress. The special effects were great."

"You think so?" Cassie replied. "I mean, the effects *were* great, but I thought the people were the best part of the movie, with all their different reactions to the situation."

"That's not a moment, though."

"Okay, I guess the moment I liked best was when the boy realized that he could talk to the tiger, that it wasn't going to hurt him at all. His reaction was priceless!"

"He's a good actor." James swung the car into her driveway and killed the engine. "Both the broad humor and the tension were handled very well, believably."

"You sound like you're thinking of hiring him."

"The thought had crossed my mind." They walked up the steps to the door, and James took her key to open it. "But I think it would be more a case of offering him a part and hoping he'd take it. He's a very hot property these days."

"*Now* you sound like a Hollywood wheeler-dealer!" Cassie laughed and disappeared into the kitchen to make coffee.

"I'm not sure I really want to be a Hollywood wheeler-dealer." James followed her, his bulk dwarfing the small kitchen.

"Oh?" Cassie added a final scoop of coffee to the basket, slid it into place and switched on the coffee maker. "What do you want to—" Her words were cut off by the pressure of James' mouth. He caught her in his arms as she turned from the counter, and she melted against him, reveling in the embrace she had been anticipating all evening.

"You know what I want," he murmured, tugging the pink scarf so her hair spilled down in an inky cascade. "I want to do this." He nibbled the sensitive spot below her ear. "And this." His lips slid down her neck to the curve of her shoulder as Cassie's head fell to the side to allow him easy access. "What I want to know, though," he breathed against her skin, "is just what you want."

Cassie looked up at him, startled, then rested her head on his chest. "I don't know," she sighed. "I just don't know." Behind her the coffeemaker beeped, signalling the completion of its cycle. She moved out of James' arms to place pot, mugs and sugar on a tray, and carried everything into the living room. She sat on the sofa, and when James took a seat beside her, she curled trustingly into the curve of his arm.

"I don't know what I want," she said again, gazing into her mug, watching the coffee swirl in lazy circles as she turned her hand. "I don't want—I *didn't* want a relationship with you. Objectively, I still think it's a mistake, but you make me want things I know are bad for me."

"You make me sound like bubblegum and soda," James complained, but there was a smile in his voice. "I promise I won't give you acne or cavities."

Cassie giggled weakly. "You make me laugh. How can I get you out of my life when you make me laugh?"

"You can't, because I won't go," James growled, and beneath her cheek Cassie felt the deep-timbred vibration of his voice.

"You have a marvelous voice," she told him. "Deep and dark."

"I like your voice, too. Low and husky and never shrill. Very sexy." He took her mug and set it on the coffee table beside his. "Poor little Cassie. It must be awful not knowing what you want." He kissed her lips lightly, then drew back.

"Do you know what *you* want?"

"Oh, yes." There was no hint of uncertainty in his reply.

"What is it?"

"Not now. Some time I'll tell you, but not now. Now I want to kiss you." Softly, tenderly, he touched his lips to her hair, her brow, her lids, her cheekbones, until she could wait no longer and twisted closer to him, reaching up for his mouth. Winding her arms around his neck to hold him close, she returned his kisses with an ardor she would have thought impossible a few weeks earlier. She had learned from James, and she sought to please him as he pleased her, teasing, nibbling at his lips before parting them with her tongue to savor his mouth, which tasted faintly of sweet coffee.

He made her want him; he could always make her want him. She was like a moth, flying into the beautiful, destroying flame. Her fingers worked quickly, restlessly at his shirt buttons until she could pull it open and slip her hands inside to caress him, boldly exploring his ribs, the heavy planes of muscle, the thick mat of hair which delighted her. He groaned low in his throat at her touch, and something deep and primitive in Cassie reveled in the knowledge that she had such power over him.

She bent to kiss him, the strong column of his neck, his small flat nipples, and he groaned again, turning, pulling her with him to stretch out on the sofa. He lay on his side against the back cushions, with Cassie facing him, prevented from falling by his arms around her, his leg thrown over hers. Held that way, protected by his strength, she felt inexpressably small and fragile, her femininity, her softness, contrasted with his hard virility.

The room was lit only by the glow from the kitchen doorway; at some point he had switched off the lamp, and as Cassie looked up at his face she saw the deep hunger he felt. Suddenly shy, she buried her face in his chest and felt him chuckle softly. His hands slid over her back, following the curve of her spine, gliding over her hips and thighs and back up her sides, tracing her waist and ribs over and over, sensitizing her until her whole body seemed to come alive for him. She gasped softly when his fingers slid beneath the hem of her pink sweater, stroking the smooth skin of her back, tracing a delicate line along the waistband of her jeans.

The arm which held her on the sofa loosened fractionally, and his hand followed her waistband to the front, brushing lightly over her navel, one fingertip sliding inside the denim with teasing insinuation. Slowly he eased the pink wool up, then lifted the sweater over her head and tossed it aside. His hand slid over her shoulders, easing her bra straps off, then following the lacy fabric to the small hook between her breasts. A flick of the fingers and it was open, and he tossed the bra aside as well.

Her small breasts swelled into his hands as he caressed her; then she arched toward him, her breath coming in shaky bursts as he bent his head to kiss her taut nipples, teasing them with teeth and tongue. She was on fire for him, blind and oblivious to anything but their mutual need, and had he chosen to take her, there and then, she could have made no objection.

He chose not to, though, repeating a scenario that had been played out between them many times in the last two weeks. He had said that he would not make love to her again until she asked him to, and, true to his word, he had not. Instead he drove her half-mad with deep, tender, passionate, tormenting kisses and caresses, and then, when she would have surrendered willingly, her need for him outweighing her hesitance, he drew back.

Now he gave her nipple a last tug with his lips as she quivered against him with urgency, then pressed his mouth into the soft valley between her breasts for a moment before rolling up to a sitting position, bringing Cassie with him. His fingers brushed over her breasts, leaving trails of fire on her skin.

"Goodnight, Cassie." He stood, buttoning his shirt, then bent and lightly kissed her forehead. "Sleep well."

She sat mute and immobile until he had let himself out,

closing the door behind him with a soft click. The room seemed colder when he had gone, and she shivered. He left her like this every night, aching and frustrated with a need only he could fulfill, a need she wished vainly that she could deny.

How on earth had this happened? Cassie hunched forward, head in hands, very near tears. How had she let things get to the point where she would seriously consider a relationship with a movie star? If there were any more certain road to self-destruction, Cassie didn't know of it, for the monsters of James' fame and money would devour her identity, leaving nothing of her self but an empty husk, living off James like a parasitic orchid, beautiful and useless.

In many ways she admired and respected him, and heaven knew she desired him, but all the admirable aspects of himself that he had showed her could not alter the basic fact of who and what he was. She wasn't willing to fight that. She knew it was impossible to have a normal life with someone of his notoriety, but something kept her coming back to him, to be kissed and touched and left needing him so badly that she had cried with the ache. She wondered if he enjoyed tormenting her this way, or if it were a torment for him, too, but one he was willing to endure as he waited for her own frustration to get the better of her.

*Why did he pick on me?* Her unfulfilled desire was turning to anger, at herself and at James. Her life had been just fine before he forced his way into it, but he had altered the pattern and to tear him out of her life now would leave a gaping hole. *Why?* She hadn't asked for someone like him, hadn't wanted him, yet now the knowledge that his time at the hospital would be over in a week brought her no joy, only a bleak depression.

He had changed her in ways which went far beyond the relatively unimportant loss of her virginity, and those changes could not be undone, however much she might wish it. He had stolen her independence, her separateness, had made her dependent on him against her will. He had stolen her placid contentment with life, leaving her unsure, bewildered, where before she had known her way.

Sometimes she thought she hated him.

His last day at the hospital came sooner than she would have thought possible, the intervening week seeming to fly past, and Cassie was appalled to realize just how depressed she was at the thought of his leaving. James brought small gifts for everyone he had worked with in the previous six weeks, all individually wrapped and accompanied by cards that he'd thoughtfully hand-signed, and all distributed at a cookies-and-coffee going-away party the staff gave for him in the fifth-floor lounge.

He had gifts, that was, for everyone but Cassie, and the omission hurt. Sitting in a corner of the lounge with coffee and one of Dee's famous raisin rocks, she hoped no one noticed that she was depressed. She was hurt that he hadn't had even a small box of chocolates for her, as he had for the candy stripers, and depressed by his cheerfulness as he laughed aloud and joked with the others. Personally, she had no desire to celebrate his leaving, and after half an hour she slipped away, leaving James to be the life of the party.

There were always charts to be updated and orders to be written, so she took her coffee and another raisin rock to the nurses' station. After pulling a chart out she dropped it on the desk and slumped into a chair, leaning her head tiredly on her hand, though her weariness was more of the mind than the body. Sighing, she began to write.

"Left the party already?"

"Oh!" Cassie's head jerked up. "Oh, Grace, you startled me."

"Sorry about that; I didn't mean to. I was surprised to find you out here, though. I thought you'd be enjoying the party."

"I don't know." Cassie shrugged, avoiding Grace's too-shrewd eyes. "I guess I'm just not much of a party person."

"Or you're just not crazy about the reason for this party, hmm?" Grace leaned against the desk, arms crossed, watching Cassie's bent head. Cassie sighed and laid her pen on the page, leaning back in her chair to grin up at the older woman.

"Grace, my love, please don't attach a lot of importance to this. I want to get out of here at a reasonable hour tonight, and if I'm going to, these orders have to be written. Besides," she indicated her coffee and raisin rock, "I brought some party with me. Dee makes great cookies, doesn't she?" She took a bite and grinned again with her mouth full.

"She sure does!" was Grace's rueful reply. "How she can bake like that and stay so skinny, I'll never understand. And you, you're just as bad, with those raisin-nut rolls you make."

"I'll bring some in next week, just for you, okay?"

"My hips are doomed!"

"Your hips are just fine, and I'm going to get my orders written and be out of here before suppertime for a change."

"If you're sure you're all right? . . ."

"Oh, Grace, please don't worry about me. I'm a big girl, and I'm fine. Really."

Grace was plainly unconvinced, but Cassie shooed her away.

"I'm fine; I'm fine. Now let me get these written, okay?"

"Okay, I'll quit playing mother hen." Grace walked back to her chair, laughing, and Cassie let her breath hiss out between her teeth.

Grace saw entirely too much. Cassie bent over her chart again, writing quickly. She hoped she'd convinced Grace that she wasn't moping, but she was afraid her efforts hadn't been overwhelmingly successful. Oh, well, not much point in worrying about the spilled milk now, and next week she wouldn't have to worry about concealing her feelings, either, since James would no longer be around. She leaned her head on her hand again, massaging her temple, where a throbbing ache had begun.

*      *      *

Despite aspirin and fifteen minutes lying on her bed with her eyes closed, the headache was not completely vanquished as she dressed for her evening with James. She stood in the bathroom, wearing the teddy she preferred to bra and panties, this one in ivory silk, drawing a careful line along her eyelids. With shadow and blusher and mascara applied, she studied the effect and was not particulary thrilled. Beneath the subtly applied blush, she was pale; there were little lines of strain around her eyes, and the smile she essayed looked stiff and unconvincing.

Tough. She shrugged. She didn't feel like a bundle of laughs tonight, and James would just have to accept that. She turned her back on the mirror and walked to her bedroom to dress. James had told her that they'd have dinner at his house, so she chose casual clothes, man-styled trousers in a light-weight, cranberry colored wool, and a dove gray cashmere sweater, V-necked and dolman-sleeved, which emphasized the gray of her eyes, making them look deep and smoky. Gold knot earrings and a gold chain in an unusual Greek key design were her only jewelry; she wore cordovan leather boots, as it was chilly, though it was already March first, and she took a cordovan leather blouson jacket from her closet when the doorbell rang.

If her greeting was subdued, if she were quieter than usual on the drive to Sunset Beach, James refrained from comment, talking easily and entertainingly about the scenes he would be shooting when he returned to the studio next week. He had completed this film before Christmas, but certain scenes had to be reshot in the studio, so he had to try to get himself back into the part by Monday.

"The worst of it is," he told her as he served the dinner, a delicious crab casserole and endive salad, "that I can't shave for a week!"

"Why on earth?"

"The scenes that didn't work out well are scenes where my character has been on a bender, comes to in a seedy hotel room and doesn't know where he is or how he got there. The shave this morning was my last for a while."

"Poor baby," Cassie mocked. "I wouldn't think you'd mind all that much, though. Isn't shaving kind of a nuisance?"

"Not really, and the first few days of a beard are itchy!"

"Just keep thinking of how soon you'll get to shave it off." Cassie sampled her casserole. "This is wonderful! Did you make it?"

"I wish I could lay claim to it, but I ordered it from a restaurant in Newport Beach. My culinary talents are adequate, but pretty basic. Steaks, spaghetti, that kind of stuff."

"For someone whose culinary talents are only 'adequate,' you do pretty well. I wouldn't worry about it much."

"I don't." He grinned. "California is full of caterers."

Feeling more relaxed, Cassie enjoyed the rest of her meal, shutting out thoughts of endings and good-byes. The rich raspberry mousse with its garnish of chocolate leaves was as exquisite as the rest of the meal, and Cassie regarded her empty dish resignedly.

"It's a good thing I don't eat like this every day. I'd weigh four hundred pounds!"

"I can't imagine you overweight."

"It wouldn't take much. As short as I am, five pounds would show."

"Don't worry too much about it. I think you burn up everything you eat in pure nervous energy, anyway." He rose to clear the table, and Cassie moved quickly to help him. "Don't bother with these; I'm just going to put them in the dishwasher."

"No bother." Cassie picked up the rest of the dishes and cutlery, then nodded pointedly toward the kitchen. "I'm going to help. Now, can we get these taken care of?"

"Aye, aye, ma'am." James about-faced toward the kitchen. "I begin to understand the origin of your nickname."

"Cassie? There's nothing to understand about—"

"Cassandra the Terrible."

"Oh. Well, it never pays to let people walk all over you, does it?"

"I try my best to avoid it," James assured her dryly. "Come out on the patio; I have something to show you." Cassie followed him out to the high-walled patio, shivering a little as a sharp ocean breeze found them. "Notice anything new?" She looked around, a little surprised at the question.

"I didn't before, but I wasn't really . . . oh, that's new, isn't it? The orange tree?"

"Mm-hm, isn't it a nice one?" James tucked her arm in his and walked over to the dwarf orange tree, planted in a large redwood tub. "It was just delivered today. I like it a lot, but I'm afraid it's a little too big for my patio."

Cassie studied the tree for a moment. "I don't think so. Anyway, it's such a pretty tree, that'll make up for a little crowding."

"Well, I don't know." James led her slowly around it. "What's this?" He reached out for a small envelope that was tied to one of the branches, took it off and held it toward the light. "It's for you." He placed it in Cassie's hand.

"Dr. C. Mills," she read aloud, then looked up at James, who stood smiling innocently down at her. "James, what is this?"

"Beats me." He shrugged. "It's addressed to you. Go ahead and open it." She gave him another narrow-eyed glance, then slid a card out of the envelope.

> For all your help, your patience, your careful explanations, for the long hours made longer by my presence and my questions, for your graceful handling of a complication in your busy life, and most of all, for all you have taught me, thank you.
>
> James
>
> P.S. I'll think of you, picking your breakfast in the morning sun.

"James?" she whispered, raising shining eyes to him. "It's for me?"

"For you, for your patio." He smiled. "I'm sorry I couldn't give it to you this afternoon, but it would have been a little awkward to gift-wrap."

"Well, I love it!" She walked around it admiringly. "It even has some oranges on it, see?"

"The man at the nursery said it will keep bearing for a while this season. The watering and feeding instructions are here," there was a tag tied to a branch, "and it'll be delivered to your house tomorrow afternoon."

"That's wonderful, James, and this," she lightly touched a leaf, "is just perfect! Thank you."

"You wouldn't rather have jewelry or something?"

"Don't be silly. Besides, you gave me this," she indicated the Greek key chain at her neck, "for Valentine's Day. And I still think it was too extravagant a gift."

"It wasn't; I wanted you to have it, just like I want you to have this tree. I wanted to thank all the people at LA General who have helped me so much. The work I do on *New Life*, both writing and performing, will be infinitely more real and more meaningful than it could have been otherwise, and though I owe a great deal to everyone on the staff, I owe the most to you. Without you I would never have learned so much, so I thank you, Dr. Mills, with all my heart."

As he spoke James had taken her shoulders to pull her close, his arms sliding around her until, as he said the last words, he bent to her upturned face and kissed her lips. Cassie swayed against him, feeling him shift his feet as he held her slight weight, kissing him, drowning in him, and swept by a wave of poignant longing for what could not be. Their time together had come to an end; she had to say good-bye to James, and that was far more difficult than she had imagined possible. She was unaware of the tears sliding down her cheeks until James lifted his head, frowning at what he saw in the glow of the patio light.

"Tears?" He lifted one from her cheek with his fingertip. "What's wrong, Cassie?"

"It's nothing. I'm just being silly." She shook her head, trying to hide from his gaze, but he took her chin in his fingers and lifted her face again.

"Come on, tell me. Is it the tree? If you'd like something else I can—"

"No, no, it isn't the tree!" Cassie choked on a sob. "James, the tree is wonderful, it really is. It's the most wonderful good-bye present in the world, and I wouldn't change it for—"

"Wait a minute." James pulled her into the light, his frown deepening. "Is that what you think? That it's a good-bye present?"

"Good-bye . . . and thank-you."

"And that made you cry." James' voice was very soft.

"I'm not crying," was her quick denial. "It's just . . . I don't know . . ." She shivered as an errant gust of wind found them, tossing a swath of ebony hair across her mouth, and James pulled her close against his side, brushing her hair back with his fingertips.

"Come inside. It's cold out here." He took her back into the warmth of the living room, pushed her onto the sofa cushions and pulled a snowy cotton handkerchief from his pocket to dry the tears from her cheeks.

"It's not a good-bye gift, Cassie. This evening is not a good-bye, not an ending for us just because my time at the hospital is ending." He smiled crookedly. "You won't get rid of me that easily."

"I'm not trying to get rid of you," Cassie muttered, and he chuckled.

"You've tried before," he reminded her. "Don't you know by now that it won't work? I said I wanted to see you, didn't I?"

"Yes, you did."

"Did I ever say that I *didn't* want to see you?"

She shrugged.

"Did I?"

"No, you never said that!" Exasperation was coming through in her voice, but James just smiled.

"Then don't try to second-guess me, okay? I'm not about to let you slip away that easily."

Cassie gazed up into his eyes, trying to read something in their green depths; then a rueful grin spread slowly across her face. "Okay." She nodded slowly. "I won't try to second-guess you."

"Smart girl," he said dryly.

"I don't understand, though."

"Understand what?"

"Understand why you won't let me 'slip away.'"

He smiled. "You will. Sooner or later, you will."

The orange tree was delivered shortly before noon the next day, with James' Mercedes following the bright green nursery truck up to the house. Cassie had already spent a significant portion of the morning studying her patio, and thought she knew where she wanted the tree.

"Don't you think that's the best place for it?" she asked James, while the nurseryman awaited the final decision, leaning on his hand truck, chewing an unlit cigar. "Or should it go over there, nearer to the house?"

"The corner looks like a good spot," James said, agreeing with her first choice. "The tree will get protection from the wind, and you'll get shade in the afternoon. Will you have trouble watering it out on that corner?"

"No, the hose reaches farther than that." She pondered the tree and the patio for a few moments, then nodded, her decision made. "The corner. It'll show the tree off better, anyway."

"The corner it is." James turned to the nurseryman, who grinned around his cigar, obviously enjoying the show.

"You know where you want it yet?"

"That corner of the patio." James pointed.

"You got it." The nurseryman wheeled the tree and tub into place, and with some assistance from James eased it off the hand truck and onto the ground. "Looks nice, don't it?"

"It looks absolutely gorgeous!" Cassie told him, and he took out his cigar to point it at the tree.

"It ain't just pretty, miss. That's a Valencia; you'll get some real good juice from it. Just sign here, Mr. Reid." He'd pulled a folded form from his shirt pocket, and when James had signed that, he produced another slip of paper. "Uh, Mr. Reid? . . ." His manner was an oddly hesitant contrast to his earlier casual amusement as he held the paper out to James. "Could you autograph this for my wife? She'd never forgive me if I didn't get your autograph after deliverin' this tree."

"No problem," James laughed. "I'm glad to. What's your wife's name?"

"Marie." James wrote quickly, then handed the paper back. "Thanks a lot, Mr. Reid. She'll really appreciate this. No kiddin', she'll love it!" They walked with him to his truck, and he was still calling thank-you's as he drove off.

"Do you know what this tree deserves?" Cassie asked as they walked back to the patio.

"What's that?"

"A toast!"

"At this hour?" James feigned shock. "Don't you know what happens to people who drink in the morning?"

"Don't give me that nonsense! You wild-living Hollywood types have champagne breakfasts all the time. Anyway, it's not morning anymore." She showed him her watch, a chrome digital which read 12:04. "I even have a bottle of something cheap and pink in the refrigerator."

"If you're offering a high-liver like me a drink, shouldn't it be better than 'something cheap and pink'?"

"You didn't bring the Rolls, did you?"

"No."

"Then don't expect *Dom Perignon!*" She dodged past him, evading the swat he aimed at her bottom, and ran into the house, giggling. The bottle of "cheap pink" wine was actually a very respectable rosé, and James nodded approval when she handed him the bottle and a corkscrew. He poured two glasses, handed one to Cassie and turned to the tree.

"Here's to Dwarf Valencia, long may it thrive!"

"Hear, hear!" They touched glasses and sipped. "Here's to Dwarf Valencia," Cassie proposed, "and all the little Valencias it can bear!" They sipped again.

"And here's to us," James said, "because we must be the only two people in California nutty enough to toast an orange tree!"

"What a wet blanket!" Cassie dropped onto the chaise longue, laughing. "You have no sense of whimsy, James."

"How can you accuse me of that, the man who gave you an orange tree? If you're really into toasting citrus trees, though, there's a grapefruit grove on the Santa Ana Freeway that you'd just love. You could toast those trees 'till 1999 and probably still have some to go!" He pulled one of the patio chairs around to sit with his feet propped on the end of her chaise.

"You nut! All you'd have to do is toast the whole grove, not each tree. That," she waved her glass toward the tree in its redwood tub, "is my orange grove. Or orange grovette . . . as in a teeny, tiny grove."

"I think all that hard work at the hospital has finally gotten to her," James informed the tree, then leaned back into his chair, eyes closed, and took a long swallow of his wine. "Would you like to have lunch somewhere different?"

"Hadn't thought about it," was the laconic reply. "Where?"

"Disneyland."

Cassie's eyes opened wide. "Disneyland? Really?"

"Why not? We've been planning to go, and we can have lunch *and* ride all the rides."

"Hmm, why not?" Cassie sat up and swung her feet to the ground. "Can you go somewhere like that without being attacked by fans?"

"Generally I can, as long as I wear sunglasses and don't call attention to myself. Ready to go?"

"Just let me get my purse." As she followed James into the house Cassie reflected that he didn't have to call attention to himself, his natural presence did that. She had seen women follow him with their eyes as he passed, and even those who didn't recognize him as James Reid recognized him as a strong man, a completely male man. Somehow she didn't think that sunglasses would provide a particularly effective disguise for that. A suit of armor, perhaps, but sunglasses? No chance.

The glasses didn't stop the looks, but she had to admit, as they walked down Disneyland's main street, that with the glasses and some actor's magic of his own, James wasn't recognizably the man so many watched on the screen. The people who looked didn't seem quite able to place him, and because they weren't sure who he was, they didn't approach him. Cassie looked around her happily, enjoying the perfect day, cool but sunny, with just enough breeze to stir the leaves on the trees.

"Where do you want to go first?" she asked, and James grinned down at her from his great height.

"You sound like a little kid. How long has it been since you were here?"

"Let me think. It must be nine years, at least. I was a sophomore in college, and I came with a bunch of girls from the dorm."

"Good grief! You live half an hour away and haven't been here in nine years?"

"You forget, I've spent a significant portion of those nine years becoming a doctor. That does tend to fill up the days."

"No kidding. I used to think actors worked long hours, but that was only because I hadn't known enough resident physicians! We'll make up for one of the gaps in your education today, Dr. Mills."

"Whatever you say, Professor. Lead the way."

Having decided to work their way around the park, riding everything once, they set off, pausing between rides for hot dogs, frozen bananas, tacos and other treats. By the time darkness was falling they had ridden a space-age roller-coaster, whirling teacups, a monorail, a carousel, mountain bobsleds, taken a jungle cruise and had made their way to an area of the park decorated to resemble old New Orleans.

"Ohh! I'm ready for a break," Cassie sighed, dropping wearily onto a park bench which overlooked a lagoon where a stern-wheel riverboat was steaming past. James slid onto the bench beside her, draping an arm along the back, and Cassie let her head fall back against his sleeve. "Where are you taking me for a little rest and food, Fearless Jungle Guide?"

James grinned down at her, his teeth a flash of white in the dim light. "How about if I take you off into the bushes and make a meal of you?" he growled softly and leaned closer, sliding his free hand up the slender line of her throat as his arm tightened around her shoulders.

"That's not exactly what I had in mind," Cassie replied in a husky whisper, watching him from beneath heavy lids.

"Too bad." The murmured words were breathed against her lips. "I thought the idea," he kissed her lightly, briefly, "had definite," another kiss, longer this time, "very definite, possibilities." Their mouths met and clung in a kiss which sparked desires both of them had kept under strict control all day. The kiss was long and deep, their bodies straining toward each other, and though their hands never moved, James' fingers caressing her throat sent little *frissons* of delight over Cassie's skin, while she felt the heavy pulse of his heartbeat accelerate beneath her hand when she lightly ran the tip of her tongue along the sensuous curve of his lower lip.

The kiss might have gone on for a very long time but for a burst of childish laughter behind them.

"Oh, gross! Kissy, kissy, kissy!" A series of loud smacking sounds was silenced when James directed an icy glare at the perpetrators, three boys of nine or ten who cackled with derisive glee as they made a scampering retreat. He watched them go, then closed his eyes with a sigh.

"Ah, the innocence of youth. Isn't it charming? I suppose I should thank them." He opened his eyes again, glancing at the people all around them. "This is neither the time nor the place. What it *is* time for is supper," he added more briskly and stood, pulling Cassie to her feet. "And we'll have it over there."

"Over there" was a buffet restaurant just behind them, with a large, open-air dining area covered by an airy canopy twinkling with tiny white lights, and a Dixieland band playing at one side. They chose a table far enough from the band to permit conversation, but talked only desultorily for a time as they ate and enjoyed the music. When Cassie pushed her plate away, James smiled.

"Now you'll see why I told you to skip the desserts."

"The suspense is killing me."

"I'll be right back." He crossed to a small serving counter she hadn't noticed before, at one side of the dining area, and returned minutes later with his hands full. "These," he set one in front of her, "are 'choux fritters,' and they're very similar to the *beignets* served in New Orleans, a sort of deep-fried cruller."

Large and round and rolled in sugar, the fritter looked and smelled delicious, and when Cassie bit into it she found it lived up to its publicity. She took another bite, savored it, then looked across at James, wide-eyed, with sugar clinging to her lips.

"This is marvelous! I could eat two, they're so light."

"Good thing I got spares, isn't it?" James set another in front of her, and she laughed.

"You're going to think I'm a terrible pig, but I'm going to eat them both!"

"I'm not going to think you're a pig; I'm going to think you're someone who works too hard and skips a lot of meals. And anyway, I fully intend to eat two of them." He popped the last bit of his first fritter into his mouth and grinned at her as she laughed, then sat back, relaxed.

Cassie nibbled her fritters, listened to the music and watched James' face in the shifting light, growing more and more thoughtful. When the last notes of the song faded away, he turned back to the table and met her intent gaze, smiling quizzically when he realized that she'd been watching him. Cassie looked down at her coffee cup for a moment, then back to his face again.

"James?"

"Hmm?"

"What . . . what is it that you want? Why do you want to see me, after all I've said, the way I feel?"

"I think you know." The quizzical smile lingered on his lips.

"I don't know if I do," Cassie said seriously. "And I think I need to."

James nodded after a moment. "I want to be your lover," he said simply.

Cassie felt herself blush and was grateful for the dim light. "I see."

"I don't think you do."

"Probably not, but I'm not very comfortable with the idea, you must know that."

"I know that, but I can give you time, both to get to know me better and to become comfortable with the idea."

"Give me time?" She studied him for a moment, half puzzled, half annoyed. "How much time do you propose to give me?"

"I hadn't thought about it." James was gently amused by her irritation, but there was no malice in his amusement. "Perhaps a month?"

"And if I'm not any more comfortable with the idea in a month?"

"Don't cross bridges before you get to them." He reached out to take one of her hands in his. "Wait and see, that's all I'm asking. Are you finished?"

"One last bite." Cassie licked the traces of sugar from her fingers, and looked up to find James watching her, his eyes dark and intent on the unintentionally provocative gesture.

"If I thought you'd done that deliberately . . ." He left the sentence unfinished and reached out to take the sugar off her lower lip with his fingertip, then touched the fingertip to his own lips as though he tasted her as well as the sugar. Cassie felt something warm and tingling start deep inside her and bent her head to conceal the quick rush of heat to her cheeks.

"Come on." James' voice was suddenly brisk as he drained his coffee cup and rose. "Let's go on the pirate ride!"

# Chapter Eight

$S$omewhat taken aback by the sudden way he had shifted gears, Cassie was nevertheless content to follow James to the ride and abandon any efforts at serious conversation for a while. He had given her a great deal to think about, but one phrase kept replaying itself in her mind: "I want to be your lover."

Standing close beside him in the line, she was conscious of every movement he made, of the warmth of him behind her as the air grew cool, and when he handed her into the slightly rocking boat that would carry them through the ride, the hint of his much greater strength sent a thrill of excitement through her. "I want to be your lover." Cassie couldn't forget that he already was her lover, her only lover.

"Relax." He bent close to be heard above the sea chanties and pirate songs on the PA system. "You're here to have fun." Cassie raised an inquiring eyebrow, and James laughed softly as their boat moved off. "Nothing has changed since this morning, you know. What I said was as true then as it is now, the only difference is that it's been said aloud. Just remember that I won't hurt you, Cassie." They rounded the first corner and the pirate songs got louder. "I won't hurt you. . . . Look over there!"

Cassie followed his pointing finger and laughed aloud at an animated pirate who was comically beckoning them into his lair. James was right, of course; nothing had changed. And since she was, as he'd pointed out, there to enjoy herself, she would relax and do just that.

The ride was an experience in witty and humorous animation, and Cassie was gasping with laughter when they emerged. "I loved the pirate's cat with the patch over his eye, and *especially* the spot where you see pirates chasing beautiful maidens, and then the chubby maiden chasing a pirate!" She giggled helplessly as they walked a few steps, then got herself under control again. "What fun, to have a job designing rides like that. But what an imagination you'd need!"

"If you like that one so much, you'll love the haunted house."

"You think I will?"

"I know you will, especially in the dark!" He finished with a sepulchral chuckle which almost sent chills down Cassie's spine, even though she knew he was joking!

"Have you ever done a horror movie?"

"Hm-mm. Do you think I should?"

"Maybe so. With a laugh like that you'd scare people to death!"

"Ahh, but I only want you, my pretty!" He laughed that laugh again, coming toward her with clawed fingers and ghoulish eyes, and she backed away, unnerved in spite of herself.

"James, stop that! You're too good at it!" He dropped the character, and she let him take her arm again. "If anyone offers you a part as a psychopathic killer, turn it down, all right? You'd be far too convincing!"

"I'm just getting you in the mood for the haunted house," he protested in exaggerated innocence.

"Get me too much in the mood and I won't go in there at all. It is kind of creepy-looking, isn't it?"

"It's a fun kind of creepy," James reassured her. "You'll love it. And anyway—"

"I know, I know! I have you to hold on to. You never give up, do you?" Laughing, she let him lead her inside.

They didn't leave the park until they had ridden a rollercoaster in the guise of a runaway train and then walked back through the New Orleans area to visit a *parfumerie,* where

James asked the perfumer to blend a perfume just for Cassie. He seemed to know exactly what he wanted, and kept the perfumer busy adding a drop of this and a drop of that until, at last, he was satisfied.

"Just put a dab here." He touched a drop to Cassie's wrist, then waved her hand in the air until the alcohol evaporated. "Now, let's see . . ." He brought her wrist to his face and inhaled, held his breath, then let it out on a dramatic sigh. "That's it! That's exactly what I want!" Cassie stood by, a little bit puzzled, sniffing her wrist and trying to decide what the perfume reminded her of, as James purchased a crystal flaçon for it.

"It's nice," she told him. "I really like it, but it reminds me of something. I can't quite figure out what it is."

"I had a very definite mixture of scents in mind, floral, and warm, like skin, and just a touch of something else."

"Yes, I can tell that." Cassie sniffed again. "But what is that something else?"

"You really want to know?"

"Of course, I do! It's something familiar, but what? . . ."

"It's that brown gunk, the stuff you scrub with."

"You wanted this to smell like surgical scrub?" She sniffed again and nodded slowly. "That's it, all right, but why in the world? . . ."

"It has a special meaning for me." He smiled as they left the park behind. "Actually," he growled in her ear, "it turns me on!"

"You can't be serious!"

"I am. Do you remember the first time I kissed you? In the on-call room when you were upset that night? You were beautiful and sexy and you smelled like this perfume, of flowers and warm skin and the stuff you had scrubbed with." They had reached the car, but James didn't immediately open the door. Instead he took her shoulders in his hands and leaned back against the car, pulling her between his legs and sliding his hands down to link behind her waist.

"I don't think I've ever," he nuzzled her neck as her head

tipped back, "known a scent as erotic," he bit softly at her earlobe and Cassie sagged weakly against him, "as that one."

He lifted his head for a heartbeat of time, and looking up at him, silhouetted against the glitter of lights, Cassie thought she had never seen anyone more beautiful. She lifted her hands to touch his face wonderingly, tracing her fingers across his brows, his cheekbones, then clasping her hands behind his neck as he kissed her mouth. Her lips parted eagerly beneath his, answering the kiss, their tongues touching, retreating, in a ritual as old as time.

When he took his lips from hers at last there was a light dew of perspiration on James' brow, and Cassie could feel his muscles tense as he exerted will over desire. He took a deep breath, dropped a kiss on Cassie's forehead and fished in his pocket for his keys. "Time to go home, Cassandra."

When they reached her house he walked her to the door, but declined to come in for coffee. "Not tonight, Cassie. I have a long drive back to Sunset Beach. Just remember," he lifted her wrist to breathe the perfume again, "what I want." He kissed her inner wrist, brushing his tongue over the thin skin in a scorchingly evocative caress, and then he was gone.

"I'm sorry to have to tell you this, Cassie, but you're named in the suit, too."

"*I'm* named? George, all I did was admit Mrs. Larrison, give the history to Alan and go home. I spent maybe twenty minutes with her, because by the time I got back from my weekend with the Traveling Clinic she'd been discharged. Why on earth am I named in the suit?"

"Everyone who signed her chart is named as a defendant." George Hammett, M.D., leaned across the conference-room table to cover Cassie's hand with his. "It's a nuisance suit, pure and simple. There's no possibility that any malpractice occurred; you and I both know that. Since Alan is the one who actually did the delivery, he'll bear the brunt of all this, but you'll have to be prepared to give a deposition, and possibly to testify."

"This is completely nuts! The suit states that an unnecessary episiotomy was done, so now she has an uncomfortable scar, and she's suing for damages for mental anguish, right?"

"That's right."

"Her baby weighed over ten pounds! It's obvious that an episiotomy was medically necessary, George."

"I know that, and the judge will realize that, but someone has convinced them otherwise, so we just have to go along with it. Before the hearing we'll review the chart and make certain of our facts, so until then you're not to worry about it, understand?"

"That's easier said than done, George."

"I know it is, but you can manage, my dear." The Chief of Staff for Obstetrics and Gynecology stood when Cassie did and ushered her courteously to the door of the conference room that they had used for their discussion. "Don't worry," he repeated. "This will all blow over."

"Thank you, George." Cassie shook his hand, smiled, said good-bye and walked away looking more sanguine and composed than she really felt. A malpractice suit, even one as obviously unjustified as this, was upsetting to face, carrying with it as it did the specter of a career ended before it had even begun. That was silly. She wasn't going to lose her license; she had done nothing wrong.

Cassie walked briskly through the hospital, wishing she'd had time for lunch before George had asked her to meet with him. It was two fifteen now, though, and she wanted to get back to the OB unit to check on Rita Davis. She found Dee Woods at the nurses' station, making notes in Mrs. Davis' chart.

"Hi, Dee. How is she?"

"Oh, hi, Cassie. Mrs. Davis, you mean? I just took her temperature again and it's not good. It's gone up some more, to 102.2°."

"Oh, boy," Cassie muttered. "Did you find out just how long her membranes had been ruptured before she went into labor?"

"Approximately twenty hours. She said her water broke in mid-afternoon, the day before yesterday, and she went into labor just before lunch yesterday. She didn't come to the hospital until late yesterday afternoon."

"She's got it, all right," Cassie said grimly, and Dee nodded, her coffee-colored face troubled.

"Postpartum infection?"

"With that history, it's almost inevitable. After her membranes ruptured she was open to infection for over twenty-four hours. We'll start antibiotics right now and watch her very carefully."

Cassie took the chart Dee handed her and began scribbling orders for antibiotics and laboratory studies, while Dee picked up the telephone and dialed first the pharmacy and then the lab, relaying the orders.

"We're busy up here, Cassie, but I'll check on Mrs. Davis as often as I can."

"Thanks, Dee, I appreciate it." Dee went to give Mrs. Davis her first antibiotic shot, and Cassie pulled several charts from the rack, reviewing the progress of patients who would deliver in the next few hours. She tried to concentrate, but Mrs. Davis' condition was cause for concern and her thoughts kept returning to that. It was an unhappy fact, but some problems in obstetrics were still very serious, despite the advances in medical science.

Infection following childbirth was no longer the frequent killer it had been in the days before antibiotics, but it was by no means a minor problem, and most of the sterile precautions taken by hospitals were aimed at preventing just such an event. Cassie fervently hoped that Mrs. Davis' infection could be quickly eradicated, but she knew that the new mother would remain in the hospital considerably longer than the usual two or three days.

No doubt she'll sue me, too, Cassie thought in an unusual burst of bitter cynicism, even though I'm worried sick about her, and doing all I can to save her life. No, she shook her head, she would not take that attitude, though some days it wasn't easy to avoid. She sighed, massaging her temples, where a gnawing ache was beginning to make itself felt.

"Hi, Cassie. How's Mrs. Davis doing?" Gail looked as wrung out as Cassie felt, her face pale beneath her freckles and shadows of strain around her eyes. She leaned against the counter and picked the chart labeled "Davis, Rita M." from the pile by Cassie's elbow.

"Not good," Cassie told her. "See for yourself." Gail read the notes and gave a low whistle.

"Not good at all." She flipped a couple of pages. "She's Dee's patient . . . good. She'll need good nursing care."

"Dee offered to spend extra time with her," Cassie said, opening another chart. "It's so busy, though, you might want to see if you can get a float nurse up here for the rest of the day."

"I know that!" Cassie looked up, startled, to find her friend glaring at her, angry spots of red staining her cheeks. "I am perfectly capable of running this unit, *Doctor* Mills, so why don't you do the doctoring and leave the Head Nurse's job to me!" She whirled around and slammed into her office, leaving Cassie staring at a closed door.

*Lord, what a day!* The tentative ache at her temples had become a full-blown pounding, and Cassie replaced the charts in the rack. She had to have an aspirin before anything else went wrong. She was halfway to the on-call room and the aspirin in her purse when there was a call from a clerk at the nurses' station.

"Telephone for you, Dr. Mills!"

"Okay." She turned and trudged back to the desk. "Could you ask Dee or one of the other nurses to sign out two aspirin from the med room for me?"

"Sure. Yours is line three."

"Thanks a lot." Cassie pushed the blinking button with fatalistic resignation, wondering what new disaster was in store for her. "This is Dr. Mills."

"And this is Attila the Hun," growled a deep voice in reply. "How's things, sweetheart?"

"Oh, hi, James." Cassie slumped into a chair. "I'm glad it's you and not something else going wrong!" It was a relief to speak to James, even through the unsatisfactory medium of the telephone. In the two weeks since he had given her that one-month deadline they had spent nearly all their free time together, whenever Cassie wasn't on call and James wasn't required at the studio or at meetings. James was her sounding-board and comforter, as she tried to be for him, and she had even given him a key to her house, so that on her call days he could come over from his office and water the orange tree. It was a relief just to hear his voice and the warming concern in it as he replied to her weary comment.

"That bad, is it?"

"Worse."

"Do you want to tell me about it?"

"I hardly know where to start." She sighed, then fell silent for a moment as Gail emerged from her office, slammed the door and stalked past her and down the hall.

"Cassie? What is it?" The concern in James' voice was sharper, cutting into that silent pause.

"It's okay, James, I didn't mean to scare you. It's just that this has been a really rotten day, and it's only," she checked her watch, "two fifty-one. I can hardly wait to see what the rest of the day has in store for me."

"Give me the highlights."

"Okay, Gail is having a bad day, and I put my foot in my mouth without realizing it, and now I'm on her list. We have a patient who's developing a potentially dangerous postpartum infection, and I'm being named in a malpractice suit."

"Good grief!" There was a pause, and then, "A *malpractice* suit?"

"It's a nuisance suit, James, but it will certainly be one, a big one!"

"And Gail is upset with you, and you also have a patient in bad shape?"

"Mm-hm."

"How are you holding up?"

"Oh, I'm okay. Everyone has days like this."

"Can I take you to dinner when the day's over? It'll give you something to look forward to."

Cassie sighed in regret. "It sounds wonderful, James, but no. I know I'm supposed to get off at five today, but if I get away before midnight I'll be amazed. We're just swamped with patients today."

"I'm sorry to hear that. I won't keep you if you're busy, though. You take care of yourself, Doc. I worry about you."

"You shouldn't worry. I'm tougher than I look."

"You must be, or you'd never have survived this long." Cassie could hear a smile in his voice. "Take care, anyway. Good-bye, Cassandra."

"Good-bye, James." Cassie cradled the receiver, but before she could stand, a nurse was hurrying toward her from the corridor.

"Dr. Mills? We need you down here."

"I'm on my way." And she was, at a run.

By the time she left—"crawled out" would have been a better phrase, she thought—it was nine o'clock, and she felt as if she'd run a day-long marathon. The drive home was accomplished in a haze of fatigue, and Cassie's only thoughts centered on whether or not she'd eaten since breakfast that morning. No, she decided after some consideration, she hadn't eaten anything. No wonder she felt so hollow. Well, she wasn't too tired to slap some peanut butter on a piece of toast, but she had a feeling that any more complex culinary effort was beyond her.

A light glowed dimly from somewhere inside as she unlocked the front door, but she wasn't especially interested. I must have left the kitchen light on, she thought. No wonder my electric bill is so high. She pushed the door open, and as she stepped inside a man walked out of the kitchen.

It was the single woman's nightmare, an intruder in the house, and Cassie uttered a strangled shriek and whirled to run back outside before she realized who it was. Heart pounding violently, she sagged against the doorframe, one hand going to her throat, feeling the racing pulse there.

"You scared me to death!"

"I'm sorry about that. I didn't mean to." Incongruously dressed in a pair of jeans, a thin sweater and a frilly apron, James crossed the room to her side. He lifted her face for his kiss, and the contrition in his face deepened. "Good Lord, I really scared you, didn't I?" He pressed his fingers to the pulse that was pounding in her throat. "I *am* sorry." He kissed her lips lightly, then the pulse just above her collarbone. "I didn't think about what *you'd* think if you came home and found someone in the house."

"I'm a product of my culture." Cassie walked with him into the living room and switched on some more lights. "I know you didn't mean to scare me, but finding someone in what you think is an empty house is a little bit unnerving these days. Why *are* you in an otherwise empty house, by the way?" She dropped into an armchair and lay back, legs stretched out, relaxed, as she slipped off her shoes.

"Since you couldn't come to dinner with me, I brought the dinner to you."

"Hence the apron." She nodded at his oddly-adorned middle, and James grinned.

"I hope you don't mind, but it was hanging in the kitchen."

"Not at all. I think pink is your color." She closed her eyes for a few moments. "You did say you brought dinner, didn't you?"

"Mm-hm."

"You're a candidate for sainthood," she said fervently. "However, there is one thing . . ."

"What's that?"

"Could we eat it? I figured out on the way home that I missed both lunch and dinner today."

"The salad's in the refrigerator, the potatoes are baked and the steaks are waiting to go in the broiler, so we can eat in ten minutes."

"Definitely a candidate for canonization. If you don't mind, I'll shower and change while you cook, though. I just feel kind of all-over grungy."

"Dinner will be ready by the time you are," James promised her, and it was. When Cassie joined him in the kitchen, dressed much as he was, in a pair of jeans and a sweater, he was forking the steaks onto plates, while the dining room table was laid with a bowl of tossed salad, a bottle of red wine and even candles in the silver candlesticks, lit and casting a warm glow over it all.

"Very impressive." She took the chair James held for her, then sniffed the aromas arising from her plate. Her stomach protested noisily. "I thought, when I was driving home, that about all I'd have the energy to fix for myself was a peanut-butter sandwich. I would certainly never have fixed anything like this!"

"It's not that wonderful," James told her as he took his seat. "Steak and salad is your basic, boring meal, and it's certainly not hard to fix, but everybody likes it, and I figured you'd be hungry, if your day was as bad as it sounded."

"Well, I happen to like steak and salad a lot, and I'm glad it's not hard to fix, because I wouldn't want you to go to a lot of trouble, and I can't tell you how much I appreciate it!"

"Your day was really a bad one?"

"The worst."

"Then we won't talk about it until you've eaten. I wish you could have been at the studio today, anyway. We were re-shooting that very intense scene where my character admits he's an alcoholic, and everything was going beautifully when a dog showed up, out of absolutely nowhere, and jumped in my lap, barking and licking my face. I fell over backwards, literally fell out of my chair, and for about ten minutes we had a real riot going, with people trying to catch the dog, running around in circles, bumping into each other, the dog enjoying the game immensely, and me lying on my back in the middle of this chaos, laughing like an idiot!"

In spite of herself Cassie was laughing, too, at the pandemonium James described. He kept her mind off the worries of her day with a seemingly inexhaustible supply of animal-actor stories until she had eaten her meal, declined ice cream for dessert and was comfortably curled up on the sofa with a cup of coffee.

"Do you want to talk about what went on today?" he asked her, and she sighed wearily.

"Just about everything that could go wrong, did. You've heard of Murphy's Law?"

"Of course."

"Well, this was one of those days."

"You said you're being named in a malpractice suit. How could that happen?"

"It's a nuisance suit, like I told you, and everyone who signed the patient's chart is being named in it. She was a patient I admitted, but I turned her over to a third-year resident, who actually did the delivery." Briefly Cassie outlined the circumstances of the case for James. "There was no malpractice, of course, and that will come out in the hearings or the trial, if it gets that far, but it's an expensive, upsetting, time-consuming nuisance for us all."

"It won't damage your reputation?"

"Not with other professionals, but it's the kind of thing that can hurt you if it gets in the papers. People tend to assume you're guilty if you're sued, even if it's later proven that you weren't guilty of anything."

"How about the patient who wasn't doing well?"

"She's definitely got a postpartum infection, and even today that's a dangerous condition. It was too soon to tell if she was responding to the antibiotics when I left tonight, but I'll call in before I go to bed to check on her."

"And you had an argument with Gail, too?"

"Not exactly. She blew up; I just stood there with my mouth hanging open. I'm worried about her." James slid closer to pull Cassie into the curve of his arm and gently massage the tense muscles of her nape with his free hand. She had told him that Gail had a personal problem, but that it was something she had been told in confidence and couldn't share with him. To her great relief he had respected her reticence and offered comfort without being curious.

"I'm sure she knows you care and that you're worried about her. When she's ready, she'll come to you."

"I hope so," Cassie sighed. "I don't think I want to talk about my problems anymore. They'll all be waiting for me when I get in tomorrow, anyway. I'd rather talk about you."

"Me?"

"Mm-hm."

"What about me?"

"How about your childhood? You mentioned that you grew up in Cincinnati, but I could have learned that much in a magazine. What was it like?"

"Very ordinary." He slouched a little lower and tucked Cassie snugly against his side. "Actually, it's only in the last ten years that my life has been out of the ordinary. My father ran a construction company; my mother was a housewife and taught singing, though she couldn't teach me very much, because I inherited my father's voice."

"Not operatic quality?"

"The pits. Dogs and little kids love my singing. Anyway, I went to public school in Cincinnati and spent a large part of each summer at my maternal grandparents' ranch. I played football and baseball in high school, and I got decent grades but nothing earth-shaking, and I went to the University of Cincinnati."

"What did you major in?"

"English literature, with a minor in history." Cassie giggled and James feigned a scowl. "Okay, smarty, what did you major in?"

"Zoology, with a concentration in organismal physiology." James stared. "Minor?" he asked after a moment.

"Organic chemistry," she replied apologetically. "I did take as much European history as I could fit in, but the pre-med requirements are stiff."

"I'm in awe," James said dryly. "The one chemistry course

I took was to fulfill a requirement, and as I recall, I had to struggle to manage a gentleman's B-minus."

"I wouldn't let it worry you. You no doubt had the better general education, instead of just science, science, science. Did you do any acting in college?"

He nodded. "Drama Society. And the high point was playing Willy Loman my senior year. I wasn't thinking of it as a career, though."

"Even so, *Death of a Salesman* is pretty impressive."

"You wouldn't think so if you'd seen it." James' mouth rose at the corners in amusement. "In retrospect I realize I was pretty awful, though I certainly wasn't inhibited onstage. I wasn't shy at all about screaming and yelling and overacting."

"What did you do after college?"

"Went to Vietnam." Something in his voice didn't encourage further discussion.

"Oh."

"Sometime I'll tell you about it, but not right now."

"Mm-hm. What did you do after that?"

"I decided to be an actor, and with the overconfidence of youth I assumed that the thespian world would immediately recognize my outstanding talent and beat a path to my door."

"They didn't?"

"They didn't. It took four years of acting classes, working construction and bartending to make ends meet, before I had anything but bit parts and walk-ons. You know the rest; it's been written about by any- and everyone."

"Yes." She thought about what he'd told her for a minute. "James, have you ever regretted it, becoming an actor, a public figure?"

"No." His answer was quick and confident, with no uncertainty. "There are drawbacks to it, of course, but any career has those. It's what I want to do. I think I have some talent for it, and I try to work hard at doing the best job I can, but at the bottom of it all, acting is what I want to do. And writing, of course."

He added the last almost as an afterthought, but somehow

Cassie thought it was more important to him than he made it seem. Every instinct she owned was telling her that James had let her into a carefully guarded area of his life, and her probe was as subtle as his admission had been.

"Writing? Like the screenplay that you came to the hospital to research?" Her question was as offhand as she could make it, and she held her breath in the moment before he answered.

"Yes, but I've written other things, too. I started in college, writing for the campus newspaper, of all things—this sounds like a dime novel, doesn't it?—but I also sold some articles to magazines. You wouldn't believe how thrilled I was to see my name in print; if I'd won a Pulitzer Prize, I don't think the high could have been any greater. I planned to become a novelist."

"What happened?" she asked softly.

"The war. I marched off to war, and when I came back, I didn't want to write, ever again, because whatever I wrote would be filled with what I'd seen and heard and felt and smelled, and I wouldn't do it." There were harsh lines carved into his face, and his eyes were shuttered; he was looking inward to bitter memories. "So I tried acting. I thought I had some talent for it, and it was a way to escape the reality I remembered, to become someone else, with that person's background and memories. It's been very therapeutic, but I haven't stayed in it this long just for therapy. I really love the work. It's exhilarating when a scene works, when you know instinctively that your portrayal of a character will move people, make them think. It's a wonderful feeling, and I don't think I'll ever tire of it."

"But you're writing, as well," Cassie observed, and James nodded.

"Yes, I am. Psychic wounds heal just like flesh wounds do; some leave scars and some don't, but the healing goes on. I can look back at what I experienced now, and the pain, though it's still there, is more distant, not so overwhelming."

"I'm glad for that." Cassie covered his hand with hers, and

he turned his palm-up to return the comforting pressure of her fingers. Looking at their hands linked together, Cassie asked quietly. "Do you still want to write a novel?"

He thought about that for a moment. "Maybe."

"Are you going to write one?"

"Maybe."

"I think you should. I bet it'd be very good. I'd buy it."

James chuckled. "My very first fan."

"Hardly. You have fans all over the world."

"They're fans of James Reid, the actor. You're talking about James Reid, the writer. My first fan."

"I'm honored," Cassie told him and yawned hugely. "Excuse me; I didn't realize I was so tired."

"I should go and let you get some sleep." James started to rise, but she caught his arms, holding him there with her.

"No, don't go just yet. I wasn't hinting. Really. It's nice just having you here." She yawned again and slid farther into his arms so that she was half lying across his lap, her legs stretched out on the sofa and her head cradled on his chest. The regular beat of his heart and the slow rise and fall of his chest as he breathed were wonderfully soothing, and she snuggled closer, rubbing her cheek against his shirt in a kittenish caress. James stroked her hair as one might stroke a kitten, letting the strands slide through his fingers, over and over.

"James?" When Cassie spoke again some minutes later her eyes were closed and her breathing slow and regular.

James thought she was asleep, and her murmur surprised him. "Yes?"

"Why haven't you ever gotten married?"

She still sounded as if she were almost asleep, and James was taken aback by the question, though he answered it.

"I think I've been looking for the kind of relationship my parents had, and that isn't easy to find. The women I meet are usually more interested in the movie star than the man." That explanation would have satisfied her, but some imp of honesty impelled him to go on, to tell her the whole truth, to open himself to her as he had been doing all evening, surprising himself with his frankness. "There was the war, too."

"The war?" Her whisper was a sleepy breath of air.

"Mm-hm. I saw so many people going through the hell of losing the ones they cared for that for a long time I didn't allow myself to care for anyone."

"I'm sorry, James."

"I know you are. Your caring means a lot to me."

"Mmm." She turned her face into his chest, breathed deeply once and relaxed into sleep.

How long he sat holding her as she slept James didn't know, but though he knew it was late, and that he should go, he was loath to leave her. Somehow she broke through defenses he didn't even know he had erected, pulled truths from him that he had scarcely admitted to himself, yet she didn't pry. It was always evident that he could refuse to answer and she wouldn't invade his privacy. Something about her made him want to let her into his life, but James wasn't altogether certain he enjoyed that feeling.

His jealously guarded independence was crumbling; he was practically throwing it away on a woman who steadfastly maintained that she wanted no relationship with him. James smiled at his own foolishness. Whatever her reasons for opposing their relationship, he knew that Cassie was bound by the same force which drew him to her, and he had a lot of faith in that magnetism. He knew she felt the attraction between them as strongly as he did, her response to his kisses proved that, and he was certain it was only a matter of time before she admitted it and gave herself to him again.

Cassie stirred and murmured in her sleep, bringing James out of his reverie for a moment. He looked down at her face, gentle, innocent and very young in sleep, remembering the night he'd met her. James didn't remember when he'd last met someone who saw him as nothing more than a colossal nuisance and, moreover, had no qualms about telling him so. Her bluntness and her antagonism had intrigued him, though he knew she hadn't meant them to, hadn't been using hostility as another woman might, to pique his interest. No, she had been simply a busy professional who didn't want to take on an additional burden for what she'd seen as the frivolous purpose of helping to make a movie.

Star-struck she definitely wasn't. Perhaps that was part of her charm, her complete lack of interest in James Reid the public figure. Her interest was in James Reid the man, and he found he was very glad of that. She moved again, and as James settled her more comfortably, he glanced at his watch.

"Damn!" he swore under his breath. It was past midnight and time for him to go. He would try to put her to bed without waking her, so he gathered her into his arms and rose carefully from the sofa. She muttered something unintelligible as he carried her down the hall to lay her on her bed, but relaxed again as he searched for her nightwear. He was highly amused to discover an almost new lace peignoir on a hanger in her closet, while on a hook behind the door hung a football jersey-style nightshirt with the legend "USC Sleeping Team" emblazoned on the back. Smiling, he left the peignoir on its hanger and took the nightshirt.

She roused when he sat her up and propped her against his shoulder, frowning fuzzily up at him as she tried to figure out what was happening.

"James?"

"Yes?"

"What're you doing?"

"Taking your clothes off."

"*What?*" She stiffened and pushed him away to sit on her own. "You are not!"

"I was just putting you to bed," he explained, smiling, amused by the contrast between the calm, capable Dr. Mills and this tousle-haired, sleepy-eyed girl. "You fell asleep, and I was putting you to bed." James showed her the nightshirt he'd gotten out.

"Oh." She reached for the nightshirt, and James put it in her hand. "I can take it from here, James."

"You're sure?"

"I'm sure." She was awake now, and her tone was very certain.

"Well, then . . ." James stalled, but Cassie rose, heading firmly for the front door. Sometimes she didn't understand him at all, but sometimes she could see right through him. This was one of the latter instances, and James grinned ruefully as he followed her. She was so tiny and lovely, too fragile-looking to be so commanding, but he knew as well as the medical students did when to give in gracefully.

"Thank you for the dinner, James." She turned to face him at the door. "It was a lovely thing to do for me." She reached up to kiss his cheek, but he caught her face in his hand and kissed her lips, lightly, but lingering to savor the taste of her, unable to resist. When he lifted his lips he was breathing quickly, and he could see the flush high on her cheekbones before she lowered her head to hide it from him.

"I was glad to do it, Cassie." She took a steadying breath and looked up at him. "Are you on call tomorrow?"

"No."

"Good."

"Why's that?"

"Because you still owe me a dinner out. I have meetings all day tomorrow, so why don't you meet me at my office? About six-thirty?"

"Sure. I'd like that."

"I'll see you tomorrow." He brushed his lips over her forehead and left, leaping down the front steps. Looking back at her silhouetted in the doorway, he called, "Lock the door!" She waved and closed the door, and James drove away, smiling.

To her relief Cassie found the next day far easier than its predecessor. Mrs. Larrison's lawyer, faced with absolute confidence on the part of the staff that they had made the right decisions regarding her care, was apparently reconsidering the suit, and George Hammett was confident that it would eventually be dropped. Mrs. Davis was responding well to antibiotic therapy and was out of danger, though her hospital stay was going to be longer than most, and after the previous day's rush of deliveries they had only one all day, and that at 10:00 A.M.

By three-thirty Cassie was sitting at the nurses' station having a soda with Grace and two other nurses who had just come on for the evening shift.

"After a day like yesterday, it's hard to believe, but I don't have anything to do."

"My heart bleeds," Grace drawled. "Can you imagine how many visitors we'll have up here tonight, with all the babies who were born yesterday? It's going to be a three-ring circus!"

"*My* heart bleeds," Cassie said, grinning, "'cause just as soon as I get Mrs. Davis' lab results, I'm gone!"

"It's not nice to gloat, Cassandra." Grace reached for the telephone as it shrilled its demand from the desk. "Fifth floor, Labor and Delivery. Yes, she's right here." She held the phone out to Cassie. "The lab."

"I'm halfway home!" Cassie sang, took the receiver and switched to a business voice. "This is Dr. Mills." She listened for a few moments. "Yes, and what's the white count? . . . It is? Great! Thanks a lot. You'll send the written results up for her chart? . . . Okay, thank you. 'Bye." She handed the receiver back to Grace, grinning broadly. "The culture is highly sensitive to ampicillin, and her white count is going back down to normal!" She swiveled around on the chair and hopped to her feet. "And *I* am going home! Bye-bye!" She skipped down the hall as Grace blew a raspberry at her retreating back.

It took even less time than usual for her to collect her things and drive home through streets not yet crowded with rush-hour traffic, and when she had showered and made up, and emerged from the bathroom wrapped in a robe, it was still only 4:30. It wouldn't take more than twenty minutes to reach James' Studio City office, no more than five or ten to dress, and that left her with an hour and a half to fill somehow. But how?

She really didn't have any chores to do at home, the five o'clock news had no appeal and neither, quite frankly, did "relaxing." She didn't want to relax; she wanted to see James and give him some good news to balance her earlier litany of horrors. Cassie stood in the middle of her bedroom for a moment, undecided, then nodded firmly and reached for the dress she'd planned to wear. She would just dress and go to James' office. If he was busy, she'd wait in the reception room, but if he wasn't, they could begin the evening early.

After she had pulled the dress carefully over her head she smiled at herself in the mirror. The dress was new, and one of the most blatantly feminine garments she had ever worn. Of deep, rose-pink silk, it had a slip-styled bodice with ribbon-thin straps, and fit close to her body, from the low neckline to three inches below the waist, where it flared into a pouffy, two-tiered skirt which just covered her knees. She loved it, felt good in it and was smiling in anticipation of James' reaction as she caught the silky black fall of her hair back on one side with a fat pink silk rose on a comb.

Her only jewelry was the gold chain James had given her and tiny gold hoops for her ears, but she was more than happy with her appearance when she finished. Mocking her own vanity, she stuck out her tongue at the mirror, then picked up her bag and shawl and went to meet James.

Both the parking attendant and the security guard at James' office building knew her face, if not her name, and admitted her with knowing smiles at her glowing expression and pretty dress. Her quick progress across the lobby was checked only when her eye was caught by a headline on one of the tabloids. "WHO IS SHE?" the bold print screamed above an obviously doctored photograph of James and a faceless woman. "James Reid has mystery 'friend'!" Unable to resist, she fished some change from her bag and bought a copy, skimming the article as she waited for the elevator.

It was a relief to find that the exclusive scoop promised on the cover was nothing more than the hardly-startling news that James hadn't been seen in the usual Hollywood hot-spots in the last few weeks. Cassie tucked the paper under her arm. She knew perfectly well that he hadn't been to those spots in the last few weeks, because she knew where he had been instead, and her smile was a bit smug at the thought that the tabloid had no idea at all of the truth.

His secretary wasn't at her desk, which led Cassie to believe that he might, indeed, be finished for the day, though she could hear the deep rumble of his voice through the closed office door. He must be on the telephone, she thought, and tapped softly on the door before pushing it quietly open.

"James, I thought I'd come early—" Her words of explanation trailed weakly away as she stared at the two people seated together on the sofa, sharing a drink, James and the voluptuous, redheaded Marise Marshall.

# Chapter Nine

or an instant Cassie was paralyzed; then she felt a flash of wild urge to turn and run from what she saw, to flee from the evidence of James' duplicity and the pain which ripped through her. But then James rose, smiling broadly, and walked across the room to meet her, his lips moving as he spoke words she couldn't understand above the roaring in her ears.

She blinked and realized that she'd misread what she saw, that her first impression of the *tableau* had been inaccurate. "Come and join us," James was saying as the roaring faded in her ears and strength returned to her shaky legs. Still smiling, he led her back to the sofa, seating her beside Marise. "Do you remember Marise, Cassie? You met at *Ma Ménage*."

"Yes." Cassie surprised herself by being able to speak. "How do you do, Miss Marshall?" She could feel a flush in her cheeks, embarrassment at her mistaken assumption, and she hoped the others didn't notice it, and hadn't noticed that stricken moment at the door. James had told her that his affair with Marise was over, had been for some time, in fact, and Cassie believed him. She didn't want either of them to think she was behaving like a jealous idiot.

"Just fine, honey," Marise was replying to her greeting. "And how is the doctor business going?" Cassie had to smile at the characterization of her work as "the doctor business," and with that smile, she began to relax. There was something essentially likable about Marise, despite her veneer of flash and glitter, and Cassie could understand why James liked her, and still saw her, though they were no longer lovers.

James brought her a gin and tonic, and she used the drink as an excuse to stay out of the conversation for a few minutes, rolling the pleasant sharpness over her tongue as she listened to them finish a discussion of film contracts and points and percentages which meant nothing at all to her. The reason for their meeting was obvious and innocuous, and that was, of course, a relief, but Cassie's initial reaction was still deeply upsetting to her.

"Thank you again, darlin'," Marise said as she set her empty glass on the low table and rose. "Will I see you Monday?"

"Sure. Same time, okay? Oh . . . and bring a copy of that contract, if you can." James rose to walk her out, and Cassie rose too, just because it seemed the thing to do.

Halfway to the door, Marise turned back and smiled charmingly at her. "I'm so glad to see you again, honey, and some time we must talk about your work. I'm so impressed. Really!"

She was, too; Cassie could see the sincerity beneath the breathless enthusiasm, and smiled. "I'd like that, Miss Marshall."

"Oh, call me Marise, please. And I love your dress! It's a Fendi, isn't it?"

"A knock-off, I'm afraid." Cassie smiled, and Marise grinned conspiratorially.

"That's the best of all . . . gorgeous and affordable. It's a great dress, anyway." She turned back to James. "I'll see you Monday, darlin.' 'Bye." She kissed him quickly and was gone in a flash of aquamarine jersey and diamonds.

Despite the other woman's kind words about the rose silk, Cassie couldn't help but feel that she paled into drabness beside the voluptuous Marise, with her masses of red hair, back-slit sheath and rather amazing figure. Cassie smothered a smile. Marise herself was rather amazing, yet Cassie felt a reluctant liking for the brash, outspoken and eminently pragmatic woman who lived beneath the colorful veneer.

What she felt no liking for at all were her own feelings, her reaction, the conclusion she had jumped to when she saw James with a woman. James was obviously puzzled by her distance during dinner, and it was almost a relief when he took her home and said goodnight, for she finally had the freedom to think. She could analyze her feelings, but the results of the analysis were not pleasing to her.

Why had she been so quick to jump to the conclusion that she had interrupted a romantic tryst in James' office? He and Marise were no longer lovers, the past was past, and they had obviously been having a business discussion today. She had no reason to feel jealous, not of a man who was only a friend.

She had fought so hard against involvement with James, yet her first impulse when she saw them had been to shriek at Marise, "You can't have him; he's mine!"

*Oh, my God.* Cassie squirmed on the sofa in distress, heedlessly wrinkling the silk dress. *He's mine.* She hadn't wanted to think those words, didn't want them to ring true. She wanted them to be outrageous, laughable, but they weren't. As much as it hurt to have to admit it, she knew it was true. She felt proprietary toward James, possessive of him, yet she had no right, and no wish, to feel that way. *How on earth had it happened?*

She massaged her temples, trying to chase away an incipient headache. She had met him with open hostility and distaste, and somehow that had mutated into . . . into what? Love? Surely not! She couldn't, mustn't love him! Not an actor, a movie star, a very wealthy, very famous man, a worldwide public figure. The whole idea was ludicrous, of course, insane, and she was insane to feel as she did about him, to be jealous of someone like Marise, who, after all, had much more in common with him than Cassie did.

Yet what could she do about it? Her calm, well-ordered life was unalterably changed, her emotions were in a hopeless, tangled mess, and she didn't know what to do about any of it. Her attitude was completely unreasonable, of course; she wanted James, and yet she didn't, but knowing she was being unreasonable didn't make it any easier to decide on a course of action. She just didn't have any idea in the world what to do about James, or about the way she felt, or about anything!

With a sigh of frustration she pushed herself off the sofa and stalked through the house to her bedroom. She might not know what to do, but at least she could get some rest. She hoped.

By the time the decision-making month James had allotted her had passed, she wasn't even getting much rest, and the idea of making a decision about her relationship with James seemed absurd. Her only respite from self-analysis was the time she spent with patients, too busy to think, and the time she spent with James, too drunk on his presence to think of anything but him.

It was one month to the day since James had given her that deadline at Disneyland when he broached the subject again. They had eaten a late Sunday lunch on his patio, then walked a long way down the beach, talking idly, watching gulls wheel and dive in the wind, enjoying a sunny day after nearly a week of rain. Finally they sat in the lee of an enormous boulder, looking out at the Pacific and a naval destroyer steaming north toward Long Beach.

"I found this in my office." James took the tabloid Cassie had bought from his jacket pocket and unfolded it to the "mystery woman" headline.

"Oh, yes, I bought that," Cassie laughed. "I know I shouldn't support that rag by paying for it, but I couldn't resist. I was awfully relieved to find out they didn't know anything."

"They didn't have a lot of facts, but they did know that I'm involved with someone."

"They construed that from your absence from the social scene, that's all."

"True." His voice changed, became serious rather than teasing. "It's also true that I'm involved, though." Cassie wasn't sure what to say to that, and dug her toes into the sand, watching intently as the grains sifted over her feet. "What I'm wondering is when you're going to get involved, too." Cassie's toes stilled beneath the sand, and she looked silently up at James. "The month is up, Cassie, but as far as I know you haven't come to a decision yet." She couldn't hold his gaze and looked back down at the sand. "Have you?" he asked after several heartbeats.

She sighed deeply. "No, I haven't. I'm sorry, James, but I'm so confused. . . ." She faltered to a stop. "I'm sorry, James."

"I'm not trying to make things hard for you, Cassie. You have to know that." Cassie glanced sideways at him and saw that he was gazing out at the water. "That rag is right," he repeated. "I am involved with you, and you know I want you to be involved with me, as well. You know what I want."

*You want to be my lover.* "Yes," she murmured. "I know."

"Mm-hm." He knew the thought which had leaped to her mind, and Cassie braced herself for his next question. When it came, it surprised her. "Do you see that ship?"

"Hmm?"

"Out there." He pointed. "It looks like another destroyer going to Terminal Island."

"Yes. I like to watch them; they look so magnificent." They both watched the ship out of sight, then James lay back on the sand, hands folded behind his head and eyes closed against the sun.

"I'm going to Santa Barbara next weekend," he said after several minutes. "Not for business, or anything like that, just to get away for a little while." Cassie stole a glance at him, wondering why he was telling her this, but his eyes were still closed and his face gave nothing away. "I want you to come with me."

In the moment of silence which followed that bombshell Cassie was conscious of the boom of the surf breaking on the beach and the thin cry of a gull high overhead, of the salt tang of the stiff ocean breeze and the warmth of the sand beneath her hands. She knew what James was asking, and the central issue was not a weekend in Santa Barbara. If she agreed to go with him, she was agreeing to become his lover.

"James, I'm not sure—"

He interrupted her admission of uncertainty. "Don't answer me now. Think about it. I'm leaving Friday afternoon at about three. You can tell me any time before then. You still have that weekend off, don't you?"

"Yes, I'm off."

"Good. You tell me sometime between now and Friday afternoon." He stood and dusted the sand off the seat of his jeans, then turned his back to Cassie as she followed suit. "Would you brush off my jacket? I know it's got to be loaded with sand."

"Of course." He was right. His jacket, a blouson style in loosely-woven wool, was sandy indeed, and she dusted her hands over the wide expanse of his shoulders, down the length of his back and across his hips until the jacket was clean. By the time she had finished her hands were trembling and her heart pounding with the force of her longing to touch him without the barriers of jacket and shirt.

"Turn around." He took her by the shoulders as her hands left his back, turned her around and returned the favor, brushing sand from the sweater she wore over a plaid shirt. The sand was concentrated on her lower back and hips, and James' hands moving over those slim curves were a sweet torment. He seemed not to notice her agitation, though, draping a casual arm around her shoulders and starting back up the beach toward his house when he had finished dusting her off.

Despite the confusion of her thoughts, she enjoyed being held close against his side, warm and protected, her already-sensitized body sharply aware of him, the play of his muscles as he moved, his hip and thigh against hers, her shoulder tucked beneath his arm, her arm around his waist so that she could feel the bunch and flex of the muscles there. Somehow she fought the demands of her clamoring body, moving away from him as they neared the house, when she wanted only to fall into his arms.

He let them in the front door, closed and locked it behind them, then walked slowly across the living room to Cassie, who stood uncertainly in the middle of the sand-colored carpet. He was smiling gently as he looked down into her nervous face.

"Don't be afraid of me," he murmured. "I won't hurt you; you know that." She nodded mutely as he took her face in his hands, sliding his fingers into her hair, gently massaging her scalp. With a barely perceptible pressure he tipped her face up, and her lips parted in anticipation as her eyes fell closed.

He teased her, touching his lips briefly to her brow, her eyelids and cheekbones, nibbling at her earlobe before finding her mouth at last. Even then he withheld what she wanted, tracing her lips with the tip of his tongue, pressing little kisses at the corners of her mouth until she linked her hands behind his neck to pull him down to her. She returned his kiss with a fervor born of her frustration, seeking his tongue with hers, savoring him, arching on tiptoe into the curve of his body, instinctively seductive.

His hands slid over her back to curve around her nape, then moved down the graceful line of her spine to cup her bottom, lifting her against him before slipping under the hem of her sweater. She was barely aware of him tugging her shirt free of her jeans, but she shivered in delight as his hands, large and warm and slightly rough, moved over her back. When his palms skimmed up her flanks to her shoulder blades he groaned softly.

"You're not wearing a bra?" he murmured against her mouth.

"No," she breathed, and he groaned again, his fingers tightening on her shoulders. Slowly, so slowly, he moved his hands in little circles on her burning skin, inching around her ribs to brush the outer curves of her breasts, retreating, returning again, sliding over her velvety skin, the slight roughness of his palms almost painfully erotic.

They still stood in the middle of the living room, clinging to each other, straining together despite the barrier of their clothing. Cassie pulled James' shirttail loose, and her hands found his skin as he reached her taut nipples, circling them over and over as she clung to him, afraid she might fall without his support. She knew it was deliberate on his part, standing in this embrace when they could be stretched out on the sofa, fighting the barrier of their clothing rather than removing it, frustration feeding their desire.

"You'll never know," James whispered when at last he lifted his lips from hers, pulled her sweater into place and wrapped his arms around her, holding her tight. "You'll never know," his voice was so husky that it was barely audible, "just how much I want you."

"James . . ." Cassie breathed his name, a world of longing in her voice and her eyes, but he shook his head.

"No, not now. I won't rush you." He loosened his arms, releasing her when she would have clung to him, seating her in a deep chair while he walked several paces away to look out the window. She could see him forcing a lid of control on his desire and struggled to do the same, though she wanted to plead with him to kiss her, to hold her.

If he'd wanted to make love to her, he could have, just as he could have on any number of evenings in the past month, when her desire had outweighed her reluctance. Sometimes she almost wished he would sweep her off her feet, carry her to bed, drunk with passion, and make love to her, relieving her of the burden of making the decision.

Which was, of course, the reason he didn't do it. It was her decision to make, and he would ensure that it was made deliberately, in the clear light of day. If she wanted them to become lovers, she would have to tell him so. As her skin cooled and her mind cleared she resented that, resented him for putting her in that position. It would be so easy to be seduced, but it would not be easy at all to make her decision about Santa Barbara.

James turned from the window to meet her frowning gaze, and she read the knowledge in his eyes. He knew exactly what she was going through and would do nothing to make it any easier for her. She would have to take full responsibility, and right now, she didn't want to. She averted her eyes, staring at the floor, and heard James chuckle softly as he walked past her to the kitchen.

"I'll make us some coffee. I think you could use a cup."

Cassie stuck out her tongue as he disappeared, feeling childish, but a bit better for the gesture of defiance. Just once, she thought, I'd like to see you shaken up, James Reid. Just once.

By Thursday afternoon she was no nearer reaching a decision and more torn than ever due to the pressure of time. James was coming to her house about nine that evening, after a dinner meeting with some studio executives, and he would expect her answer then. Would he be willing to wait until Friday? she wondered, then shook her head at her own foolishness. If she didn't know by nine o'clock that evening what she wanted to do, there was no reason to expect she'd know by Friday morning, so she might as well make up her mind.

"Easier said than done," she muttered, and left the on-call room for the nurses' station and Gail's office. Gail had seemed in a better state of mind the last few days, a little remote, perhaps, but maybe she could help. Cassie tapped on Gail's office door, heard a muffled, "Come in," and pushed it open.

"Hi, Gail. Are you busy?"

"For once, no." Gail leaned back in her chair and smiled, the warmth of the expression almost eclipsing the strain in her face. "What is it? Some patient problems?"

"No," Cassie dropped into the chair beside the desk. "Some *me* problems."

"Oh-oh. Some *you* problems . . . and some *James* problems?"

"It's that easy to tell?" Cassie grimaced in self-derision. "So much for maintaining an impassive façade, huh?"

"Don't get all shook up about it. Remember, I'm the only one who knows there's more between you and James than a handshake. If there's a problem, and it's not with a patient, then it must be with James. After all, you wouldn't get shook up if your car needed a brake job, would you?"

"Probably not."

"So okay, just chalk another one up to my extraordinary powers of perception and tell me what's wrong." Gail was smiling, sympathetic, the friend Cassie knew so well, and Cassie did as she was told.

Briefly she outlined what had happened between her and James from his first day at the hospital to what he'd said he wanted, and her own misgivings and desires, finishing with his invitation to Santa Barbara.

"So now he's asked me to go with him for the weekend, and we both know what it means. I don't know what to do, though; I just don't know."

"You don't know whether you want to be lovers, or you don't know what will happen to you if you do?"

"Either . . . or both. I don't know that, either!" Cassie threw up her hands helplessly.

"You do have it bad." Gail was wryly sympathetic. "Let's take it one question at a time. Do you want to make love with him?"

Cassie blushed and looked down at her sensible white shoes. "I don't kn—"

"Cassie . . . be straight with yourself, if not with me. Do you want him?"

"I . . ." She took a deep breath. "Yes, I do."

"But you're afraid of what will happen?"

"Yes." This answer was quick and certain. "I'm scared to death of that."

"Scared of what? I don't really see that things would be so

very different, and it's not as if your life is a shambles now, is it?"

"Well, it's—"

"Cassie it's obvious how you feel about him," Gail interrupted again when Cassie started waffling. "And it boggles my mind that you've held back this long. If you didn't want to make love with him, if you honestly didn't want him, you wouldn't have anything to decide. You'd just have said no when he asked."

"I guess so," Cassie sighed. "Yes, of course that's right; I just didn't want to admit it."

"Then why are you torturing yourself this way when you love the man?"

"Love. . . ." Cassie shrugged. "I care about him, certainly, but love him? I don't know if that's what I feel."

"Of course you love him. What else could it be? It's not the physical relationship you're afraid of; it's the emotional involvement. Maybe you're too close to it to see this, but the emotional involvement already exists."

Cassie heard Gail's words as if from a great distance as their import sank in. *Of course you love him.* So it was true, then. After all her initial hostility, all her resistance, she did, indeed, love James Reid. God, it was a disaster.

"Cassie? Are you okay?" Gail's softly spoken words interrupted her thoughts.

"Gail, I don't *want* to love him!"

Gail looked at her disbelievingly for a moment, then laughed. "Do you think that matters? Cassie, you're my friend and I love you dearly, but you're human just like the rest of us. You're just as susceptible to falling in love with a handsome, rich, sexy, gentle, famous, compassionate, intelligent, talented man as anybody else, and not wanting to doesn't have a lot to do with it. He's fabulous, and he's obviously crazy about you. How could you help but fall in love with him?"

"I tried hard enough not to!" Cassie said tartly, and Gail laughed again.

"I don't think that matters much at this point. Maybe you don't want to be in love with him, but think about it. How would you feel if you caught him with another woman, for instance?"

Cassie thought about it and swallowed hard. "I wanted to strangle her," she admitted, and Gail gasped in shock.

"You found James with a woman? I don't believe it!"

"It wasn't like that, really. She's an actress, a friend of his, and when I saw them in his office, I thought the worst."

"But his office? You know James wouldn't do something so tacky!"

"I didn't know anything. I just saw her, and I thought, 'He's mine. You can't have him.'"

"I rest my case." Gail sat back and folded her arms across her chest.

"Okay, so I love him. Now what?" Cassie demanded.

"Now you go to Santa Barbara."

"But what if it's a big mistake?"

"Then you learn from it. Life is full of mistakes, Cassie, and most of them aren't all that awful."

"I do love him," Cassie whispered after a pause. "I think things would be a lot simpler if I didn't, but I do love him."

"Do you want to make love with him?"

"Yes," she said in a husky whisper. Then came a long pause. "I'll go with him."

"I don't think you'll regret it."

"Even if I do, at least I won't have been guilty of hiding from life." She looked down at her hands for a moment, then looked across the desk at Gail. "You don't pull your punches, do you? Why aren't you a psychiatrist?"

"Because I'm such a dynamite OB nurse, of course." Gail grinned, and they laughed.

"Can I return the favor?"

"Hmm?"

"Have you seen a specialist yet?"

A shuttered wariness dropped over Gail's face. "Not yet."

"To quote someone I admire very much, 'Why are you

torturing yourself this way?' Surely it would be better to know the truth?"

"And if the truth is that I can never be a mother, what then?" Gail's voice rose angrily, and Cassie spoke soothingly, placatingly.

"Gail, you can't assume the worst when you don't know. You're aware of all the things that can be done now—"

"I don't want to talk about it!" Gail bit out. "Okay?"

"Okay. I'm sorry I pried." Cassie rose, looking sadly down at Gail's bent head. "You know where to find me if you do want to talk."

"Yeah." Gail managed a wan smile. "In Santa Barbara."

James was late that evening, and by the time he rang the doorbell Cassie had discovered that nervous people really do pace the floor. She jumped at the sound of the bell, one hand going to her throat, where her pulse raced madly. This was ridiculous! She took a deep breath, ran her damp palms down her jeans-clad thighs and muttered "Calm down," to herself as she walked quickly to the door.

"Hi, James." She smiled, holding the door wide for him. "You look tired. Was it a bad meeting?"

"Hi." James kicked the door shut with his heel and took Cassie in his arms, her head resting on his chest, his face against her hair. "Mmm, you feel good." He rubbed his cheek over her hair, then kissed her lips lightly and walked into the living room with an arm around her shoulders. "Let's just say the meeting was . . . ah . . . not especially cordial." Cassie remained on her feet when James dropped onto the sofa.

"Would you like coffee? Or a drink?"

"Coffee, please. I let them order me two martinis, which was stupid, because I don't even particularly like martinis, and I don't think I need anything else alcoholic."

"Coffee, it is." Cassie grinned. "Do you want any food with that?"

"Please!" he groaned. "After an endless meal of bad French food? I may never eat again!"

"Coffee, no food. Be right back." She was laughing as she vanished into the kitchen, and returned minutes later with a coffee tray. "Here you are." She handed him a cup, and settled back beside him with her own. "What happened tonight?"

"An argument," James said dryly. "And, in a way, you were responsible for it."

"*I* was? How on earth?"

"You taught me so much. Every time they suggested another tired old cliché for the *New Life* screenplay, I fought them tooth and claw, and by the end of three hours they weren't at all happy with me."

"Should I apologize for being a good teacher?" James shook his head, grinning. "Okay, I won't apologize. Will they put the clichés in, or will you win in the end?"

His grin widened. "Ordinarily we'd probably fight our way to a Mexican standoff and end up with a compromise nobody liked, but I do have some leverage in this case."

"And what's that?"

"They want me to star in it." His voice was smug. "I can always play the prima donna and just stay home buffing my nails and admiring my profile if they won't go along."

"You fraud! You know you wouldn't do that!"

"Ah, but they don't know that, and that's what's at issue."

"I had no idea you were so underhanded."

"I'm full of surprises." He smiled, and reached out to pull her against him, his arm around her shoulders holding her close. "How about you?"

"How about me?"

"Do you have any surprises for me?"

"Oh."

Cassie hesitated, and James dropped his head back to look up at the ceiling as he elaborated. "Will you come to Santa Barbara with me?"

"I . . ." Her voice was very soft. "Yes, I will." She'd been half afraid that he might gloat, but he gave no immediate sign that he had even heard her reply, except that his arm tightened around her shoulders.

"I'm glad," he said simply, and Cassie laid her head on his shoulder, happy just to be close to him, the tension draining from her now that she'd committed herself. James seemed content with that quiet closeness as well, holding her, toying with her hair, letting it run through his fingers like black silk. "You feel good," he said after they had sat for a time. "I relax when I'm with you; you make the problems unimportant."

Cassie didn't know what to say to that; in a rush of shyness she buried her face in his chest and felt him chuckle. With gentle fingers he turned her face up to kiss her willing mouth. She was drowning in him, oblivious to anything else, the room around her fading away as she returned his kisses, daring to part his lips and explore his sweetness, savoring the coffee-taste and warm man-smell of him. Now that she had made the commitment to go with him, she would have surrendered willingly to him, but he drew back just when Cassie was certain he would love her.

"Shall I pick you up here, or at the hospital?" he asked in a husky whisper. Cassie blinked owlishly up at him, the haze of passion clearing slowly from her eyes.

"I . . . I'll be here," she whispered. "I'll come home and change. What should I wear?"

"Something casual. Jeans, like these." He ran his hand over the curve of her hip and thigh. "Bring that pretty dress, though, the dark pink one."

"The rose-colored one? The one Miss Marshall liked?"

"That's the one." He smiled. "And Marise wasn't the only one who liked it." He stood, pulling her to her feet with him. "It's time for me to go, I think. I'll see you tomorrow at three, okay?"

"Okay," she whispered.

"Tomorrow." He kissed her quickly, teasingly, and was gone.

As she stood there alone reaction set in, and she began to tremble, slightly at first, then harder, until her teeth were chattering. What had she done? James was going to show up tomorrow at three, expecting to load her and her suitcase into his car, drive her up to Santa Barbara and take her to bed. What would he do? Would he take her to dinner first, or would he expect to go directly to bed? Would he stage a traditional seduction scene, with champagne and candlelight? And could she handle something like that, or would she completely humiliate herself and get the giggles?

Somewhere in the back of her mind she knew she should have faith in James, knew that he wouldn't embarrass her or make her uncomfortable, but she had no such faith in her own *savoir faire*. She could only hope, and hope fervently, that she did nothing really stupid.

Those worries were still with her when James drove up at 3:02 the next afternoon, though she did her best to hide them. She wore a pair of snug-fitting jeans and a dolman-sleeved velour sweater in deep emerald green, cowboy boots and a brown leather blouson jacket. Her small suitcase was waiting by the door, the rose silk dress carefully folded with layers of tissue paper. She was ready and waiting before James arrived, sitting on the sofa, sipping a glass of iced tea, struggling to be calm, though her nerves felt like overwound springs.

She hardly knew what to say when she opened the door to James, but he spared her the necessity of making conversation. Dressed much as she was, in jeans, boots and a V-neck sweater with no shirt underneath, he looked comfortable, casual and devastatingly handsome, the reddish highlights gleaming in the deep brown of his hair as it was stirred by the breeze, and he smiled warmly when he saw her.

"Hi." He brushed a casual kiss across her lips and looked past her to the suitcase standing in the hall. "Is that your stuff?"

"Yes."

"Anything else?"

"Just my purse." She took it from the hall table. "And I'm ready."

"Okay." He picked up the case. "If you don't mind my being rude and hurrying you, I'd like to leave right away and beat the freeway traffic."

"Of course." She followed him to the car, waited while he placed her case in the trunk beside his own and let him seat her in the luxurious comfort of the Mercedes. "Decided not to take the Rolls today?" she teased as he started the engine, and he grinned.

"It's not that you don't deserve the Rolls, but I want to blend into the crowd, as it were."

"Is that why you don't have vanity plates? Something like 'JAMES 1' and 'JAMES 2'?"

"Precisely. Nothing but good old California numbers on my license plates."

"Well, maybe you blend in with the Sunset Beach crowd in this car, but as you may have noticed, it sticks out like a sore thumb on my street."

"Maybe so, but not the way the Rolls does. I do enjoy driving that car, but at times it makes me more conspicuous than I want to be. This," he patted the steering wheel, "is practically the California State Car."

"And here I thought the California State Car was a dune buggy."

"Good point!" James laughed, accelerating up an on-ramp to the Ventura Freeway. "Speaking of which, look over there!" He pointed to just such a vehicle, brilliant in candy-apple red and chrome, and driven by a blond, tanned young man who could only be a surfer. Their easy banter made the two-hour trip pass quickly, but as they drove through the lovely seaside town of Santa Barbara, Cassie's tension returned, along with increasingly lurid speculations about the luxury hotel she had no doubt James was headed for and the scene which would be set there.

Her confusion increased when James drove straight through town, past several hotels, and followed the coast highway west toward the hamlet of Isla Vista. She had almost steeled herself to ask where they were going, even if she did sound dumb, when he turned onto a narrow, unmarked road which wound down toward the ocean. It threaded its way through clumps of wind-twisted pines and a few hardy palms, past massive boulders and finally, halfway down the slope to the sea, ended in front of a low, sprawling, adobe building.

Cassie saw no sign or other identification on the beautifully landscaped grounds, but James pulled up before a massive oak door, killed the engine and turned to smile at her.

"We're here."

"This is going to sound silly, but where is *here?*"

"*Las Brisas del Mar,* my favorite inn. A college buddy of mine owns it. He bought this place ten years ago, when it was a rundown dump, renovated it and re-opened it as a small inn. I think you'll like it."

"I'm sure I will; it looks lovely." Cassie was relieved of the need to say more by the emergence of two smiling young men from the inn, one to collect their luggage and the other to park the car.

In short order she and James were ushered inside, across a cool, tile-floored lobby with a high, black-beamed ceiling and a small fountain splashing musically in the center, while groups of plantings in terra-cotta tubs provided alcoves of privacy for leather sofas and armchairs. Cassie saw a dining room through an archway, and a swimming pool glimmering aquamarine in the late afternoon sun, as they were led to their suite, which was at the end of one of two long wings that led from the main area of the inn toward the ocean. Her impression was of calm, serene comfort everywhere.

Their suite followed the theme of adobe-style simplicity, with dark beams and white walls, tile floors softened by thick rugs in the blues and reds of the west, and invitingly comfortable furnishings. In a switch which made Cassie laugh aloud, the bathroom was opulently luxurious, with a sunken tub, complete with Jacuzzi jets, and a window overlooking the Pacific, partly screened by some more luxuriant plants.

"Oh, James, you have to see this! A sunken tub looking out over the ocean! It's too much!"

"You don't like it?" He came to the bathroom door, smiling at her astonishment.

"Oh, of course, I like it! It's beautiful! It's just a surprise, after the restraint everywhere else."

"Well, Tom thought he should put something a little bit extraordinary in here, since people come to get away from the everyday."

"This certainly accomplishes his objective! It's so . . . so . . ." She shrugged. "It's gorgeous! Your friend . . . Tom . . . should be congratulated."

"You'll have a chance to do that, if you like. We can join him and Janice for dinner tomorrow."

"Why, yes, I'd like that." Cassie left the bathroom and walked, rather quickly, across the bedroom to the sitting room, feeling that she could face James with more equanimity there than in a room dominated by a massive oak bed. "I'd like to meet someone who's been your friend for so long. I haven't met very many of your friends, after all, while you've met practically everybody I know! Who knows what deep, dark secrets I might learn?"

"An ulterior motive, huh?" James began to stalk her, arms outstretched, and she backed away, giggling. "You'll pay for that, my pretty!" He feinted to the side, and Cassie dodged behind a chair, laughing harder.

"You'll never catch me, you know," she teased. "I'm too quick and crafty!"

"We'll see." He lunged at her, and she leapt back, barely escaping, only to realize that she had literally backed into a corner. The hearth blocked her escape to the left, and James and the chair finished the job of hemming her in. Her heart began to beat in hard, heavy thumps as she read in his eyes the payment he would exact.

He had reached out for her when the interruption came in the form of a loud knocking on the door. James halted abruptly, then straightened when the knock was repeated.

"Saved by the bell. Don't think you'll get off so easily the next time, though," he warned Cassie with a half-smile, and moved away to answer the door.

There were several levels of meaning in that caution, and Cassie was trying to unravel them as she came out of her corner to sit in the armchair she'd been hiding behind. She wondered just what James had in mind for the "next time." She wondered if she were eager to find out . . . or afraid.

# Chapter Ten

$\mathcal{T}$hank *you*, sir!" The bellboy pocketed what must have been a generous tip, and James closed the door, smiling across the room at Cassie as he held a good-sized wicker basket in his hand.

"What's in there?"

His grin widened. "Our dinner."

"In a basket?" Cassie walked over to see.

"Not just any old basket," James corrected her, "but a picnic basket, to be precise. And I know exactly where I want to have it, so let's go."


"This was a wonderful idea!" Cassie leaned back on the sand and looked around at the little crescent of beach James had brought her to, smiling unselfconsciously. "I'm afraid I ate too much, though."

"If you're fishing for compliments," he grinned, "you already know you're a long way from fat. Have another peach."

"No, please! It was all delicious, but I really can't eat another thing." It had indeed been delicious, a gourmet variation on the picnic dinner, with a country *paté* and crusty bread, cold chicken in a spicy sherry-and-ginger sauce, endive salad, and fruit, cheese and homemade shortbread for dessert. "Let me help you put that away."

She rolled to her knees, facing him across the basket as they re-packed the dishes and leftovers, but when she reached for the blanket they'd been sitting on, he shook his head.

"Leave it here for a while. We don't have to go back just yet." He moved the basket out of the way and sat her beside him. "Relax."

"I can, can't I?" She stretched her legs out and leaned back, bracing herself on her arms, gazing out at the fading glow in the western sky. "It's funny to think," she said after a moment, "that there's nowhere I *have* to be, nothing I *have* to do, and no one even knows where to find me. You have no idea how liberating it is to realize that if there's an emergency they'll just have to handle it themselves."

"That they will." James lay back on the blanket. "All you have to do is relax," he reached one hand up to massage her neck, "and unwind," the gently probing fingers moved to her shoulders, "and enjoy yourself."

Cassie was enjoying herself. As James' hand moved down her back she leaned forward, head down and relaxed, practically purring as he found and released little knots of tension, and finished by running his hand rhythmically up and down her back.

At the end of a neck-to-waist caress his hand slipped around her waist and he eased her down beside him, her head cradled on his arm as she gazed up at the darkening sky. She sighed deeply, wriggling a little closer to his comforting warmth, and his arm tightened around her.

"You know, I wish I knew something about astronomy so I could identify the stars and constellations. About the only one I can ever find is the Big Dipper."

"*Ursa Major,*" James corrected her, "or the Great Bear, if you want to be colloquial about it. Actually, it's not dark enough to see much right now, and there'll be fog later. That, over there," he pointed to the west, "is Venus, though, and over there, to the southeast, is Jupiter. They're brighter than most stars, so they appear in the sky before it's fully dark."

"That's interesting. So the 'evening star' is really a planet?"

"Mm-hm."

"I'll have to get a book and read about it, when this residency is over and I have some free time for a change."

"When will that be?"

"July first." There was a smile in her voice. "After four long years I'll be a board-eligible OB-GYN, and I'll take the Boards the week after Thanksgiving."

"When will you go into practice?" There was a certain soberness in James' tone that Cassie didn't quite understand.

"July first," she replied. "I can practice as an OB once I'm residency-trained. The Board certification just guarantees that I'm qualified."

"Do you know where you'll be practicing?" His voice still held that wary undertone.

"Right in LA. I've already accepted a position with George Hammett's group." She could feel the tension drain out of James and turned her head to peer at him in the darkness. "Is something wrong?"

"No." The wariness was gone. "I just didn't know you'd be finishing up so soon."

"I'm Chief Resident. You have to be in your last year for that, and most residencies start on July first and end on June thirtieth. So I'll be done in three months." She explained it succinctly, surprised that he hadn't known. "Why does it matter?"

"It doesn't, really, except insofar as I should congratulate you for being so nearly finished." He laughed softly at himself. "I guess I just envisioned you working at the hospital indefinitely."

"Please! Anything but that!" Cassie laughed and rolled back to look up at the sky. There was more involved in James' questions than he'd said, but she was unwilling to press, still a little wary of him.

"Don't worry," he said, so close to her ear that she felt the soft touch of his breath. "I wouldn't curse you to a lifetime of on-call." He rolled slowly toward her, easing his body over hers as he gathered her into his arms. "I don't want you to work so hard; I want to take care of you." He threaded his fingers into her hair, cupping her skull in his hands. "I want . . ." He breathed the unfinished wish against her lips, and as they parted for him, he took her mouth.

Her tension and awkwardness long since vanquished by James' charm and his provision of the unexpected—a picnic when she'd anticipated champagne and caviar—Cassie gave herself up to him, winding her arms about his neck to hold him close, pressing sensuously into the curve of his body as pleasure flowed through her. Warming and melting her from within, the pure sensual enjoyment of holding James, kissing him, rendered her oblivious to anything else, but when he eased the velour top upward, running his hands over her stomach and ribs, she began to shiver uncontrollably.

"You're cold." He tugged the sweater back into place. "Let's go inside." Cassie was beyond caring where they went; she only wanted to be with James, and she made no protest as he slipped her leather jacket around her and gathered up the basket and blanket. They walked back to the inn through a rapidly-thickening fog, but Cassie didn't feel the chill or damp, though moisture dewed her skin and beaded on her hair. In silence, meeting no one, they reached their suite and slipped inside, and when the door closed out the rest of the world James took her in his arms again.

"You're wet," he muttered against her hair. "Come with me." He led her to the opulent bathroom that had so amused her earlier, seated her on one of the plushly-carpeted steps leading up to the enormous tub and turned away to rummage in cupboards, from which he produced a towel and a comb. "Take off your jeans and your sweater." Cassie looked up at him with stricken eyes, and he smiled more gently. "You're wet all over from the fog. Do you have a robe in your suitcase?"

"Yes, I . . . I do."

"I'll get it." He tactfully left her to undress, opening the door just far enough to drop her white peignoir on the counter. "Come and dry your hair by the fire when you're ready," he told her. "It'll warm you up."

"All right." She heard him moving into the bedroom, probably to get out of his own damp clothing, and her heart began to pound. It took her no time at all to peel off her damp jeans and sweater and hang them on a towel rod, and after a moment's hesitation she did the same with her bra and quickly toweled herself dry. Oddly, she didn't feel cold anymore, despite the damp hair which clung to her neck and back. She was warm all over, whether from the wine which had been packed with their picnic, or from something else, she didn't know, but her cheeks were flushed and her eyes bright in the large mirror as she slipped the peignoir around her and tied its sash.

James was waiting for her, seated on the raised hearth when she appeared, towel and comb in hand. Dressed in only a pair of jeans, he looked big and male and a bit intimidating, with the firelight gleaming on his chest and shoulders while his eyes were shadowed and mysterious. She hesitated in the doorway, suddenly shy, until he smiled and patted the stone beside him.

"Come and sit down." He turned her so that her back was to him, allowing him to reach her hair, and then he rubbed it with the towel before taking the comb. With slow, smooth strokes he began to comb it, the fire's heat drying it as he let it run through his fingers like black silk, and a heady lassitude crept through Cassie. His touch on her scalp, her neck, her shoulders, was evocative of other touches, and when at last he laid the comb aside she turned eagerly into his arms.

His kisses burned with a long-frustrated need; his hands were rough with an impatience he fought to control, until Cassie's own impatience communicated itself to him. Having consented freely to come to him, she abandoned shyness and dissembling, letting her trust in him take her past nervousness or embarrassment. She loved him. Though the admission had been dragged out of her, it was nonetheless true, and she gave herself to him completely, with the openness and generosity of love.

James' arms were bands of steel around her, crushing her

to him. One hand twisted in her hair as he plundered her mouth, but Cassie couldn't lie passively against him. Her own hands were busy, sliding over the smooth, hot skin of his chest, his shoulders, exploring the muscles of his back and arms and taut, flat abdomen until he groaned something against her mouth and swung her up against his chest to carry her into the bedroom.

She felt no embarrassment when he laid her across the wide bed and slowly untied the sash of her robe to spread the thin white fabric out to either side of her, only gladness and a certain pride that the sight of her body pleased him. He stood above her, gazing down at her in the dim light filtering from the sitting room as he unfastened his jeans; then, in a quick, fluid movement he stripped them off and knelt beside her.

Slowly, carefully, he reached out to brush a stray lock of hair off her forehead; then his hands outlined her, tracing the lines of her face, down her throat, along her collarbone. Lightly he skimmed his fingertips over her breasts, the nipples tightening beneath his touch; then his hands moved on, down her ribs, across her waist, circling her navel, then over her velvet-skinned belly and down the slim curve of her thighs. She felt as if she were being worshipped, adored, and she reached up to touch James as he knelt by her, adoring him in turn.

He held himself very still as she half sat up to smooth her hands over his chest and shoulders, reveling in the warmth and hard strength of him. She could feel the muscles of his abdomen contract beneath her fingertips, and when she daringly let her hands follow the line of dark hair which trailed past his waist he groaned, then reached out to catch her to him as he collapsed on the bed.

They needed no words; all was said with lips and hands and bodies as they kissed and caressed, each delighting in pleasuring the other, struggling to prolong the anticipation until they could wait no more. Cassie shuddered as James moved to cover her body with his, all her senses focused on him, the scent of his skin, the taste of his mouth, the smooth skin and rougher hair of his body against hers. She gasped as he took her, and then they were one, joined in a quickening rhythm which wound them tighter and tighter in a spiral of need and finally burst in a whirling ecstasy.

Cassie returned to earth slowly, aware of small, discrete sensations: the heavy thud of James' heart contrasting with the rapid beat of her own; the dampness of their cooling bodies; the rasp of hair on smooth skin as he slid his leg along hers; and the wetness of tears on her cheeks.

"Tears?" he whispered, wiping her cheek with his fingertips. "Why, Cassie?"

"I don't know." Her words were barely audible, her face hidden against his shoulder. "I just . . . it was just . . . it was beautiful."

"*You* were beautiful," he murmured into her hair.

"I was afraid."

"Afraid? Of what?"

"Of being too naïve, too inexperienced. I was afraid I wouldn't know how to please you, how to make it special for . . . for you."

James chuckled softly, pulling her more closely against him. "Poor Cassie, you mustn't worry. It will always be special, because you are special. Very special." He lifted her face from his shoulder and kissed her softly. "Don't hide your face, my darling; you must never be shy or embarrassed with me." He hugged her close against him for a time, his hand moving idly, soothingly, up and down her spine, from the nape of her neck to the soft curves of her bottom as she lay, spent, beside him. When she moved it was to look up at him, her heart shining in her eyes.

"I think you're very beautiful, James," she whispered, tracing the hard, exciting line of his mouth with her fingertip, catching her breath in pleasure when he trapped the finger in his teeth.

"I think *you're* very beautiful, too," he growled. "And I'm going to show you just how beautiful you are." Their lovemaking this time was languorous and slow, without the almost painful urgency they'd felt earlier, and when at last the quaking rapture consumed her, Cassie cried James' name over and over as she clutched him to her. Exhaustion was swallowing them up, but before she gave in and let the warm wave of sleep submerge her, Cassie thought she heard James murmur, "Goodnight, my love."

She awoke with the feeling that she was still in the middle of a lovely dream of making love with James and sleeping in his arms. Then she moved, stretching luxuriously, and realized that she was, indeed, sleeping with a man, with James. He was awake and watching her, his eyes heavy-lidded, his mouth curved in a sleepily sensual smile, which widened as their eyes met.

"Good morning."

"Good morning," she replied, and blushed as he moved closer, acutely aware of their nakedness beneath the blankets, feeling very small and vulnerable beside James' strength, yet very aware of her power over him. Deliberately she turned toward the heat of his body, nestling close as his arms closed about her and running her hands up his chest to caress his jawline, rasping over the shadowing stubble. "Oohh," she pursed her lips in a little *moue* and brushed her hand over his cheek, "you're scratchy."

"You want to see how scratchy?" James accepted her teasing challenge, kissing her lips lightly, then, so suddenly that he took her by surprise, he buried his face in her neck, laughing as she struggled halfheartedly to free herself.

"James, stop it!" she gasped between giggles. "Please, that tickles! Stop it, James!" She squirmed and wriggled and then she was no longer laughing and neither was James, as his arms crushed her to him and his mouth came down to claim hers. Their lovemaking was eager and urgent and exhausting, and they slept for a time afterward, awakening to find the morning almost gone.

"What time is it?" Cassie asked drowsily, and James reached across her to the nightstand for his watch.

"Hmph," he grunted in surprise. "Eleven forty-two."

"You're kidding!" Cassie groaned and closed her eyes for a moment. "I was planning an outrageously extravagant breakfast for myself, but it's practically lunchtime!"

"Nothing like a little decadence for a change of pace." James grinned, and she rolled her eyes at him in reproach. "If you want an outrageous breakfast we can have eggs Benedict and crêpes Chantilly in bed, with orange juice and champagne."

Cassie groaned again. "I don't think I'm ready for quite that much decadence, thank you. And what an awful combination! Remind me never to let you choose a breakfast for me."

"You wouldn't want strawberries and hollandaise in the same meal?"

"Yuck!"

"And champagne?" James drawled, laughing as she buried her face in the pillow.

"Please, no more! What I'd really like, since it's practically noon already, is a nice, hot shower and then a nice, big lunch in that gorgeous restaurant."

"Your wish is my command." James kissed her hard, then flung back the covers and walked, unselfconsciously naked, across to the window. He lifted the curtain aside, and Cassie watched him as he stood silhouetted against the light, big and strong and handsome and tender. His body was beautiful, magnificently sculpted and utterly male, wide shoulders tapering to narrow hips, strongly-muscled legs and arms, a body of lean, hard planes and angles, contrasting excitingly with her own smooth-skinned curves and softness. She felt her cheeks warm a little at the memory of just how exciting the contrast was, how he could make her feel. All her earlier misgivings and hesitancy seemed foolish now, and she couldn't understand why she had waited so long to love James in the fullest sense.

"Your idea's sounding more perfect all the time." He dropped the curtain into place and turned back to Cassie. "It's pouring outside."

"Raining? I thought the weather was supposed to be good this weekend."

"So did I. As a matter of fact, I had good-weather things planned . . . like walks, and picnics on the beach."

"Somehow, I imagine you have a contingency plan." She smiled. "I have great faith in your organizational capabilities."

"Blind trust . . . I like that in a woman." James shrugged into a deep brown velour robe and brought Cassie's over to her. "How does a game sound?"

"Depends on the game, I guess."

"Cards?"

"What? Gin, cribbage, euchre?"

"You choose."

Cassie grinned. "Can you get your hands on a cribbage board?" She pulled her peignoir around her and slid out of bed.

"Sure. I warn you, though, I'm tough."

"Big talk, but wait until we add the points up. You may not be talking so big then!" She slipped past him and into the bathroom. "*And* I get first dibs on the shower!" She giggled and closed the door in James' surprised face.

"Again?" James glared at her across the cribbage board. "You win *another* one?"

"Afraid so." She scribbled on the scorepad, then held it out to James, who muttered something rude under his breath. "You owe me twenty-seven dollars and forty-five cents."

"I want a rematch," he growled, but Cassie laid a quelling hand over his as he began shuffling the cards for another game.

"James, I've lost track of how many we've played—"

"And of how many you've won!"

"You won some, too."

"Yeah, but you're twenty-seven dollars ahead."

"This'll teach you not to gamble, and aren't we supposed to meet the Fredericks at eight?"

"Mm-hm."

"Well, it's seven-fifteen already, and I do need a little time to dress."

"Oh." James checked his watch. "Okay, we'll stop for now. I warn you, though, I'll have that rematch!"

"Whatever you say, O Great One." Cassie bowed deeply, then had to dodge to avoid the swat James aimed at her bottom. They had lingered over a delicious lunch of red snapper Veracruz and other Mexican specialties, been invited to join the Fredericks for dinner at their house, a short distance from the inn, and then had spent the rainy afternoon in a series of hard-fought cribbage games. Cassie smiled to herself as she carefully mascaraed her eyelashes, amused by James' competitive nature. She liked to win when she played games, but James had that male drive to conquer and didn't enjoy losing at all.

When she joined him in the sitting room, wearing the rose silk dress, with a deep pink silk flower holding one side of her hair back while the rest of it cascaded around her shoulders, his eyes were lit not with competitive fire but with a glow in their green depths which made her feel warm all over. She paused in the center of the room, and James crossed the distance between them to lay her white cashmere stole around her shoulders.

"You look very beautiful," he murmured, his voice husky as he draped the soft folds of white around her. Holding the shawl, he pulled her gently toward him and kissed her mouth, lightly at first, as if he'd intended only a brief caress, but then, as her lips quivered and softened, his arms came around her, crushing her against him as his mouth slanted over hers, hard, demanding, passionate. He was breathing raggedly when he released her, but Cassie knew that her own heartbeat was as rapid as his, her eyes as bright with desire.

"Damn!" he muttered, backing half a step away, still holding her right hand. "Why did we waste the afternoon on games?" He groaned the words, then raised her hand to his lips to press a kiss into her palm, his tongue flicking out to scorch the sensitive skin. Cassie swayed toward him, sharing his need, but a chiming from the mantel interrupted them rudely. James swore again and straightened, with a rueful grimace as he glanced at the insistent clock. "Eight o'clock and time we left." They moved toward the door. "Just don't forget that we have some unfinished business."

Cassie felt a throb of excitement at the promise in his eyes, but she only smiled and lowered her eyes demurely as she preceded him out the door. The rain had stopped as night fell, though the lowering sky and heavy, chill air promised more to come. They walked through a cold mist to the Fredericks' small house, really a bungalow in the same style as the inn, but Cassie was unaware of the cold, her whole being alive to James' presence beside her. She had an idea that the dinner they were going to might seem very long indeed.

They hadn't even reached the bungalow's front door when it was flung open, spilling a pool of golden light onto the flagstoned path. A tall, slim woman dressed in emerald green satin stood in the doorway, smiling and calling to them to hurry in out of the cold.

Janice Fredericks was around Cassie's age, twenty-nine or thirty, and stunningly lovely, with a fine-boned, naturally blonde beauty which spoke of exclusive boarding schools and "breeding." Cassie wasn't surprised to learn from the conversation later in the evening that Janice was a professional model, but she *was* surprised by the other woman's breezy, down-to-earth friendliness and utter lack of pretension. Tom Fredericks, pouring sangria as he stood at a liquor cabinet in the living room, was much the same height and size as James, tall, toughly built and lean, with closely cropped, frizzy-curly sandy hair and very pale gray eyes in a weathered, smiling face.

Despite her interest in meeting James' friends, Cassie had been surprised to feel a stab of nervousness when the tall, lovely Janice appeared in the doorway. Neither of the Fredericks gave her a chance to be ill at ease, though, welcoming her with the same warmth they showed James. By the time she was seated on a loveseat, with a glass of delicious sangria in her hand, she felt herself among friends.

"So, what have you been doing with yourself lately, Jim?" Tom leaned back on the sofa and grinned as Cassie looked up at James.

"Jim?"

"Old friends have privileges," he told her in a dry tone. "Nothing out of the ordinary," he replied to Tom. "Just re-shooting some scenes, writing that screenplay. That's about it."

"Except, of course, for squiring lovely lady doctors around town," Janice interjected. "Or is it 'mystery ladies'?"

"You read that thing?" Cassie laughed, and Janice nodded sheepishly.

"I always look at the headlines in the checkout, you know, and when I saw that one about James, I just had to get it."

"I know. I passed it on a newsstand, and I couldn't resist, either. I had to find out what they knew!"

"Not much. Just that James hadn't been in three or four particular restaurants for a few weeks. Big deal!" Janice rolled her eyes.

"You already knew those rags promise a lot more than they deliver," Tom pointed out. "But we have Jimmy here to give us the real scoop. Come on, Jim, tell us how you've been."

Together Tom and Janice drew James out about the work he'd been doing, both of them fascinated by the *New Life* screenplay and the unusual research he'd done for it. Cassie listened and sipped her wine, outwardly involved only in the conversation, while with every fiber of her being she felt James beside her.

They sat close together on the loveseat, James' arm lying along the back behind Cassie, his fingers resting lightly on her bare shoulder, moving now and then in an absent caress which sent thrills of excitement through her. His thigh pressed against hers, the warmth passing unimpeded through his slacks and the thin silk of her dress, any slight movement emphasizing his size and strength. She was conscious, too, of his scent, a subtle mix of spicy cologne, soap and the muskiness that was his alone, a powerfully erotic combination.

Cassie thought James was unaware of the tension she felt, but when he addressed a remark to her, turning to look down at her, she saw an intimate message in his eyes, a promise to be kept later, when they were alone. He leaned close to brush a kiss across her cheek and whispered, "I like your perfume; it does things to me," then turned back to the others to smoothly reply to a question of Tom's, while Cassie tried to calm her racing pulse and slow her quick, shallow breathing. A small, private smile lingered on her lips, though, because she had deliberately worn the perfume James had had created for her—the one with the hint of surgical scrub.

It was almost a relief to go into the dining room and take her seat at the table. Cassie didn't know how much more she could take of the near-torture of James' closeness and apparently casual touch; he was driving her insane, as he was all too aware. Cassie was torn between begging him to stop it until they were alone and fighting fire with fire, teasing him as he was teasing her.

They were seated facing each other across the table, and Cassie smiled meaningfully at James, leaning forward slightly and moistening her lower lip with the tip of her tongue. She nearly laughed aloud at his reaction. First he looked startled, shooting a glance at Janice and Tom as they emerged from the kitchen, dishes in hand, to see if they had noticed, then hungry, sexy, as he focused again on her moist lips, the swell of her breasts, emphasized as she leaned toward him, and finally rueful, as he met her gaze again and saw the teasing amusement there. She would pay for it later, Cassie knew, but the joke had been worth it, proving that James wasn't as unaffected as he seemed.

"I hope you're hungry." Janice smiled as she set a vast *paella* in the center of the table, flanking it with crusty bread and green salad, while Tom refilled their glasses with wine. "I think I may have gotten a bit carried away with the quantities of this."

"I'm starving," Cassie assured her, "and it looks marvelous." She breathed the savory fragrance appreciatively. "And it smells glorious!"

"Just as long as it tastes the way it's supposed to." Janice served them, then turned to Cassie as they began to eat. "I was fascinated to learn that you're a doctor. Has it been difficult for you, as a woman in a mostly-man's profession?"

"Not terribly difficult. There are always the bad jokes and the tasteless remarks, but when people realize that you're serious about your work, and that you don't intend to take advantage of your sex to get special treatment, it's no worse than it is for the men."

"Which, I gather, is pretty bad anyway."

"Well, it has its moments."

"And its hours," James put in dryly. "Very, very *long* hours!"

"Are the hours really as long as you hear?"

"Longer!" groaned Cassie and James in unison, and Cassie explained what her work week entailed. Between bites of delicious chicken, sausage, shrimp, mussels and saffron-flavored rice, colorful with peas, artichoke hearts and tomatoes, she told them about her twelve years of training, college, then medical school, then residency. She was warmed by their obviously sincere interest.

"So you'll be finished with your residency this summer," Tom said. "What then?"

"Then I go to work for my living." Cassie grinned. "And study for my Boards, of course, to get my certification. I'll practice as what's called a 'board eligible' or 'residency trained' obstetrician until I pass the Boards for my specialty, at which point I'll become 'board certified.' I always think," she added with a grin, "that that sounds like milk or something. *Certified.* As if I should have a seal of approval stamped on my forehead."

"When do you take these Boards?" Janice asked. "It is an exam, isn't it?"

"It certainly is an exam! It's given the week after Thanksgiving this year, so for me it'll be turkey and textbooks."

"It's such a tremendous amount of work. Did you always want to be a doctor, or was it something you decided when you were in college?"

"No, I wanted to be a doctor from the time I outgrew the desire to be a ballerina. That's how I ended up in LA, actually. There is no medical school in Wyoming, so when I applied to colleges, I applied to those which had medical schools, and I ended up at USC."

"Do you miss Wyoming?" Janice asked, and Cassie pondered the question thoughtfully for a moment.

"Not in the way you'd think. My parents were in their forties when I was born, and both died while I was in college. I'm nostalgic for the way I grew up, but most of my friends moved to larger towns, and I have no relatives in Wyoming, so there's not much to go back for. LA is really my home now, and I like it."

"You're not going to complain about smog and crime and traffic?"

"It's a big city; big cities have problems. Anyway, there are also beaches and the Hollywood Bowl and more things than I can name to do, and beautiful mountains and better weather than Wyoming."

"Yes, that could be a factor."

"You have to experience a Rocky Mountain winter to fully appreciate the luxury of *not* shoveling snow. If I want to see snow, I can just drive up to Big Bear, look at it and then come home. Delightful!"

"Isn't it! Tom's a native Californian—"

"A native Encino-ite," Tom interjected.

"Native Encino-ite, but after ten years here, my memories of Boston winters are still vivid!"

"No more snow shovels!" Cassie laughed.

"No more galoshes!" from James.

"No more mittens!" Janice contributed, and Tom raised his glass for a toast.

"To California." The others lifted their glasses, only to break into derisive hoots as he added, "After all, it produced me!"

"Oh, puh-leeze," Janice drawled, and rose. "On that note, I'll go get the flan. I think the shrimp have gone to his head."

"Or the wine," James pointed out. "That did occasionally happen to him in college, you know."

"I wasn't used to Cincinnati winters," said Tom, aggrieved. "And no one is really interested in boring old stories, are they?" As he and James began a humorous argument, Cassie joined Janice in clearing the table.

"You don't have to do this, you know," Janice pointed out when Cassie followed her into the kitchen with plates in her hands. "I don't want you to feel you have to work for your dinner."

"You'd rather I stayed in there and listened to an inane discussion of college peccadilloes?"

"Good point. There's a regrettable amount of college jokester left in those two." Janice stacked the plates and cutlery on a tray, then took a golden-topped caramel custard from the refrigerator.

"They're wonderful together, though. Half big, tough men, and half little boys."

"Men are all like that. Sometimes I think it's the little-boy half that makes us fall in love with them."

"I don't know." Cassie considered it. "It may be the strength, the ability and desire to protect us, that we need."

"I'm so glad James found you!" The fervency in Janice's voice startled Cassie. "You're so right for him—your own person, instead of another hanger-on. You're just the kind of wife for him, and he's needed someone like you for a long time. I think he's been lonely without even knowing he was, but now he seems different, more at peace."

"Janice, I'm not sure it's the way you think," Cassie said hastily, appalled that the other woman had drawn the conclusion that she and James were going to get married. Nothing could be farther from the truth! "I mean it's—"

"Oh, I've embarrassed you! I'm really sorry, but I get carried away sometimes. Don't worry." Janice grinned conspiratorially. "I won't say anything else dumb. Would you bring the dishes, please, and I'll take the flan?" Helplessly Cassie followed her into the dining room.

The situation wasn't improved by the glance she and James shared when she passed through the doorway. He looked up, laughing at what she suspected was a rather rowdy joke, and his face stilled at the sight of her. As Cassie paused, strangely breathless, she saw his eyes widen and darken with a message she couldn't mistake. An answering heat rose in her cheeks, and she smiled slightly, lowering her eyes to the tray she held as she set it carefully on the table. When she looked up she was dismayed to see indulgent smiles on the Fredericks' faces.

They were both convinced that she and James were on their way to the altar. They had correctly read that look, but had added their own interpretation to it, one which Cassie wished impotently she could correct. Obviously she couldn't dispute it without causing everyone a great deal of embarrassment, but knowing what James' friends were thinking kept her on edge while they ate the delicious flan and then took their coffee into the living room.

Though she managed to participate in the conversation, laughing in the right places and even making a witty comment now and then, when she and James at last took their leave she had no idea what topics had been discussed. She waved and called good-bye, but when they were out of sight Cassie pulled the soft folds of her shawl more closely around her shoulders and, head down against the chill fog, hurried toward the inn.

"Slow down," James cautioned, slipping his hand under her elbow. "You'll break your leg on these stones."

"Yes, I'll be careful." Cassie slowed her steps to a more decorous pace, but stiffened when James touched her, still on edge.

"Is something wrong?" James frowned at her, unable to read her expression in the darkness.

Cassie shook her head. "No, there's nothing wrong. It's just kind of cold, with the fog." Her explanation was pitifully weak, but James appeared to accept it.

"We'll get you inside, where it's warm, then. Come on." He put an arm around her waist and quickened their pace, half-carrying her along beside him. There was a fire crackling in the hearth of their sitting room, coffee in an insulated pot, with chocolates and rich cookies on the tray, and through the open door Cassie could see that the bed had been turned back invitingly. James walked in, looking around himself appreciatively, then smiled down at her. "A nice welcome back, isn't it?"

"It's lovely." Cassie smiled, feeling herself beginning to relax now that they were alone again. "So warm."

"Warm enough to take this off?" He helped her out of the shawl and poured coffee, handing her a cup, along with a mint cream and a piece of shortbread.

"Candy and shortbread after that wonderful dinner?" She leaned back against the sofa cushions, slipping off her high, strappy sandals and tucking her feet beneath her. "I'll get back to work too fat to fit into my clothes." She bit into the delicate shortbread, daintily removing stray crumbs from her lips with the tip of her tongue. "But I don't care. This is too delicious to miss."

James laughed at her smug expression. "You look like a well-fed, self-satisfied cat, you know."

"Do I? I feel like one, warm and comfortable, as if I could stretch the way a cat does—one bone at a time."

"If you do," James slid closer and his voice dropped, "I want to help." He set her cup aside.

"Oh, really?" Cassie looked up at him, a slanting, consciously provocative glance. "How would you help?"

"Mmm, I could get this out of your way," one of the narrow ribbon straps slid off her shoulder, "and this," the other strap followed, "and this. . . ." He kissed her shoulder, then the curve of her neck and the little hollow at the base of her throat, teasing and tasting as Cassie melted into his arms, her previous edginess forgotten, swept away by an overwhelming surge of need and desire and longing and love.

It no longer mattered what anyone else thought; there were only the two of them now, and what they shared. As James eased down the zipper at the back of her dress, Cassie was busy with his tie and shirt buttons, as eager for the touch and taste of him as he was for her, for the magic they would share. When he gathered her in his arms to carry her to the bedroom she clung to him, winding one arm around his neck while she nibbled the angle of his jaw and slipped her free hand inside his shirt to caress the broad plane of his chest.

"Cassie, stop it," he groaned. "You're driving me crazy."

"Mmm, I know." She reached up to softly nip his earlobe. "I want *you* to drive *me* crazy," she whispered, and he growled low in his throat, his arms tightening around her.

"I want to love you." He kicked the bedroom door closed behind them. "Just to love you."

And he did.

# Chapter Eleven

There." Cassie set her small suitcase by the door. "I think I got everything back in there, but it seems heavier this time." She looked around her, at the warm, firelit sitting room, the bedroom they had shared, at the window, where driving rain and a dark sky made it seem later than three o'clock on a Sunday afternoon. "I know it's time to get back to the real world," she sighed, "but it's so lovely here that I hate to leave."

"We don't have to leave right this minute." James patted the sofa cushion beside him. "Come and sit down; I want to talk to you."

"Oh, okay." Puzzled by the gravity of his manner, Cassie complied, and he took her hands in his, studying them for a moment before raising his eyes to hers.

"I'm very glad you're staying in LA." Cassie waited for him to elaborate. "I hadn't thought about the fact that your residency will be over so soon; if you mentioned it, the fact that you can only become Chief Resident in your final year never penetrated. It's not very intelligent of me, but I think I imagined you working at LA General indefinitely, and when I realized that you'll be done in only three months I was shaken, and even a little bit scared."

"But why on earth? I'd have thought you'd be happy for me, happy that I've almost finished."

"Ordinarily I would be, of course, and I am, but I was afraid of what would happen after that. It wasn't unreasonable to imagine you might intend to go back to Wyoming and practice there. You never told me the things you told Janice and Tom last night, about how much you like Los Angeles.'' There was a faintly aggrieved note in his voice, which Cassie didn't really think was justified.

"You never asked," she pointed out reasonably. "But if you had, I'd have told you the same thing. I like Los Angeles; I can do useful work here, and I'm planning to stay."

"I'm glad," he said again, and, while flattered, Cassie still didn't understand his portentous tone. "I'm glad, because it makes it easier to ask you this." Ask me what? her eyes queried, and he gave an almost imperceptible nod.

"Cassie, I want you to marry me. Will you?"

Cold washed over her; she was suddenly so cold that it seemed she must be made of ice, frozen to the very core of her being. This couldn't possibly be happening; her shocked and astonished mind simply refused to accept it. No, he couldn't possibly be serious. She shook her head slowly and told him so.

"You can't be serious, James. You *can't* be!"

"Why not?" He grinned. "There's no law against it. And just to show you how serious I am, this is for you."

Speechless with horror, Cassie watched him reach into his pocket and withdraw a small velvet box, watched him open it and hold it out to her, the solitaire diamond inside winking balefully up at her. Though it wasn't ostentatiously large, the emerald-cut stone in its elegantly simple setting looked huge to Cassie, huge and foreign and terrifying in its obvious purpose.

"James, no," she said again, recoiling from the engagement ring. "This is impossible. You can't . . ." She shook her head in a quick, almost panicky movement. "It's impossible!"

"Of course it's not impossible. You're single, I'm single, and I want you to marry me. No problem."

"James, *listen* to me!" His smile began to fade as the desperation in her voice and her face got through to him. "This," she waved a hand at their surroundings, "us, this weekend, has been fantastic; it's been perfect. We can have a relationship this way, just the two of us, with no one else involved.”

“But why, when we could be married? You’d rather be known as the mistress of an actor than his wife?”

“I’d rather not be known at all! As your . . . your lover, or your mistress, if you like.” She reddened, stumbling over the term. “I don’t have to be known as anything! I can be me, my own person with my own career, which we both know is very demanding, and my own identity. Married to you, I’d be a public figure, my identity, my *self*, swallowed up in your celebrity.”

“That’s nonsense!” James burst out. “And you know it! Cassie,” he went on more quietly, “I want you to be my wife.” He reached for her left hand, to slip the ring onto her finger, but she snatched her hand away.

“No!” She stood and jerkily walked several steps away. “James, please don’t do this!”

“Why?” James was beginning to believe her; she could see the dawning comprehension in his face, but he still thought he could change her mind. “Why won’t you marry me, Cassie? I’m a good catch, or so they tell me. Successful, not too terribly old, I can support you comfortably.”

“I can’t believe this!” Cassie glared at him, outraged by what she saw as an insult. “I can’t believe you’d think I would marry you for your money, or . . . or for reflected success! I can support myself just fine, thank you very much, and I’ll make my *own* success!”

“Then why?” James barked, coming to stand before her, and they glared at each other.

“Because of what *you* are and what *I* am. Look at you . . . look at me. Look at your house, beachfront property in Orange County. Look at mine, on an ordinary street in Burbank. Look at your car . . . no, cars.” She smiled with a touch of bitterness. “A Mercedes and a Rolls, and my five-year-old Toyota. Look at your work, your life, and then look at mine. Think about it, James; those are two different worlds we live in. I can’t marry you.”

"Can't," he asked slowly, "or won't?"

"Take your pick!" was her quick retort, and James drew an angry breath which hissed between his teeth.

"It may have escaped your notice, but we've been very successfully blending those two worlds for quite some weeks now. Why should marriage make that suddenly impossible?"

"Because marriage is official! Because when you get married people find out about it!"

"Well, what do you expect? Am I supposed to hide you away as if I'm ashamed of you? I *want* people to know how I feel about you. I love you, Cassie, and I'm not ashamed of it."

"We were thrown together by chance, James. In the normal course of events we wouldn't have met in a million years! We've become very fond of each other, and—"

"*Fond* of each other?" James snorted derisively. "I *love* you, Cassie. I went past 'fond of' a long, long time ago!"

"Okay, but marriage is different. I like what we've got between us now, but—"

"Do you love me?" James' question brought her up short.

"Do I—?"

"Do you love me?" He insisted on an answer.

"I . . . yes, I love you."

"You do?"

She flushed slightly, but answered honestly. "Yes. Yes, I do."

James gave her a long, level stare, then nodded, grim-faced. "But not enough to marry me," he said flatly.

"Marriage and loving you are two entirely different issues!"

"Not ordinarily, they aren't. People meet, fall in love, get married. One-two-three."

"People meet and fall in love, but you can't be so naïve as to include marriage as a mandatory third step, especially not in a town where women sue for palimony with monotonous regularity."

"Cassie, be reasonable. I don't want a 'pal,' I want a wife. You."

"James, I want to love you, but I don't want to be swallowed up by the juggernaut of your life and work."

"That's ridiculous!"

"Oh, right, descend to slinging insults! I can see that this is going to be a reasonable discussion." Cassie turned away, only to be jerked roughly back. James hauled her around to face him, his fingers biting into the soft flesh of her upper arms. His face was thunderous, and Cassie felt a tremor of fear at his anger and greater strength. It must have shown in her face, because James grimaced and released her.

"You're right, there's no point in name-calling." He shrugged helplessly. "I lost my temper; I'm sorry."

"I know; it's okay. You have a temper like mine—awful." Cassie managed a weak smile, and James laid his hands on her shoulders again, gently this time, and drew her close.

"I do love you, Cassandra," he said softly, and kissed her with a tender, deliberate thoroughness. She couldn't resist his tenderness and clung to him, trying with her kiss to tell him how much she loved him in return. She didn't want to hurt James, and she did love him, but she couldn't marry him. He would understand, eventually; she'd make him understand. Slowly he broke the kiss, touched her lips lightly with his fingertips, then straightened, letting his breath out in a sigh. "I guess," he said at last, "that it's time to go."

"I almost hate to leave." Cassie looked wistfully around her. "It's so beautiful here. This has been wonderful, James. Thank you for bringing me." He kissed her upturned lips, a quick, hard kiss.

"I wanted you to come." He took their jackets from the closet and held hers out as she slipped her arms into it. "I wanted you with me."

Cassie felt warm all over from the warmth in his eyes and smiled happily. James was wonderful to be so understanding, to see her point of view and accept it. She was lucky to love him.

"Cassie?"

"Mm-hmm?"

"I know that I took you by surprise with this proposal, and I'm sorry. I'll give you time to think it over."

The warmth faded away. "What do you mean, 'give me time'?"

"I'll give you time to think over my proposal. Time to get used to the idea."

"There's *nothing* to think over."

Cassie spoke the words very distinctly, but James only shook his head in mild amusement at her recalcitrance and carried their suitcases to the door. His hand was on the knob when she caught his sleeve and jerked it away.

"What are—?"

"James, *listen* to me!" He turned, anger growing in his face again as she went on. "I'm not thinking about anything, James. I already told you how I feel. That's that."

"Don't make a snap decision. You'll regret it later."

Cassie stood toe-to-toe with him, glaring up into his thunderous face. "Watch my lips, James. This is not a whim. I don't need time to think about this, because there . . . is . . . nothing . . . to . . . think . . . about! And that's final!" She jerked open the door and stalked out.

The engine sputtered and died in her driveway, leaving a deafening silence. Neither of them had spoken since they left the inn, staring stonily out the windows throughout the drive back to Burbank. James carefully removed his key from the ignition and sat back in his seat.

"I forgot to ask," he said stiffly, "but do you need anything from the supermarket? I can run you back to the store if you're out of milk or anything."

"No," Cassie replied to the hands she held folded in her lap, "I don't need anything."

He nodded and slid out of the car, and they walked, silent again, to the front door and inside. "I'll check the house," he said, telling rather than asking, and Cassie waited by the door as he turned on lights and looked into rooms to make certain nothing had been disturbed. "Everything looks okay."

"Thank you," Cassie said stiffly. They stood facing each other in uneasy silence, until both spoke at once.

"I'd better go," James said, as she began to thank him for the weekend, and they fell silent simultaneously.

Cassie shrugged and spoke first. "Thank you for the weekend, James. The inn is lovely, and so are Tom and Janice. It was wonderful."

"All except the ending?" he asked sardonically. "Never mind, you haven't done the expected in all the time I've known you; there's no reason to start now."

"James—" she began to protest, but he turned away.

"Oh, good night, Cassie." His tone reflected his exasperation. "I'll call you." He took two quick strides away from her, then paused, head down and shoulders hunched, before wheeling around. In only one long pace he returned to her, caught her in a rough embrace and kissed her. It wasn't the tender kiss she loved, but bruising, angry, punishing, taken for his own pleasure with no care for hers. In a strange way his strong emotion was exciting, though, the depth of his anger parallel to the depth of his caring, and after her first instinctive withdrawal she found herself responding in kind, returning his kiss with a fierce demand of her own.

When they moved apart at last they were both breathing raggedly, and James leaned heavily on the doorpost for a moment, then wiped a hand over his face and straightened. "Good night, Cassie," he said again, without expression, and this time he did go, leaving her standing in the doorway, watching his taillights disappear down the street.

Obviously nothing at all had been settled, and obviously James still intended to "give her time" to come around to his point of view. She frowned at the corner around which he'd vanished, stepped back into the house and closed the door. James seemed fond of "giving her time" to change her mind. He'd given her time to get to know him, with that month he'd stipulated at Disneyland, and he'd gotten his way in the end. She had come to know him, to rely on him, to love him, and when he gave her his ultimatum, asked her to go to Santa Barbara, she had agreed.

No doubt he fully expected the same thing to happen this time, she thought, annoyed by his self-confidence. He couldn't know it, but if she'd been aware that he intended to propose marriage to her, she never would have gone with him. He also couldn't know that this time his strategy would fail.

Against her will she had worked with him at the hospital, had continued to see him, had fallen in love with him, had finally pushed aside her qualms and misgivings and become his lover, and she liked things the way they were. Looking back at her fears and her indecision, she had no idea why she had waited so long to love James. It seemed so right, as if they belonged together, and the weekend had been almost a honeymoon. Almost. She wanted to love James, but Cassie did not intend to make the mistake of marrying him and giving up an identity of her own.

She wondered what he meant by "giving her time" this time, how he would try to persuade her to marry him. Cassie flicked off the living room lights and smiled into the darkness. Whatever his tactics, they were sure to be interesting.

His tactics weren't just interesting, they were amusing, entertaining, highly diverting. He didn't pressure her or even mention his proposal for several days; instead he courted her with gifts. They weren't expensive gifts, but charming; a funny mug reminiscent of their day at Disneyland, a bunch of daisies in a brightly-painted vase from an Olvera Street Mexican market, a gaudy plastic key-chain in the shape of the initial C. Every day there was another gift, waiting for her on her desk, or delivered by messenger, or even, in the case of a massive, succulent Persian melon, waiting on her patio when she carried her morning coffee outside.

She laughingly thanked James for each new surprise when she saw him or they spoke on the telephone, and finally asked why he didn't present them in person.

"Too banal," he laughed, and took another bite of the melon they were having with prosciutto as a first course while two thick steaks sizzled on his barbeque grill behind them. "I don't ever want to bore you, Cassie, and I don't want you to think I'm trying to pressure you unfairly." He pushed his melon rind away and leaned back, fixing her with his penetrating green gaze. "However, now that the subject of pressure has come up, I'll ask you again. Will you marry me, Cassie?"

The silence seemed to stretch out endlessly, broken only by the hiss and sputter of the meat on the grill, until Cassie finally looked up, directly into James' eyes. She shook her head sadly. "No, James. You know that, and you know my reasons."

He held her gaze for another long moment, then nodded slowly. "I think the steaks are done." He went to check, and when they resumed their meal the topic was not raised again. Cassie was happy just to be with James, for in the week since they had returned to Los Angeles their meetings had been all too brief. Now it was Saturday evening, and after working all day at the hospital Cassie had driven down to spend the evening with him in Sunset Beach. When the meal was over they returned, by unspoken consent, to the living room, and Cassie sank onto the comfortable couch while James put a tape in the stereo and quiet music filled the room.

A heady excitement began to creep through her veins. She wanted James to make love to her, wanted it badly, and he was setting the scene, with soft music, the privacy of this room, the two of them alone together. She'd been waiting for this, for him, all week, and when he came to sit beside her, she snuggled happily into the curve of his arm.

She kissed him eagerly, turning her body to fit against his, winding her arms around his neck, revelling in the feel and strength and scent and taste of him, and in the anticipation of what was to come. A coil of tension deep inside her was winding tighter and tighter, her need growing as he carefully eased off the sweater she wore and pressed her back onto the cushions, lying half above her as they loved each other.

When his hands and lips stilled, when he moved away, her first thought was that he intended to take her up to his bedroom. She sat up, close beside him on the couch.

"James, do you want to go upstairs?"

"No." The terse answer was almost shocking, and Cassie recoiled slightly.

"But, James. . . ."

"No," he said quietly, not angry, but firm. "We're not going upstairs, and we're not going to make love."

Cassie could only stare blankly at him as the heat of passion ebbed away. "Not . . . make love?"

"No."

A horrible thought came to her.

"Then it was all just a way to get me to bed? And you did that, and now you don't want me anymore?" Her voice was rising toward hysteria, and she became suddenly aware of her near-nudity. Frantically she scrambled for her sweater and jerked it roughly over her head. "My God, you must be the most despicable, disgusting—"

"*Stop it!*" His angry bellow cut her off. "That's not it at all, and I *do* want you!"

"Then why?"

"Because I want you on my terms . . . I want to marry you." Cassie slowly relaxed and sat back, looking at James as if she were certain he'd lost his mind. "No, I'm not crazy. As a matter of fact, I had some doubts about you."

"What?"

"Not that you were crazy, but just that you don't seem to know what you want."

"I know perfectly—"

"For instance, when you were so upset about our making love that first time, having been a virgin, I thought you were waiting until you married, and when you came to the inn with me, I thought I knew how you felt. I thought if you loved me, you'd be happy to marry me, but you threw that back in my face. Now I know what *I* want, which is to have you as my wife, but you don't seem to know what you want."

"I *said* I—"

He cut her off as if she hadn't spoken. "You made the rules last time, so I'm making them this time. We won't make love until we're married."

Cassie stared incredulously at him. "You're bananas, you know that?"

"Not at all, but I do know what I want."

"So do I. I want to love you, to make love with you."

"Not until we're married." His expression held nothing so crass as smugness, but there was a certain calm assurance there that set her teeth on edge.

"You know what this is, don't you? It's blackmail."

"I prefer to think of it as incentive."

"My God, you're conceited!" Cassie was losing the tenuous grip she had on her temper, but James stayed calm.

"No, I'm not, but I'm in love with you, Cassie. If you love me the same way, eventually we'll agree."

"Even though you're trying to manipulate me into agreement? That's hardly fair."

"Fair doesn't matter in this. I'll use whatever means I have at my disposal, including manipulation." He was infuriatingly calm, even smiling slightly as he said, "And I'll win in the end."

"We'll see about that!" Cassie snapped.

"Yes, we'll see. We'll see each other in church." As usual, James had the last word.

After that, whenever they met, or even spoke on the telephone, James asked her to marry him, and whenever he asked, Cassie refused. Sometimes he simply listened to her negative reply and changed the subject, but sometimes they argued, and it was one of these arguments which brought matters to a head late in April. James lay back on the chaise longue on Cassie's patio, watching the sun filtering through the orange tree's leaves and toying with a glass of iced tea. They had just finished lunch, and Cassie, pleasantly relaxed, was slouched comfortably in a chair, watching James watch the tree.

"Will you marry me, Cassie?"

"No, James, I won't." She said it as part of their ongoing game, lightly, with a half-smile.

"Would you at least do me the courtesy of taking this seriously?" James' voice was heavily sarcastic, his face frankly angry as he sat up to look across at her. "Because I guarantee you, Cassie, it's serious to me!"

"It's serious to me, too, James." Cassie half smiled, trying to tease him out of his anger. "You know I want to love you, if—"

"I'm not so sure about that!" he snapped, interrupting her rudely. "I'm not sure at all." He rose and paced to the edge of the patio, then swung around to confront her. "You *said* you wanted to love me in the fullest sense, but I don't buy it anymore."

"What do you mean, you don't buy it?" Cassie sat up very straight, her own temper rising at his deliberately scathing tone.

"I mean I don't buy it! You said you wanted to love me, but it was a lie! You want to sleep with me, but you won't commit yourself to anything more than that. You won't take the leap of faith it requires to tie your life to another person's."

"It takes more than a leap of faith to tie two lives together. It takes some kind of common ground, too."

"I thought we had that between us. I thought we shared a lot of common ground. Why are you so hung up on externals, anyway? I thought we shared more than superficial ties!"

"You were wrong, then, weren't you?" Cassie snapped, pushing herself out of her chair and stalking agitatedly across the patio. "Maybe there's nothing between us at all! You're a movie star, and I'm a doctor; you're wealthy and I'm anything but; you're world-famous, and I'm not and don't want to be." She shook her head and looked down at the grass, shoulders slumped. "Our lives and our life-styles are so different," she said sadly. "Too different for us to ever build a lasting relationship. You're like a shooting star, James, flashing across the night sky. It's beautiful, exciting, but it's too far away to touch or catch, and it's gone as quickly as it comes, leaving nothing but a memory." She turned to face him, a mute appeal for understanding in her eyes.

"You would be my lover, though, wouldn't you? If I let you?" Cassie met his gaze steadily, but her cheeks reddened in a silent affirmative. "Damn!" James struck his palm with his closed fist. "You don't want love, Cassie, all you want is sex! And if that's all you want, then I'm not for sale!"

"James, that's not what I meant!"

"Isn't it?" His tone was openly insulting. "Isn't it? I'll get out of your life, Cassie, just like you wanted me to that first night at the hospital. I was a fool to try so hard to win your confidence, wasn't I? I guess I was a fool ever to let myself become involved with a little coward like you!"

He stood glaring down at her for a moment, then backed a step away. "Good-bye, Cassie. Maybe you'll find that nice, safe, boring niche you seem to want." He swung around and was gone, walking out of her backyard and, it appeared, out of her life.

He didn't mean it, of course; he couldn't mean it, she told herself. He would change his mind; sooner or later he would change his mind. Her shocked brain refused to accept the idea of a future without James, and as she gathered their lunch dishes to carry them inside, she tried to persuade herself that he didn't mean what he had said, that he would give in. Somewhere, deep inside, she knew the truth, though: that James didn't say things he didn't mean.

The day stretched endlessly before her, empty without James to help her fill it. That made her angry, because she had spent many Saturdays happily alone before she met James; surely she could occupy herself now. Laundry, shopping and a great deal of unnecessary house cleaning served to pass the hours until she could reasonably go to bed, but then there was nothing she could do to stop her thoughts. Over and over she heard James' words, reverberating in her brain, and the phrase which returned with increasing frequency was "a little coward like you."

Coward. The accusation cut deep, for Cassie had certainly never considered herself a coward. She had made her way in a difficult and demanding profession, had done a good job in what was considered a man's field. How could he call her a coward? How *dare* he call her a coward? She was growing angry, and she nurtured that anger, for it was more comfortable than the sense of loss she had felt before.

When Cassie returned to the hospital on Monday she was still convinced that she had made the right decision, but James' hurtful accusations couldn't be dismissed from her mind as easily as she would have liked. Absorbed in her thoughts, she didn't notice the big, blond man standing in the hall outside the Clinic examining rooms.

"Hi, Cassie."

She wheeled around and smiled at Steve Anderson, surprised to see him. "Oh, hi, Steve! I didn't see you there; I'm sorry."

"That's okay." Gail's husband grinned. "You looked like you had a lot on your mind."

Cassie shrugged off her preoccupation. "I'm still sorry I ignored you. Are you here to see Gail?"

"Not exactly. I'm here *with* Gail. She's seeing Dr. Thompson."

"She is?" Cassie hardly dared to hope, but Dr. Thompson was the infertility specialist she had recommended to Gail weeks ago. "Is she having a workup done?"

"Mm-hm." Steve grinned, a fellow conspirator.

"Well, when did she decide to do it? And how did you convince her?"

"I didn't convince her to have the workup done." Steve smiled again. "I just convinced her that it's her I love, not whether or not she can have a baby. She decided the rest for herself."

"Oh, Steve, that's wonderful!" Cassie reached up to quickly kiss his cheek. "Have you been here long?"

"Not too long today, but this is her third appointment."

"Really? She's never said a word to me about it."

"I don't think she wanted to talk about it until it was all over, but this should be the last visit. The news will either be good or bad, but at least it will be news." Beneath his smile and easy manner, Cassie could see the strain of waiting and wondering, and she felt a surge of sympathy.

"Do you want some coffee, or maybe breakfast? The cafeteria's open."

"I'm fine, but thanks for the offer. I want to be here when Gail's done, anyway."

"Okay. Well, good luck!" She held up crossed fingers and grinned as she walked away, though the grin faded when she was out of Steve's sight. She fervently hoped that whatever Gail's problem was, it would turn out to be something readily correctable. There were many things that could be done for infertility, but there were still some problems that couldn't be solved.

She smiled grimly to herself. There were always problems which couldn't be solved; she and James could attest to that. Of course she was certain he would eventually understand her reservations, understand why she couldn't marry him, but it might be a long time before he returned to her. It might be never, a little voice pointed out; James was not in the habit of saying things he didn't mean, and he'd said a very definite good-bye.

Determinedly she pushed the unpalatable thought aside, unwilling to believe that James had taken himself out of her life permanently. Nevertheless, it was a very long day, and Cassie felt strangely abandoned and lost. With no visit or telephone call from James, and the evening looming emptily ahead of her, she even felt disinclined to leave for home, and at six o'clock was still at the nurses' station, dictating discharge notes.

"I'm impressed," Grace drawled, looking down at Cassie's

head bent industriously over her work. "They aren't going to believe it in Medical Records when they get all these tapes to transcribe. How far behind were you, anyway?"

"The oldest one was . . . let's see, just over three weeks." Cassie flipped through the stack of folders. "And I am now up to six days."

"It's no wonder you get all those nasty messages telling you to complete your records, considering that discharge summaries are supposed to be done within forty-eight hours. Is this unexpected fit of industry in response to one of the Records Department's more pointed reminders?"

"If you mean did they tell me to shape up, or else, no. I still get the routine threats and accusations. I just decided to use my free time this evening and get caught up, that's all." Cassie could feel Grace's assessing gaze on her and shifted her shoulders uneasily. Grace had long since figured out what was going on between Cassie and James, and though she had scrupulously kept their secret, she was interested and concerned, and far too astute for Cassie's peace of mind.

"No date with James tonight?" Grace asked when they were alone.

"No." Cassie's terse reply didn't invite further comment. Grace shrugged after a moment and returned to her desk, but Cassie was aware of the speculative glances that were sent her way as she doggedly read one summary after another into the tape recorder. They really wouldn't believe it in Medical Records, she didn't quite believe it herself, but even a dictation marathon was preferable to the long, lonely evening she faced at home.

"Cassie, what on earth are you doing here so late?"

"Discharge summaries, and I could ask you the same," she replied to Gail's surprised query. "Aren't you supposed to be off duty at five?"

"The Head Nurse's work is never done," Gail quipped. "I had a couple of things to stick around for, anyway, but you surprise me. Discharge summaries? They'll—"

"—never believe it in Medical Records," Cassie finished

the sentence in chorus with her friend. "So I've been told." She tipped her head to the side, studying Gail's face for a moment, seeing a glow there which had been missing for too long. Gail's cheeks were flushed, her eyes sparkled with excitement, and she clasped her hands together as if she were holding herself in check.

"Cassie, can you come into the office when you have a minute? I'd like to talk to you."

"I can come now." She flicked off the tape recorder. "I'm only one day behind now, and I don't want to overdo it. If I catch up they might expect me to stay that way." She followed Gail into the office and closed the door. Now that they were alone, Gail hardly seemed to know where to start, so Cassie said, "Gail, I saw Steve in the Clinic today."

"You did? Then you know? . . ."

"I know you went to Dr. Thompson for a workup, and I'm *so* glad!"

"You don't know the half of it!" Gail stepped forward, eyes bright, a smile breaking through, and clasped Cassie's hands in hers. "He did the last of the tests today, and I've been waiting for the results, and he just called!"

"Well, *tell* me!"

"It's just my tubes, and he wants to do surgery next week, *and* he says it has an eighty percent chance of success!"

"That's *fantastic!*" Cassie shouted, and they flung their arms around each other, hopping up and down in delight. "Oh, Gail, that's wonderful. It's more than wonderful; it's . . . it's . . . Oh, I don't know what it is! It's super-wonderful!" She stood back, holding Gail at arm's length, grinning up at the taller woman. "When is the surgery scheduled?"

"It's scheduled for Monday, and—"

"Monday? That soon?"

"Yes, and he thinks he can correct it pretty easily."

"Terrific! Well, what, exactly did he say?"

They sat facing each other across the desk, and for a few minutes the air was thick with the Latin and Greek of medical terminology as Gail explained what Dr. Thompson planned. Finally they both sat back and grinned at each other.

"I feel a little silly." Gail reached up to touch her face. "But I can't seem to stop grinning like a nut."

"Don't try to stop; it suits you. I'm glad to see you happy again, and it's made you look terrific all over," Cassie teased. "You have cute little pink cheeks and everything!"

"What a disgusting image! Cute little pink cheeks? Yuck! I'm just glad . . . and nervous at the same time."

"About the surgery?"

"Yeah."

"I don't think you'd be normal if you weren't a little bit nervous, but you know as well as I do that the odds are all in your favor."

"Yeah," Gail said again, then added quietly, as if scarcely daring to hope, "and in a year or so, I could be having a baby." Her wide smile broke through again, and Cassie laughed softly.

"You're 'blooming' already, aren't you?"

"I feel like it, just because I feel so relieved to know what the situation is at last." They sat in silence for a moment. "What about you, Cassie? You don't look too great today. Do you have a cold or something?"

"No, I'm okay." Cassie did as well as she could at producing a convincing smile. "I'm just a little tired."

"More than a little, and more than tired, I'd say."

"Oh, you would, would you, Dr. Freud?"

"Yesss, I vould," Gail said, aping a German accent. "Is something wrong between you and James?"

Cassie stared at her friend blankly for a minute, then shrugged, resigned. "In another life you were a gypsy fortune-teller, right? Or was it just a mind-reader?"

"Nothing so exotic. Just a friend."

"Well, there's nothing wrong between James and me anymore," Cassie said tiredly, "because there's nothing between us at all. We said good-bye, or, rather, James said good-bye, and it appears that he meant it."

"Oh, Cassie, I'm sorry. Are you sure it's really over? Maybe he's just angry and he'll change his mind."

"I doubt it."

"It can't be all that bad, surely. What made him so angry, anyway?"

"Look, Gail, I don't mean to be rude, but do you mind if we don't get into it now?"

Gail looked at Cassie's closed, tense face, and nodded. "Of course I don't mind. Just remember, if you need someone to talk to, Auntie Gail is here."

"I know, and thank you."

"If you're not busy tonight, can you have dinner with Steve and me? I feel like you deserve to be part of the celebration, after all the times you gave me a talking-to."

"Thanks for asking, but I think this celebration is for you and Steve. Invite me to the baby shower, though, okay?"

"Consider yourself invited."

"I'd better get going, Gail. You and Steve have a lovely evening, won't you?"

"Okay," Gail promised. "I'll see you." Eyes troubled, she watched Cassie walk away, a small, strangely lonely figure in greens and a lab coat.

# Chapter Twelve

$\mathscr{P}$roviding moral support for Gail and coping with the pressure of her own work was all that kept Cassie going as the loneliness sank in. James had obviously meant what he said, for he'd taken himself completely out of her life, not calling, not communicating in any way since the night he'd hurled that word at her—coward—and walked away.

She'd have liked to deny that his absence left a void in her life, but the tedious evenings spent with only the banality of television re-runs, the dull cafeteria meals, the emptiness of her days, all made a mockery of her brave thoughts. She did her work, dealt with her patients, but she missed the spark James had brought to her days with his probing questions, his congratulations, his comfort when she needed it. She ate enough to maintain life, but food had no savor, and her diet of peanut-butter sandwiches and fast-food hamburgers left a lot to be desired. She hardly slept at all, having even lost the ability to fall asleep at will which had so amused James, and her nights were restless at best.

The only ray of brightness in the unrelieved gray of her life was Gail's surgery, which went with textbook smoothness. Cassie had waited with Steve outside the operating room, playing gin rummy for pennies until Dr. Thompson came out to give them the good news, and then he'd insisted on taking her to lunch at a local Chinese-Kosher delicatessen. Fong's was, as he pointed out, probably the only spot in the Western Hemisphere where one could have wonton soup and a pastrami on rye, and they toasted the success of the surgery with cream soda.

"I want to thank you, Cassie," Steve said as they walked back to the hospital, and she looked up at him in surprise.

"What for?"

"For talking to Gail, for having the courage to disagree with her and make her angry at you when you saw her hurting herself by her own attitude. She didn't say anything to me at the time, but later, when we talked about it, she said you'd really been blunt with her, and though she wasn't too happy about it at first—"

"*That's* an understatement!" Cassie rolled her eyes, and Steve laughed.

"Yes, well, later she realized that you'd made her think about her options, even when she didn't want to."

"I'm just glad she didn't decide she never wanted to talk to me again!"

"You know better than that, kiddo!" Steve draped an arm across her shoulders as they walked. "I wouldn't let her write off my unofficial little sister, now, would I?"

"You'd better not, unofficial big brother!" Cassie poked him playfully in the ribs, and they both laughed again as they paused across the street from the hospital, waiting for the traffic light to change. Cassie's gaze slid idly over the passing traffic until one car caught her eye and she froze. She stood with Steve's arm around her and watched James drive past, watched him watching her, his face hard and cold.

Somehow she managed to keep smiling, to reassure Gail, still fuzzy from the anesthetic, that all had gone well, managed not to betray her feelings, but inside she was screaming. James had never met Steve, didn't know he was an unofficial brother, husband of her best friend, and Cassie knew exactly what construction he had put on what he'd seen. The icy distaste in his face had told her very clearly.

Though she tried to force James from her mind by burying herself in her work, it wasn't easy to ignore the reminders of him all around her. Driving along the city streets she saw advertisements for his latest film; passing newsstands she saw his name in tabloid headlines; she heard speculation about him on the television entertainment news. Rumors were rampant and inescapable about him, rumors that he had become difficult to work with, temperamental, even unreliable. The scandal sheets, less inhibited by the constraints of journalistic ethics, ran luridly detailed accounts of his suddenly active and public social life, of glittering nights on the town with a series of starlets, and even dark hints of a drinking problem.

The man thus chronicled, even allowing for hyperbole and exaggeration, was so unlike the man Cassie had worked with, shared her thoughts with—loved—that Cassie didn't know what to believe. Whether this was the real James, the temperamental playboy, or whether it was the other James, the man she'd known, Cassie was no longer sure.

Had she ever really understood him, or understood herself? Her self-doubt grew along with her loneliness, as did the realization that she could not just command herself to stop loving him.

Love like this was new to her, frightening in a way, for she needed him the way she needed air to breathe. She needed to see him, to talk to him, to touch him. Bit by bit, as the days passed, and then the weeks, all the sensible reasons she had for refusing to accept him on his terms were being shown to be nonsense in the face of the strength of her love and longing for him.

Could she have made a terrible mistake? The idea seemed absurd at first, but grew stronger and stronger until it could not be dismissed. It was too late for her to change things, though. She couldn't just go to James without a rag of pride and beg him to take her back . . . could she?

"Sit down." Cassie obeyed Gail's curt command, dropping into the hard chair beside her office desk. "Here." Gail handed her a styrofoam cup of black coffee, then sat back and folded her arms. "Okay, what happened between you and

James, and what do you intend to do about it? And I'm not asking you to tell me; I'm *telling* you to tell me."

It was late May; over a month had passed since Gail's successful surgery, and she was completely recovered, both physically from the surgery, and emotionally from the depression and doubt which had plagued her. She was once again the Gail Cassie knew, quick-witted, funny and perceptive, sometimes a little too perceptive.

"Gail, there's really nothing to talk about."

"Don't pretend with me, Cassie. You look like you've had all of fifteen minutes of sleep in the last month, and you're too skinny, so why don't you tell me what went on between you and James, and why it's eating you up this way?"

Cassie hesitated for a long moment, trying to decide, glanced at Gail's face, noted the determination there and sighed in mixed relief and resignation. "Okay, you know how I felt when I found out James was going to observe." Giving in to her own need to talk, to sort out her feelings by putting them into words, she outlined for Gail all that had happened, her words pouring out faster as she remembered the hurt and the bitterness and the doubts. When she had finished she sat back, studying her hands, waiting for Gail to respond.

"Just exactly why," Gail asked after a thoughtful pause, "why did you refuse to marry James when you were, and are, in love with him?"

"Because if I married him I'd end up losing myself."

"Losing yourself?"

"My *self*." Cassie emphasized the single word. "I'm *me* right now; I have a difficult, demanding career, a job with George Hammett's group starting in July, a life of my own. If I married James I'd be the wife in the background, a pale shadow standing behind him, the object of pitying speculation every time he had a new co-star. Would my patients have faith in me as a competent obstetrician, or would the notoriety of being Mrs. James Reid get in the way? Would George appreciate a member of his group attracting that kind of media attention? And would James understand how important my work is—or would the demands of our conflicting careers come between us?" As she repeated her reasons aloud Cassie was aware that they were not nearly as compelling as she had once thought.

Gail was less diplomatic. For a moment she considered what Cassie had said, then snorted derisively. "You gave me some advice, advice that I didn't want to hear at the time, so I'm going to return the favor and give you some advice *you* may not want to hear."

"I'm not sure I like the sound of this."

"Chicken! Just sit there and listen, okay?"

"Yes, ma'am."

"Okay. If you let a man—not a movie star, but a *man*—like James Reid get away from you just because you're intimidated by his money or his fame, or because you're too proud to marry a wealthy man and take the chance that some uninformed gossip might say you married him for his money, if you let him slip away for those reasons, without trying to work out a compromise, then you're a fool!" She shoved her chair back and stood, leaning over the desk and scowling at Cassie.

"And as for that nonsense about your patients and George Hammett? For heaven's sake, Cassie, grow up! Women about to have babies don't care who you're married to; they just want you to take good care of them. And who was it who arranged for you and James to meet in the first place? George Hammett, that's who! Why on earth should George object to you and James marrying? It looks to me like he was matchmaking, anyway."

Gail sighed heavily and dropped back into her chair. "Cassie, if you let your pride get in the way of your happiness, and of James's, just because you're afraid of the problems which might arise, then he was right to call you a coward."

Coward. The word echoed and re-echoed in her mind that night as Cassie paced around her living room, agonizing over the action she was considering. She had made herself a meal, but like so many meals recently it had only been picked at, then returned to the kitchen for a decent burial, while she carried a cup of coffee into the living room, and sat down to think. She hadn't been able to sit for long; her internal restlessness seemed to demand some sort of outlet, so she was pacing, but eventually she began to get on her own nerves.

"Oh, sit *down!*" she said aloud after another circuit of the room. "Sit down and think about this." She dropped onto the sofa, curled her feet beneath her and picked up her cup, cradling it between her hands to capture its fading warmth.

Could she do it? Could she go to James with her heart in her hands and beg him for a chance to try again, to reconsider his proposal? What would he do? Could she bear it if he threw her capitulation back in her face as she deserved? It would be his right, but could she bear the humiliation?

And could she make it work, even if he agreed? When James had called her a coward he hadn't been referring to her professional side, she knew, and she had to wonder if perhaps he had more insight than she did. Cassie hadn't had a serious relationship with any man since her freshman year at college, and that had been little more than a teenage crush on both sides. It had ended by mutual consent as the school year ended and they went their separate ways. When they met again the following September he had a new girlfriend, Cassie had a heavy course load, and neither of them seemed to feel any nostalgic longing for what had been.

She had absorbed herself in a heavy pre-med schedule, then in medical school, and finally her residency, too busy, she told herself, for a romance. So there she was, twenty-nine, single by choice, and terrified that she was incapable of sustaining a long-term relationship. *No, let's be blunt, Cassandra. You're scared you don't have it in you to make a marriage work, and because you're scared you ran like a thief when James proposed. You really are a little coward, aren't you?*

And yet, was she willing to abandon her pride to the extent of begging James to take her back? Could she do that? She bent forward, elbows on knees and head in hands, struggling with herself, with her pride. Her pride. It meant a lot to her, that pride, that proud independence she had fought so hard to maintain. But why was it so important?

After long minutes of thought she straightened suddenly, an arrested expression on her face. What was the purpose that pride served? Was it no more than an issue to hide behind, a convenient concealment for her real fear of her own inadequacy? Was she so afraid of dipping a toe in the pool that she couldn't even be honest with herself?

Pride. What good was it? As far as she could figure out, the only thing her pride was doing for her right now was robbing her of the chance to be with the only man who would make her life complete. It was very late, her grip on calm, rational thought was less firm than usual, and Cassie berated herself fiercely. All the time she'd wasted, all the hurt she'd caused in the name of a meaningless, useless, destructive pride . . . *What kind of fool am I?* she asked herself.

She had no choice, she realized, no choice but to go to him, if she was to have any self-respect at all. She would see him and talk to him, and if he no longer wanted her, she would have to live with that rejection. The important thing was to put her empty pride aside and go to him.

With her decision made she was eager to implement it, but a glance at the mantel clock put paid to that idea. It was 3:30 A.M., and calling James at this hour was not the way to rebuild bridges. Somehow she would have to contain her impatience until morning, and she went to bed with her mind full of plans, fears and hopes.

Her plans were frustratingly difficult to put into action the next morning, though. There was no answer when she telephoned James' house as early as she dared, then twice more, until she was certain he was gone for the day. She then called his office, but the secretary who answered the telephone was infuriatingly unhelpful, not recognizing Cassie's name and refusing to reveal his whereabouts. Cassie muttered an unladylike epithet as she banged the receiver down. She hesitated a moment, then rapidly dialed another number.

"March," said a brusque male voice when she was put through to James' manager.

"Hello, Jonathon. This is Cassie Mills."

"Oh, yeah, the lady doctor. How ya' doing, kid?"

"I'm doing fine, Jonathon." She smiled at the phone. Jon's insistence on retaining the New York accents of his youth never failed to amuse her. "I have a little problem, though."

"Oh, yeah? What's that?"

"Well, I need to get in touch with James today, and I don't know where he is."

"He didn't tell you?" Jon's voice was more cagey, not so openly cheerful, and Cassie laughed in what she hoped was an easy manner.

"He probably did tell me, but you know how it is," she lied. "I didn't write it down, and now I can't seem to remember what—"

"What studio?" Jon supplied, and Cassie took quick advantage of that bit of information.

"Yes. I can't remember which studio he said. He's there today to—"

"To shoot that 'lost weekend' scene?"

"Yes, that's the one! If you could just tell me which studio he's at, I'd really be grateful. I'm just so absentminded sometimes. . . ." She let her voice trail off on what she considered a nauseatingly kittenish note, but it seemed to do the trick.

"No problem, sweetheart." Sweetheart? "He's at the studios on Warner and Olive in Burbank. I don't know which sound stage, but they can tell you that at the gate."

"That's great. Thank you, Jon; I really appreciate this. James will think I'm a little bit ditsy, but at least I'll be able to find him."

"I wouldn't worry about it, kid. Ditsy is kinda cute, ya' know?"

"Sure, Jon. Thanks again." She hung up, half amused, half disgusted with herself for using such tactics, but entirely satisfied with the end result. Not only did she know where James was working, but the studios weren't more than ten minutes from her house! It was unheard-of for Cassie to leave work early, but that day she did, thanking providence that the Labor and Delivery unit wasn't busy.

At home she changed into beige slacks and a short-sleeved cotton sweater in a shade of lipstick pink which always made her feel just a bit more brave, then drove directly to the studios without giving herself a chance to change her mind. The guard at the gate was willing to admit her when she said she was a doctor, and Cassie even stooped to using a rather spurious explanation of business with James to learn the location of the sound stage he was shooting on. Her principles were certainly going down the drain today, she thought, but it was all in a good cause.

She just hoped it would be a successful cause. Her determination, conviction and optimism were evaporating as she locked her car and walked across acres of parking lot simmering in the dazzling noon sun. The red light above the sound stage door wasn't lit, so she eased the heavy door open and slipped inside, pausing to lean against the wall while her eyes adjusted to the dimness after the brilliance outside.

She paused to collect herself, as well, because despite her conviction that she was doing the right thing, it was impossible for her to face the prospect of humiliation and rejection without qualms. She had to do this, she *had* to, but her hands were shaking, palms damp, and she swallowed hard before pushing herself away from the wall.

Blinking in the gloom, she picked her way carefully over the thick cables snaking across the concrete floor toward a small set in one corner of the vast stage. Overhead the ceiling was lost above gridwork thickly festooned with lights and the hanging apparatus for scenery and other equipment; the huge stage was artificially chilly, and the only well-lit spot was the set, where a tumult of activity was focused. A scene was apparently being set up, and Cassie hung back in the shadows, watching as reflectors, lights, cameras and microphones were moved and adjusted by a group which looked, to her unaccustomed eye, to be little more than an undirected mob.

She supposed a busy delivery or operating room seemed similarly out-of-control, but she was nonetheless surprised when the hubbub died down and the mob resolved itself into a crew. James appeared then, striding onto the set and taking his place without speaking. He waited impassively while lighting and sound levels were checked; then silence descended on the stage.

Cassie watched from her corner, scarcely daring to breathe, as the take was shot, riveted by James' performance. She had been told by Jon what sort of scene he'd be doing, but she hadn't anticipated the effect his talent would have on her, even with the distractions of cameras and crew. His poignant, wrenching soliloquy, spoken by a man struggling with his life, held her spellbound, enthralled by his transformation into that confused, tortured man. She blinked, startled, when the director shouted "Cut!" and returned her to reality.

James walked a few steps off the set, out of the glare of the lights, while the crew set up for a different camera angle, and as he left the brightly-lit circle he saw Cassie. She had stepped out of her secluded corner, and the movement caught his eye, bringing him sharply around to peer past the cameras at her. He froze for an instant, then waved away a makeup man who was pursuing him and walked across to her.

In makeup and costume, James was a stranger to her. Two day's growth of beard stubble had been emphasized with dark makeup, his face artificially sallowed and aged. There was glycerine on his forehead and upper lip, simulating perspiration, and his hair had been oiled and disarrayed. Even his eyes were a stranger's, red-rimmed with eye pencil, cold and indifferent as he looked down at her.

"What are you doing here?" he demanded without so much as a hello.

"I . . . I wanted to . . . to talk to you," Cassie stammered, her poise slipping badly in the face of his coldness. "I need to—"

"James!" she was interrupted by a peremptory bellow from the set. "We need you over here!"

"As you can see," James jerked his head toward the set, "I'm busy today."

"I can wait until you're finished," she offered, but he shook his head in a brusque negative.

"I'd rather you didn't." He swung away from her and strode back to the set.

Cassie stared at him in disbelief. She had been afraid that he would reject her once he had heard what she had to say; she hadn't anticipated his being unwilling even to hear her out. She looked across to the set, but James had already turned away as the makeup man dabbed more glycerine across his brow, uninterested in her presence. Well, now you know how he feels, she told herself.

A frozen numbness was seeping through her, and Cassie turned jerkily on her heel to hurry away, head down to avoid the further humiliation of tripping over something. She had nearly reached the door when she collided with someone and looked up in surprise at Marise Marshall.

"I'm terribly sorry," she apologized breathlessly. "I wasn't looking where I was going, Miss Marshall."

"Miss? . . ." Marise looked startled, then peered more closely at Cassie's face. "It is you, isn't it? James's doctor, Cassie?"

"Yes, that's right."

Marise's expression changed from surprise to recognition to a sort of wary antipathy Cassie thought she understood. "Well, well, Dr. Cassie. I didn't expect to see *you* here. Why did you come?"

"You don't have anything to worry about," Cassie said wearily. "I only came to talk to James, and he was too busy."

"After all you put him through, honey," Marise retorted tartly, "I'm not surprised he's 'busy.'"

"I suppose you're right." Cassie shrugged, that cold numbness preventing her from feeling, or showing, any emotion. "At any rate, it's you he'll want to see, you he wants, not me." It hurt to admit that, even through the numbness, but Cassie saw no apparent reason not to be honest. Marise only stared at her, though, and after a moment that fact penetrated Cassie's apathy.

"He wants me, you said?"

Cassie nodded.

"Well, that's news to me, honey, and to Harry, too." She held up her left hand, adorned with an enormous diamond, and Cassie frowned, perplexed.

"You mean you're? . . ."

"Harry and I are getting married next week." Marise smiled as she said the words, a smile of pure gladness, without the shading of artifice and calculation which seemed to color most of her remarks. "It's on Sunday, at Temple Beth-El, if you'd like to come." Her grin was one of girlish amusement. "Harry was real impressed with you, a lady doctor!"

"Well, thank you," Cassie said weakly, taken aback by the casually extended wedding invitation. "Uh . . . congratulations, and . . . and best wishes." Painfully aware of how awkward and gauche she sounded, Cassie turned to walk away, but Marise stopped her with a hand on her arm.

"Wait a minute." Cassie reluctantly obeyed. "Why don't you stay and talk to James when he's done with this scene? It can't take too much longer, and I'm sure he'll be glad to see you."

"No," Cassie replied dully, very cold again. "He doesn't want me to stay. He doesn't want me." She pulled free of Marise's hand and fled.

The wavelets washing around her feet were as icy as the wet sand, and her feet had long since been numbed by cold, but Cassie walked on, indifferent to the presence of others on the beach, fishermen, runners, an elderly woman filling a paper sack with bits of jetsam. She had no idea how far she'd walked, miles, probably, from the lot where she'd parked her car in Pacific Palisades. It had been early afternoon then; now it was sunset, and she watched the sand turn rosy orange in the fading glow as she retraced her steps.

Her emotions seemed locked away behind an unnatural calm, but her mind still worked, albeit slowly. She had realized, as she trudged along the sand, that she had lost James, completely and irreversibly, and had lost him entirely through her own callous stupidity. She had fallen in love, but she'd refused to be honest with herself about what that meant. She'd pretended that it was enough for them to be part-time lovers, hiding their relationship as if she were ashamed of it, never thinking how degrading a situation like that would be to both of them, but especially to James.

She had been unforgivably, unbelievably selfish—and cruel —in her disregard for James' feelings, never caring or even considering how badly he might be hurt by her panicky defense of her independence. James had said he loved her, and more than that, that he wanted to marry her. He had opened his heart to her, and she hadn't even been tactful, not to mention sensitive. She had reacted with horror, had thrown his offer back in his face in about as insulting a manner as could have been conceived.

The fact that she regretted it bitterly now was no consolation at all. The bitterest things in the world were probably regrets, and just about the most useless. Regrets wouldn't make James love her again; they couldn't turn time back and make things the way they had been. The only thing one could do with regrets was learn to live with them, somehow.

A chill fog was creeping in off the water and dusk was becoming night. Tiredly she slogged across the deep, shifting sand to the parking lot, dusted off her feet and climbed into her car to go home. It was odd to be so calm while knowing that pain and tears awaited her, but all Cassie felt when she swung her small car into the driveway was cold and tired and longing for a shower.

She didn't bother to pull into the garage, just parked in the driveway and hurried into the house, going first to her bedroom to peel off her clothes and drop them in an uncharacteristic heap on the floor, and then to the bathroom to sedate herself with hot water.

She stepped under the spray and leaned back against cool tile which quickly warmed as hot water beat on it, thinking of nothing at all until she realized, in momentary surprise, that tears were streaming down her cheeks. How long she stood in the shower and wept Cassie was never sure, but when she emerged she had no tears left to cry and her skin felt shriveled and pruney from moisture. Drained of emotion and enervated by the steamy heat, she blotted herself off, unwound her hair from the towel which had kept it at least somewhat dry and pulled on a thick terry robe.

A rush of steam followed her from the bathroom into the hall, but as it cleared she could detect another scent, the enticing aroma of fresh coffee. And that made no sense at all, because she hadn't made coffee when she came in. Puzzled, and a little bit apprehensive, she moved quietly down the hall and peered cautiously into the living room. What she saw there brought her around the corner and into the room, gaping in astonishment.

"It took you long enough to get out of that shower," James commented, pouring coffee from the pot on the low table before him. "Here's your coffee."

Cassie slowly crossed the room to take the proferred mug, noting the manner in which he had made himself at home. The coffee filter and kettle stood on the kitchen counter, his leather jacket was draped over a chair, and he had apparently been reading a magazine while he waited for her. She accepted the coffee mug, sat in an armchair which was at an angle to the sofa and James, and sipped gingerly at the scalding brew before speaking.

"How did you get in here?"

"Through the front door." He held up a key. "You never took this back." She had forgotten the key's existence, but James hadn't, and after all that had passed between them, he'd felt free to walk in, uninvited and most certainly unwanted.

She felt something begin to penetrate the emptiness inside her then. It was anger, but at least she was feeling something, and she welcomed it. "I'll take that back now," she snapped, holding out her hand for the key, which James dropped into her palm with a shake of his head and an infuriatingly complacent smile.

"Don't you want to know why I came here?"

"Not particularly." She was pleased with the cool steadiness of her voice. "I just want you to leave. Now," she added, in case he had missed the point.

"No." James' refusal was as calm and as firm as her statement had been, and Cassie looked full at him for the first time since she'd walked into the room, for the first time since they'd parted.

*He looks older.* The thought leaped unbidden to her mind, but that first impression was accurate. For the first time since she'd known him, James looked thirty-nine, the lines in his cheeks and brow more deeply carved than she'd seen them, his eyes shuttered, wary and tired. Then he smiled that irritating, bland smile, and her anger reasserted itself.

"Look, James, it's late, and I'm tired, and I don't feel like being sociable, so why don't you just go home?"

"Not just yet." He lounged back on the sofa, and his eyes changed, hardened. "This afternoon you said you wanted to talk. Let's talk."

"After this afternoon," Cassie said coldly, "I don't think we have anything to talk about. I don't recall inviting you here tonight, either, never mind offering you coffee, so will you please just leave?"

"No, I won't." James' voice was calm, his expression mocking. "You wanted to talk, so we're going to talk. And, just because I'm such a swell human being, I'll make it easier for you and ask the first question." He paused, and his voice was very cold as he said, "Why were you at the studio today?"

Cassie stood abruptly and moved away, her back to him. "It doesn't matter why I was there, not anymore."

"I think it does, and you're going to tell me."

"No, I'm not!" Cassie struggled to keep her voice level. "I'm not going to tell you anything, because there's nothing left to say."

She didn't hear him move, but when he spoke it was from just behind her. "Are you sure you won't tell me?" Cassie edged slightly away from him, shaking her head, but she was grabbed and spun roughly around to face him. "If that's the way you want it . . ." he growled, and took her mouth in a hard, almost desperate kiss.

In the first moments she resisted him, struggling against his superior strength, but his arms were bands of steel around her, crushing her against his body. She could feel every bone and sinew and taut muscle of him as his mouth forced hers, leaving her helpless to fight him. And then she no longer wanted to fight him.

Her emotions were as highly wrought as James', perhaps more so; she had wanted, needed, his touch for so long, and now she was in his arms, the scent of his skin in her nostrils, the taste of him on her lips, and she clung to him with a furious intensity. Feverish with passion, they kissed and caressed, and then James startled Cassie by leaning backward with her clasped in his arms and falling onto the couch.

She hadn't caught her breath when James moved again, turning them both, pressing her into the sofa cushions as he half covered her with his body. She arched upward against him, her hands moving over his back, exploring muscles which tensed at her touch, then slipping up to caress his neck and twist into the thick waves of his hair as he pushed her robe off her shoulders and found her breasts with his seeking mouth. A little whimper of pleasure escaped her when he captured one taut nipple, tugging gently, sending waves of delight through her. Cassie groped for the buttons of his shirt and felt the rough denim of his jeans rasp erotically against her thigh as he moved slightly to help her. She quickly opened the shirt, sliding her hands over his chest and then around to his back to cling to him as he kissed her mouth again.

It was only when he sat up to shrug out of his shirt and his hands went to the buckle of his belt that the cold breath of sanity returned to blow away the fever gripping her, and Cassie realized what she was doing.

"Oh, no," she moaned, and scrambled away from James, struggling to pull her robe on. He reached for her again and she struck his hands away. "No!" Her voice was sharp, near hysteria. "No, I won't . . . I can't do this!"

James sat back very slowly, watching her, his eyes cold and blank. "You were happy enough to 'do this' before," he reminded her, and Cassie flinched from the icy fury in his voice.

"Well, I'm not happy about it now!" she cried, her voice breaking. "I won't just fall into bed with you! I won't be your mistress!"

There was a moment of thunderous silence, and then harshly, shockingly, James laughed.

# Chapter Thirteen

*C*assie couldn't have been more stunned, more hurt and humiliated, if he had struck her. His humorless laughter beat against her as she fumbled her robe closed and tied the belt, and she was fighting back tears when the laughter stopped. He seemed very big and threatening, sitting there, watching her with contemptuous disinterest as she covered herself. She shrank from the cold anger she saw in his face, and might have spoken, but he didn't give her the opportunity.

"You didn't feel that way a few weeks ago," he pointed out with cruel accuracy. "You didn't feel that way at all. A few weeks ago you wanted nothing more than to be my mistress; you practically begged to be my mistress, and when I asked you to be my wife, you threw that back in my face like an indecent proposition. Well, maybe," he leaned closer to seize her shoulders, his fingers biting painfully into her flesh, "maybe I've changed my mind. Maybe I do want you to be my mistress, and maybe I want you now!"

*"No!"* Cassie strained away from him. "James, stop this!"

"Why should I?" he growled. "You wanted to be my mistress and you'll get your wish!" The icy chill of panic ran through Cassie as she saw the hunger in his face. This was not the James she knew; this man with the burning, devouring eyes was a terrifying stranger, and he was going to take her, regardless of her wishes. She struggled harder. "James, you can't rape me!"

"Oh, no." His soft chuckle was in no way amused. "It wouldn't be rape at all, would it, Cassandra?" She closed her eyes and turned her face away, unable to bear the look in his eyes, aware that it would do no good to struggle, humiliatingly aware that what he said was true—it wouldn't be rape.

He made no move to carry out his threat, though. After an endless moment she heard his breath whistle out between his teeth; then his hands left her shoulders and the couch springs shifted as he rose. Slowly, cautiously, she sat up, huddled into her robe as if it offered some frail defense. She didn't want to look at James, but a force outside herself impelled it. The terrible rage had left his face, but his eyes were implacable, frigid, glacial, boring into her soul.

"I want you to tell me," he said very quietly, his careful words dropping like stones into the pool of silence around them, "why you were at that studio today."

Cassie had promised herself that pride and insecurity and all her other defense mechanisms would be cast aside when she confronted James, but not until that moment did she truly let them go. She stood, moving carefully around the coffee table to face him from a distance of some four feet. She gazed at him with bleak resolve.

"I was there . . ." Her voice was a cracked thread of sound, and she cleared her throat. "I was there because I wanted . . . I needed . . . to talk to you. I had to tell you that you were right about me. I was a coward. I was afraid to live." She shrugged helplessly and turned away to gaze blindly across the room, unwilling to see what must be in his eyes. "I was afraid to marry you because we live in different worlds. You're a star, you're known all over the world, and I'm not even finished with my training yet. I was afraid that my life would be swallowed up in yours, that my *self* would be swallowed up. I thought the inevitable conflict between our careers would drive a wedge between us, that a Hollywood marriage couldn't last. Worst of all, I didn't think *I* could make a marriage last."

She wheeled around to face him. "An apology is inadequate for what I did. I know that. I didn't have enough faith, enough trust in the love we shared to believe that it could withstand the stresses. I didn't have the courage to commit my life to yours. As you said, I was a coward."

"And now? How do you feel now?"

Cassie hesitated, head down, looking at her bare toes curling into the carpet. She took a deep, rather shaky breath and committed herself. "I love you," she said softly, afraid to say more, to ask anything of him. James reached out to take her chin between his thumb and fingers and gently raised her face. Cassie's eyes widened at the sight of his expression, at something she'd been afraid to hope for.

"Do you love me enough to make sacrifices and compromises? Do you love me enough to abandon your pride and let love and trust take its place? Will you take me on whatever terms I might set?" He was asking a great deal, but Cassie knew that without him her life was empty and incomplete. There was no question what her answer must be.

"Yes, I love you that much," she whispered. "I love you more than anyone else in the world, and—"

Her words were smothered beneath James' lips, and as his arms closed around her, she flung hers around his neck, kissing him with all the love and longing she had held within her for so long. She didn't realize that she was crying until timeless minutes later when James drew back, frowning at the wetness on her cheeks.

"Cassie?" He wiped a tear away with his fingertip. "Why are you crying?"

"I don't know." Her voice broke on a choked sob, smothered laugh. "I just love you so much . . . I . . ." She gave up, too overwhelmed to speak, and buried her face in James' shoulder, feeling, rather than hearing, his soft laughter.

"That's okay. I think I know what you mean. Come on." He kept an arm around her shoulders and steered her toward the kitchen. "Let's make some more coffee. What we have is cold, and we have a few more things to discuss."

"Do we have to *discuss,* James?" Cassie smiled provocatively up at him, sliding a hand inside the shirt he had pulled on but left open. "I can think of lots of other things to do."

"So can I," James growled, and pinned her against the kitchen doorframe for a hard, exciting kiss. "However," his voice was huskier than it had been before the kiss, and beneath Cassie's hand his heart beat as rapidly as hers, "we still have some things to talk about." He led her into the kitchen and sat her at the table, where she watched him make coffee and fought the disquiet she felt at his insistence that they talk. When he set the pot and mugs on the table and took the chair opposite her, his face was sober, and Cassie's unease increased. He stirred his coffee for a moment, watching its black-brown swirl in the cup, then looked up at Cassie.

"Did you mean all the things you said, up at the inn, when I first asked you to marry me?"

"I . . ." Cassie stopped and traced a squiggle on the tabletop with her finger. "I think I did," she said carefully. "It had been very difficult for me to admit what you meant to me, and to decide to come with you on that weekend. I should have anticipated what you had in mind, I know. I should have been more perceptive; I should have tried to understand you and your feelings, instead of being so wrapped up in myself, but my *self* was all I was concerned about. I'm sorry, James," she finished brokenly, her face anguished. "I'm so sorry I hurt you."

"I wonder if you know how it hurt?" James said, very quietly. "I know you didn't at the time. You had some idea of me as a *macho* Hollywood ladykiller, and even after all the time we'd known each other, that was still a large part of your impression. I know you weren't expecting a proposal, and I took you by surprise; that was my mistake. It was also my mistake to assume that you'd be pleased by a proposal. I never told you this," he leaned back in his chair, studying the kitchen light fixture, "but I had some dumb, romantic notion that you'd been a virgin at twenty-nine because you were saving yourself for marriage. It came as something of a shock," he said dryly, "to discover that whatever you were saving yourself for, it wasn't marriage."

"I wasn't 'saving myself,' at least not consciously. It's just that the only serious boyfriend I ever had was when I was eighteen and a freshman in college. We never made love, we were both so young, and when we broke up neither of us was heartbroken. After that I was so busy that I just never got close enough to a man to become . . . intimate. The older I got, the less likely I was to do something impulsive, to jump into involvement, and it just never happened." She hesitated. "Until I met you."

"And then you did have a relationship and the sort of involvement you'd avoided for so long." James lifted his mug and drank, and Cassie glanced up to see a gleam of amusement lighting his eyes as he studied her. "You fought it tooth and claw every step of the way, didn't you?" Cassie gave him a speaking look. "Why did you fight so hard, Cassie? Am I so awful?"

"No, of course you aren't."

"Then, why? All those other reasons don't add up to enough."

"They don't, do they? I guess the basis of it all was the fact that I've never been able to sustain a long-term love, or had the opportunity. I didn't . . . I don't know that I'm capable of it."

"Does anyone know that they're capable of a long-term love? There aren't any guarantees, Cassie; you just love and trust and do your best." James held her gaze for another long moment, then asked, "Can you do that, Cassie? Can you love me and trust me and commit yourself to me?"

"I . . . I think I already have."

James began to smile.

"Will you marry me, Cassie?" Her eyes widened and she stared at him, too stunned by his generosity to take it in. James misinterpreted her reaction. "Those are my terms," he said coldly. "You'll be my wife or we'll say good-bye now."

"Oh, James, of course I'll marry you!" Cassie flung herself into his lap, winding her arms around his neck. "I didn't think, after all the stupid, cruel things I said and did, I didn't think you'd still want me!"

"Not want you?" The look in James' eyes made Cassie blush. "Darlin', I'll want you when I'm ninety, and you know it." His arms tightened, pulling her securely onto his lap, one hand sliding over her hip to hold her thigh, moving against the soft fabric of her robe in an absent caress. "I wonder, though, if you'll still want me enough to make all the compromises."

"Oh, yes, I'll still want you." Cassie had tipped her head back to look up into his eyes, her own wide and brimming with the love she felt for him. "More than anything in the world."

"And the compromises? What about them?"

Cassie could have given a flip answer, but she didn't. She had thought about this; it was important to both of them, and she wouldn't pretend otherwise. "I think we can make the compromises together. We both have demanding careers, but so do lots of other people. The fact that we're both busy will only make the time we have together that much more precious."

"Mmm." He bent his head to nuzzle her ear, her neck, and Cassie let her head fall back to allow him free access, loving him, loving the way he made her feel, safe and protected and desired. "I've thought about something else you said."

"What's that?"

"That I'm a 'shooting star,' that I'm somehow outside the world of normal people. I don't find that especially flattering, and I want to know if you still think I'm a different type of person than you or anyone else."

"No, you're not. I let myself be intimidated by your world, by the celebrity and the money and the Rolls-Royces of that world, but you're not that world. You're James, who grew up in Cincinnati and spent his summers on a ranch and probably played Little League."

"Second base."

"Like I said. The externals aren't you; *you* are you, and you are the man I love." Her voice dropped. "The only man I'll ever love." James kissed her, as she'd known he would, a kiss of infinite tenderness, but when she expected the tenderness to turn to passion, James drew away.

"You have to understand that if you accept me, you're accepting all those distasteful aspects of my life, too. Can you live with the loss of privacy, the fans and the press who will pursue me—us, the fact that the tabloids will keep right on printing their 'exclusives'?"

Cassie smiled slowly, confident in the security of his love. "Let them print what they want. You and I will know the truth." She paused, then cried, "Oh, James, I can accept anything as long as we're together! These last weeks have been so miserable without you, without you to talk to, and laugh with . . ." her eyes began to darken as she turned on his lap, pressing closer to the warm breadth of his chest, ". . . and make love with."

The words were a breathless whisper against his cheek, and she turned her face the merest half-inch to find his lips, to run the tip of her tongue delicately along their firm line until he muttered something unintelligible but vehement and covered her mouth with his. Cassie rejoiced in his ferocity, twisting her body to press against him, her robe falling open as James tugged at the belt.

"You're so beautiful," he breathed against her throat. "Tiny and perfect and beautiful." His hands spanned the naked skin of her waist, his fingers almost meeting, and he lifted her to half kneel on his thighs as he found first one rose-tipped breast and then the other with his seeking mouth. He tormented her, delighted her, tracing delicate circles around her taut nipples until she whimpered with need, her fingers twisted in his hair, holding him tightly to her. When she could bear the gentle torture no longer she raised his lips to hers, sliding her legs off his to dangle on either side of the chair as she kissed him.

James shuddered as she rubbed her breasts lightly across his chest, and she did it again, intoxicated by her own power to inflame. The women in romantic stories never seemed to be aggressive, but Cassie was discovering an unsuspected wanton within herself and rather liked it. With a last, lingering kiss she dragged her lips from James's and slid off his lap. Standing very slim and straight before him, she shrugged the robe off her shoulders and let it slip to the floor, shivering as his burning gaze moved over her.

"James?"

"Hmm?" His voice was thick.

"Take me to bed, James." Cassie spoke softly, her voice husky. "Make love to me, please?"

Slowly, never taking his eyes from her face, James rose and reached out to her, and only when she stepped into his arms did he release the tight rein he'd kept on himself and lift her into his arms to stride down the dark hallway to her bedroom. He laid her gently across her bed, and it was only a matter of seconds until he had stripped off his jeans and joined her. Cassie let herself roll toward him as the mattress dipped beneath his weight, and she felt his arms close around her, encircling her securely.

"You drive me crazy, do you know that?" he growled, cupping her bottom in a large hand and pressing her to him, his own urgent desire obvious.

"Mm-hm, and you should know what you do to me!" Cassie whispered in his ear, then bit the lobe gently and heard him groan again.

"What do I do to you? Do I drive you crazy with this? Or with this?" He loved her slowly, worshipping every inch of her until she begged him to take her, and their joining was fierce, almost desperate, after the long weeks of loneliness and frustration. Cassie lost herself in him, in the pure sensual joy of their oneness, and when the spiral of passion in her wound to the breaking point and exploded in waves of release she felt faint with the power of it.

They lay closely clasped in each other's arms for long minutes afterward, little aftershocks of pleasure shaking them as they slowly relaxed.

"I was so afraid," James murmured after a while, "that you wouldn't change your mind. The idea terrified me, and more than once I was tempted to come to you and tell you I had to have you, on whatever terms you set."

"Why didn't you?" Cassie looked up, but could see only his profile in the dim light filtering from the kitchen.

"Because I knew it would be a mistake. A surreptitious, clandestine relationship, sneaking around, dissembling, hiding the truth, would be degrading to both of us. You're not the type of woman for that; I knew it, and I had to hope you would discover it, too. The waiting was awful, though." His arms tightened around her as if to hold her by force. "I was angry at you, too, for being so pigheaded, for keeping us apart. I'm sorry I was so cruel to you tonight, though. You didn't deserve that."

"I think I did deserve it. And I'm sorry James; I—"

"Shh, it doesn't matter anymore. It's all over, and I love you."

"And I love you."

"And I'll love you forever."

"And I'll love you forever and ever and ever," Cassie giggled, then waited to see where James would take the game next.

"I'll love you," he said thoughtfully, "as long as there are stars in the sky."

"Shooting stars?"

"Certainly."

"You know, that's another thing I was wrong about."

"What?"

"Shooting stars. I thought you couldn't catch them."

"And you can?" he asked, a grin in his voice.

"Mm-hm. Why did you keep my door key?"

If James was puzzled by the non sequitur, he didn't let it show.

"I just never got around to returning it, I guess. No," Cassie felt his headshake, "that's not true. I couldn't give it back to you because it was something that connected us. I couldn't sever that last tie."

"So you were caught, just as I was. That's one less shooting star in the sky, because I've caught it, and I'll never let it go."

"Promise?"

"Promise."

"Good. When will you marry me?"

"Gee, I hadn't thought about it. In July, when my residency is finished?"

"Sooner."

"Well, how about the end of June? June weddings are nice."

"Nope. Not soon enough."

"James, I have to have some time to plan this! When do you want to get married?"

"This weekend."

"This *weekend!*" She shot up to a sitting position, staring down at him. "James, that's insane! We can't possibly get married this weekend! There are a million things to do, and—"

"Hush, woman, and come here." He pulled her down onto his chest. "Everything will be worked out, but I'm not waiting weeks on end to marry you."

"But we can't—"

"We can, and we will." His lips closed on hers, and Cassie made no more protests.

# Epilogue

Twenty-two months later, a headline in the entertainment section of LA's largest paper read:

## JAMES REID HAS *NEW LIFE*

LOS ANGELES—Star of the newly-released feature *New Life*, as well as author of the screenplay, James Reid has another "new life" in his care today. Reid became a father yesterday evening, when his wife, LA obstetrician Dr. Cassandra Mills-Reid, gave birth to a healthy, 7 lb. 2 oz. daughter at LA General Hospital.

Interviewed at the hospital, Reid said mother and daughter are doing well, and he wishes to thank all his fans for the cards, gifts and good wishes they have sent.

## MORE ROMANCE FOR
## A SPECIAL WAY TO RELAX

Six new titles are published every month. All are available at your local bookshop or newsagent, so make sure of obtaining your copies by taking note of the following dates:

# DECEMBER 14

# JANUARY 18

# FEBRUARY 15

# MARCH 15

# APRIL 19

# MAY 17

## November Special Editions
## Available Now

### Storm Over the Everglades
### by Patti Beckman

Lindi MacTavish agreed to handle her family's newspaper in Florida, but she soon found she wasn't able to handle brooding Travis Machado, the paper's mysterious managing editor.

### Lover's Choice by Laurie Paige

Meli wanted a husband, and Tor offered to help her find one. But how could he follow through with his plan when his burning kisses told her he never planned to let her go?

### Golden Illusion by Ginna Gray

Claire Andrews was determined not to be a figurehead senator. She fought to show Matt Drummond that she was cool and capable, but soon she couldn't hide the explosive passion only he aroused.

## November Special Editions
## Available Now

### Shooting Star by Lucy Hamilton

When Cassie, a resident in obstetrics, met film star James Reid, their attraction was immediate and deep. But how could their love survive when their lives were on such different paths?

### From The Flames by Kathryn Belmont

Full of humour and passion, Jack Clancy drove away the loneliness that had haunted widow Marie Russo's nights. But the mystery surrounding her fireman husband's death threatened to destroy them both.

### No Strings by Diana Dixon

Used to women who put a price on everything, Christian was unable to believe that Allana would offer her love freely. But as she painted his portrait Allana captured his soul—and his heart.

# Coming Next Month

## The Law Is A Lady by Nora Roberts

When Phillip Kincaid was scouting loctions for his film he didn't expect the long arm of the law to point him in the right direction. But Victoria Ashton, town sheriff, was just the woman he'd been waiting for.

## The Other Woman
## by Elizabeth Neff Walker

Courtney certainly seemed to fit the stereotype of the "other woman." But when Eric Collins pursued her, she was swept off her feet like a young girl—right into a storybook romance.

## Come Lie With Me by Linda Howard

Therapist Dione Kelley helped Blake Remington to walk again. So how could she believe his words of love when she knew they were only spoken out of gratitude?

# Coming Next Month

### Saturday's Child by Natalie Bishop

What was Jarrod doing on the set of the soap opera Brynne starred in? He *couldn't* want her back again—not when he had made it brutally clear that he didn't need an actress complicating his life.

### Strictly Business by Kate Meriwether

When her father announced a contest, there was a made scramble for Roxie's hand by the VP's of his company. Moody Todd McKendrick was the front runner, but why couldn't he be a bit more enthusiastic about winning her?

### The Shadow Of Time by Lisa Jackson

Mara had believed that Shane Kennedy was dead, killed in Northern Ireland. Now he was back— and his bitterness at her apparent desertion vied with the passion still raging between them.